SPEAKING HER MIND

"I prefer to think of myself as realistic, but if I seemed unduly hard, so be it."

"Thank heavens your fellow men are less rigorous in their judgment, or else there would be no more marriages."

"Since you have no interest in marriage, Miss Lovelace, I don't suppose it matters to you one way or the other."

"I don't believe I said I had no interest in marriage, Captain Buchanan. Simply that I have no current interest in finding a suitor. There, each of us has put the other in his place."

"So you hope to marry eventually?"

"If I find the right man. Not one who believes that we women are so contrary and superficial."

"Could there be any creature so rare as the right man?"

"Of course. But I shall leave it to you to work out what his character and ideals must be. It will tax you a little, I daresay, since such a man would be very different from yourself . . ."

Books by Madeleine Conway

SEDUCING SYBILLA

THE RELUCTANT HUSBAND

THE ERRANT EARL

ROSAMUND'S REVENGE

Published by Kensington Publishing Corporation

ROSAMUND'S REVENGE

MADELEINE CONWAY

ZEBRA BOOKS
Kensington Publishing Corp.
www.kensingtonbooks.com

ZEBRA BOOKS are published by

Kensington Publishing Corp.
850 Third Avenue
New York, NY 10022

All Kensington titles, imprints and distributed lines are
available at special quantity discounts for bulk purchases
for sales promotion, premiums, fund-raising, educational
or institutional use.

Special book excerpts or customized printings can also be created to fit specific needs. For details, write or phone the office
of the Kensington Special Sales Manager: Kensington Publishing Corp., 850 Third Avenue, New York, NY 10022. Attn:
Special Sales Department. Phone: 1-800-221-2647.

Zebra and the Z logo Reg. U.S. Pat. & TM Off.

First Printing: January 2005
10 9 8 7 6 5 4 3 2 1

Printed in the United States of America

For Alex, Emily, Poppy, Jonny, Georgina,
Joe, Simon G., Amy, Tom, Simon H., Becci,
Ray, Fae, Mike, Ollie, Nell, Jamie,
Charlie, Talia, Will, Tammy, and Lawrence.
Thank you for encouragement and inspiration.

ONE

The approach to Cheveley concealed the house and its grounds successfully. The road was lined with beech and birch, the trees curving over the pathway so that it seemed that you were driving through a tunnel of greenery until you burst into open parkland dotted with great oaks and chestnuts, the latter laden with great candles of pink and white blossom sometimes as early as March, but more often in April.

A lone horseman galloped breakneck along the road toward the house one spring morning before expertly slowing down his mount to turn into the stable yard to the right of the house. He slipped from the saddle and it was only when he started to move slowly toward the house that one realized that he was no young buck but a gentleman in late middle age. In the saddle Mr. Anthony Veasey was still a powerful rider, but out of it, he was a weary fellow of not quite three score summers.

He made his way indoors, familiar with all the corridors and byways of Cheveley, where he had grown up, and where he still visited almost daily. He had news today, news that he was eager to share with his brother and his two nieces. He did not notice the freshly laid runner in the corridor, but a new watercolor of the Scottish lochs did catch his eye, largely for its utter inaccuracy. Hero had been painting again. Well, his news would soon put an end to that sort of wishy-washy pastime and the walls of Cheveley would be spared any further insipid daubs exhibiting the girl's lamentable want of imagination and excessive fondness for Scotch mists and heather.

As he stumped along the corridor, a maidservant came hurrying toward him, paused and turned to patter back toward the parlor. He entered hot upon her heels, in time to hear her announce him.

"Mr. Anthony to see the family." She bobbed and turned, bobbed to Anthony Veasey and returned to her original errand. This allowed Leonard Veasey time to come to the parlor door and hold out his hand to his brother.

"Anthony, you look hot with news. I daresay Matilda has the wit to bring us some tea, or would you prefer some ale?"

"I shall take the catlap. First let me see my nieces. How are they this fine day?"

"Much as we were yesterday and the day before, Uncle. How do you?" Rosamund Lovelace rose and came to kiss her uncle with a fondness that belied her ironic tone.

"Sharp-tongued as ever, Rosamund? I do well, I thank you. But you will thank me before my visit is out." He turned to little Hero, Leonard's daughter, took her hands and led her to the window. "You look well, my dear, pretty and plump as a partridge. The image of your dear mother. I have news that would delight her and will, I hope, delight you also."

"Dear Uncle Anthony, we need no news from you; it is a pleasure to see you. Come, take a seat here, and we shall hear you out as soon as the tea is come."

Matilda had indeed had the wit to prepare tea and crumpets for her master's brother, for a tray was prepared nigh on daily in anticipation of his visitation. The family was chatting idly about some proposed party in the neighborhood when the tray was brought in, but Mr. Anthony was jigging up and down with the anticipation of sharing his news. As soon as he had swallowed his first crumpet, wiped the butter neatly from his lips and taken the first sip of his tea, he sighed with pleasure and dropped his hands to his knees, turning his keen brown eyes from his nieces to his brother with the air of a wise little finch. He did not have long to wait. Leonard Veasey expectantly leaned forward in his easy chair.

"Well, Brother, what is this momentous news?"

"Colonel Fitzgerald is returned from the Continent at long last. Brackenbury Park is to be reopened this very week. Furthermore, he is accompanied by several of the coming men in his regiment." Anthony sat back with an air of accomplishment, as though he had brought the colonel into the Veasey drawing room with his mere words.

"He has been long enough in his return. First we were told he would be back in September, then after Christmas. Why, it is now past Easter and he is not back yet." Rosamund bent once again to the handkerchief she was embroidering. But Hero was more interested in her uncle's information.

"Who is with him, Uncle, have you any notion?"

"I believe a young lieutenant by the name of Wemyss, whose acquaintance you have already made, puss." Anthony Veasey patted Hero's hand, then turned to Rosamund and said, "I understand he is to bring a large party with him, some six or seven officers from his regiment."

"Oww!" Rosamund sucked the finger she had inadvertently pierced with her needle, then shook it. "Will Captain Buchanan be in Fitzgerald's train? I daresay we may have to put up with his presence, for he seems to hang onto the colonel's coattails quite shamelessly."

"Hold your fire, niece, he is not yet amongst us. Keep your powder dry so that you may fire at will once he is present and ready for your barrage." Anthony Veasey winked at his niece, whose expression was fierce, whether in contemplation of her ruined kerchief, now spotted with her blood, or in anticipation of the arrival of Captain Buchanan.

"Be warned, Hero, he'll have led astray Lieutenant Wemyss. Captain Buchanan is incapable of resisting temptation, in whatever form it takes, and a green lieutenant ripe for corruption will be irresistible to him."

"Why, Rosamund, you have so jaded a view of the captain, one is tempted to conclude that you wish to reserve him for your own attentions." Anthony leaped to take the rare opportunity to needle his niece.

"My attentions are reserved for less flagrant rakeshames than Buchanan. He is a block, and I am quite happy to use a block to mount my horse, but not for any civilized intercourse. If the captain has had the ear of the lieutenant, your romantic Valentine will have been deafened by his babble and will be quite unable to hear the worthwhile speech of more sensible folk."

"You are sharp, my dear. Temper your steel a little. A delicate piece of weaponry can be more deadly than a heavy sword." Leonard softened his criticism by patting his niece's hand. She smiled up at him.

"You are quite right, Uncle Leonard. I fear that I rose to Uncle Anthony's bait, and he must be congratulating himself even now on my readiness. No trout was ever so easily caught."

"I do not recall Captain Buchanan. Rosamund, have I ever met him?" asked Hero.

"Of course you have, my dear, although he has not visited these parts for many years now. You must have been just fourteen, I think. It was one of the first times you were allowed to come down from the nursery, about the time that Colonel Fitzgerald came into Brackenbury Park. Captain Macdonald stayed with us, and Colonel Fitzgerald came to dinner with Captain Buchanan. Then they came to shoot in our covers." Rosamund was astonished that Hero had forgotten Captain Buchanan, who must have impressed a delicate child with his burnished masculinity and saber-edged wit.

"What does he look like? I really cannot recall him, although his name is familiar."

"He is of more than middling height, fair, with a somewhat craggy visage which appears to attract many females. You would probably remember his eyes; all the ladies seem to recall them, though I am not sure why."

"Is his accent very Scots?"

"Not very. I am astonished you do not remember him with some trepidation. His tongue is as sharp as his eyes and he seeks out victims for what he considers to be humorous gems at every given opportunity." Rosamund sipped at her own tea, hoping that her cousin would drop this tedious topic of conversation. "Tell us, Uncle Anthony, how did you hear this intelligence?"

"You remember, niece, Mrs. Bradshaw's sister is at the Park. They are all of a fluster there, I may tell you, for they have not been asked to accommodate so large a party for years now. I don't believe the colonel has ever had any sort of party at the Park. But then, he's been only two or three times to the place since coming into the property. Still, didn't we dine there the last time he was here? That must have been, what, 1811, 1812? Over four years ago."

"Yes, that is right, Uncle, because I was too young to attend, even though Rosamund did say she'd watch over me."

"You're a stickler, Brother, but it's as her mother would have wished. I don't like to see schoolroom misses out and about. It doesn't do." Anthony polished off the last of his crumpets and continued. "I must say, Rosamund, you were coming into bloom that year. I quite thought the colonel would declare an interest in you. And you have improved in looks with every year that has passed. It's not your face or your figure that frightens off the young men."

Rosamund quirked a brow at her uncle before bending her head to her embroidery frame once again. She knew well enough the reason that the colonel had never shown the slightest sign of affection for her. But that was not a tale for her family. "I daresay you will tell me why I frighten off the men and how I should not frighten off the men. I am glad that Uncle Leonard is less determined to offload me on the next passing suitor."

"You know if I had my way, you'd have been married these five years and with two or three children for us to coddle."

"I must have inherited your own discrimination, Uncle Anthony. You've never found the right woman and seem to have made a happy enough life for yourself."

Anthony grinned. "Ah, I found the right woman, but my brother had seen her first, and I never met another to match her. But I never had so sharp a tongue nor so fierce a glare as you have cultivated, Niece. Neither you nor I suffer fools gladly, but you make it a little too obvious when you have encountered one. Still, there's no need for you to marry, certainly, and if you're happier caring for your uncles, we shall profit by your attentions, particularly once our little Hero has flown the nest. She is so obliging and restful that someone will snap her up as soon as he has the opportunity."

"Provided he is called Valentine Wemyss, Hero will allow him to snap her up with alacrity." Rosamund reached over and patted her blushing cousin's hand. "He has been a most attentive correspondent these four years."

"But he mentioned nothing of coming to Brackenbury Park." Hero bit her lip, uncertain now.

"Perhaps he wished to surprise you." Rosamund knew that the male sex sometimes behaved in unaccountable ways. It was a little baffling that Lieutenant Wemyss had not mentioned his plan to come to Oxfordshire with the colonel. She did not pursue the topic further. It had been some time since the lieutenant's last letter. He had written regularly, once a month or every six weeks ever since he had met Hero in Edinburgh four years previously. He was attached to a Scots cavalry regiment, as were Colonel Fitzgerald and Captain Buchanan, but his family had land and holdings all over Britain. Rosamund had never met Lieutenant Wemyss, but she had heard all about him, had shared in his letters and listened to her young cousin rhapsodize about his manifold virtues and bountiful good looks. Hero had drawn the young man while in Edinburgh and had used her sketches to paint a miniature of Wemyss, who from her somewhat sketchy artistic abilities seemed to be dark and dashing.

In all honesty, Rosamund was astonished that the correspondence had lasted. Hero was a dear child, but she was endowed with neither the looks nor the personality to make her stand out in any way from any of the hundred or thousand young girls whom the lieutenant must have encountered over the years. Rosamund loved her cousin dearly; the girls had been raised as sisters and she could listen for hours as Hero prattled about making jams and bottling tomatoes, or her latest purchase. But nothing could disguise the fact that Hero was a thoroughly pleasant but somewhat insipid girl. Early on, Uncle Anthony had drawn Rosamund aside, when she was nine or ten, and pointed out that playing pranks on her little cousin would afford her no satisfaction.

"Hero is like my dear brother, Leonard, in character. They are stalwart folk with little imagination but some sensitivity. It doesn't do to test your wit on her, for she will never be quick in understanding. But she is loyal and loving, and these are characteristics of more value than a quick tongue and a sense of the ridiculous. If you feel you are wading in treacle, my dear, take me aside and I will test your mettle."

Since then, Rosamund had learned to cherish her cousin, even when Hero's prattle seemed inconsequential and repetitive. But she was also mightily relieved when they had some time apart. Both girls had been sent to visit their Aunt Lydia in Edinburgh during their sixteenth summers. Aunt Lydia was the youngest surviving sibling of their family, an afterthought, and closer in age to the girls than to her brothers and Rosamund's longdead mother. Her Scottish husband was very well connected in Edinburgh society, as well as being warm in the pocket and wide in his business interests. Mr. Macdonald was also connected with the army, and in particular the regiment in which the Veaseys' neighbor, Colonel Fitzgerald, served, for his own brother served in it also, so there were always regimental men in and out of the Edinburgh house. It was in Edinburgh that Hero had first met Lieutenant Wemyss, and where

Rosamund had first set eyes on Captain Buchanan, although he had then been a lieutenant, she remembered.

Eight years! It seemed hardly possible that so much time had passed. She had been a silly girl at sixteen. She looked back with wry amusement at how certain she had been in her opinions and her behavior. Aunt Lydia must have had a trying time of it, trying to smooth out her rough edges. She had arrived in Edinburgh entirely convinced that she would be the toast of the town, that she was up to every trick and game. At times, Rosamund winced when she recalled the forward, precocious minx she had been. But Rory Buchanan had cured her of playing games and flirting outrageously.

Colonel Fitzgerald had paid a call on the Macdonalds a day or so after Rosamund's arrival in Edinburgh. With him had come a young, merry lieutenant with dancing blue eyes, a high forehead, a stubborn jaw and a wild crop of blond hair. Rosamund had not noticed him initially, absorbed as she was in cutting out a silhouette she had made of her Aunt Macdonald and unmoved by the arrival of a neighbor from home, one moreover too old to excite the interest of a girl. Then she had heard a mellifluous voice make its compliments to her aunt. She had looked up into keen sapphire eyes and her heart had skipped in a satisfyingly poetic fashion.

"And here is my little niece Rosamund Lovelace, the daughter of my eldest sister."

"I would more readily have believed her to be your sister, ma'am." Lieutenant Buchanan had winked at Rosamund as he took her hand and bowed elegantly over it.

"You are a rogue, Lieutenant, and well you know it. Do

not turn her head now. My brother Veasey will never agree to admit an impoverished cavalry officer into the family. Rosamund, be sure to avoid any entanglement with this gentleman. He has a great deal of address, but do not be taken in by that. He is a shocking flirt with no intention of being captured by any of our ladies."

"Ma'am, you malign me! Why, my heart has been captured at least once a week since I was in Edinburgh; you have such lovely exemplars of the fairer sex in residence here."

"You're like a butterfly, flitting from flower to flower, never settling on one." Lydia Macdonald turned to her niece. "You are warned, my sweet, you may dance occasionally with the lieutenant, for to be seen with him does no one any harm, but you must not form a tendre for him."

But it was too late. Rory Buchanan had been presented to Rosamund as forbidden fruit, and she must needs pick the apple and taste it. She next saw him at the assembly halls the following night and did dance with him.

"How do you like Edinburgh, Miss Lovelace?"

"I like it very well, Lieutenant. There are wonderful shops and a great deal to see and do. It is a most romantic location." Rosamund unaccountably found her conversation drying up, fearful as she was that she would sound dull and commonplace.

"Have you climbed Arthur's Seat yet?"

"Not yet. Aunt Lydia tells me that we shall do so very soon, and picnic at the summit and see the panorama of the whole city laid out before us. I never saw so great a place." She bit her lip. Now she must seem a gauche country mouse.

"I thought so too when I first came here, but one soon becomes accustomed to the racket and the size. You will be quite blasé by the end of the summer and will return home to be confounded by the stillness of the country."

"I hope I will not put on town airs. It is tiresome when one's companions return from a stay away all puffed up with customs which it is ridiculous to preserve in the country. But I am sure I will never quite accustom myself to town hours."

"You must, else you will lose that bloom that so becomes you. You would not look so well hollow-eyed and weary. It is a style which suits older ladies, but young girls should be fresh and full of life." He bowed to her as the dance ended, led her back to Mrs. Macdonald and excused himself. Rosamund followed his path through the crowd. Aunt Lydia noticed and tucked her hand in the crook of Rosamund's arm, leading her away from the other chaperones with whom she had been sitting, and wheeling her niece toward Mr. Macdonald, standing with several men of the city.

"How was your dance with Mr. Buchanan?"

"Very pleasant."

"I hope you will find your next partner as pleasant. Allow me to introduce to you to Mr. Fleming. He is the son of Mr. Macdonald's business partner and has just recently completed his studies at the university. Hector, here is my niece from England, Miss Lovelace."

Hector Fleming was a gawky young man with very pink cheeks. He stammered and blushed as he bowed and asked for the pleasure of the next dance with Miss Lovelace. Rosamund could not help glancing toward Lieutenant Buchanan, who was making up a set with his next partner, a very soignée young woman in the grays and purples of half-mourning, but bedecked with feathers and lace. She

had neat teeth, showing to great advantage as she laughed
at the lieutenant's badinage.

Rosamund exerted herself to converse with Mr. Fleming, who would never compete with the lieutenant in flair
and dash but who deserved her consideration as a familiar
of her uncle's circle. She managed to put him at his ease,
and he began telling her with great animation about his
studies in the law, the amusements that might be had in
Edinburgh and how he was to join the esteemed firm of
Macdonald and Fleming come the autumn and travel to
Hamburg. All the while, she kept watch over the lieutenant
and his lovely companion. She wondered who the lady was
and whether she herself would ever achieve such elegance.
She half wished that some distant relative had died that she
might herself take on the hues of half-mourning.

Once she had danced with Hector Fleming, he was
eager to present her to his friends, and she did not find
herself short of partners for the rest of the evening. The
young men of Edinburgh were happy to encounter an
agreeable stranger who seemed to have no airs, a dainty
way on the dance floor and conversation that was neither too frivolous nor too serious, despite Rosamund's
notable disadvantage in being English. So she danced
and flirted and widened her acquaintance in a manner
that pleased her aunt and uncle. But all the while, she
kept a covert eye on the lieutenant. She ascertained his
movements in and out of the ballroom, she monitored
his associates, noting that there were many women
among them, she observed his demeanor and his bearing. She could find nothing to disgust her in any way.
He danced with grace, his figure was given greater dignity by the crispness of his uniform and he seemed to
delight and amuse his friends, whether male or female.

***

The planned expedition to Arthur's Seat was the next occasion during which Rosamund had the opportunity to observe the lieutenant at close quarters. There were to be two carriages: in one would travel Aunt Lydia, Rosamund, Hector Fleming and Hector's sister Flora. In the other would come Aunt Lydia's dear friend Mrs. Helen Fleming, Mr. Fleming, Mr. Macdonald and Mr. Fraser Geesin, a friend of Hector's from university and Miss Flora's acknowledged suitor. There was the constant prospect of rain, but the expedition was to proceed nonetheless. They neared the hill and the carriages deposited the party about an hour's walk from the summit, sufficient to raise an appetite for the sumptuous picnic lunch the Macdonalds had arranged but not requiring excessive exertion of the ladies.

The youngsters soon drew ahead of their elders. Flora and Rosamund had struck up a healthy friendship, while Mr. Fleming and Mr. Geesin were full of the comradely banter born of a shared boyhood and all the pranks and mischief associated with that. The three young Scots vied in telling amusing tales to their English visitor of misdemeanors and narrow escapes, pausing only to point out landmarks and particularly fine prospects. It was a beautiful day, a little chilly for June, with a wind blowing in off the North Sea but with blue skies scarcely marred with cloud and the landscape jewel green from the rain that had threatened the whole enterprise.

"Look, Miss Lovelace, that is where we took the horses although we were not meant to be riding at all, but deep in our Latin primers." Mr. Geesin pointed to a flat stretch of land where they could see horses exercising even now. "I believe those are chaps from the Royal Northern."

Rosamund could not help wishing she could see Lieutenant Buchanan on horseback. She had just finished reading the poem that had taken Edinburgh by storm that year, *Marmion,* and though she had found stretches of it very dull, she had been quite taken, as were so many, by the ballad of young Lochinvar, sweeping his bride off into the night. It had increased still further the romance of a cavalryman. There was talk also of the Royal Northern British joining Wellesley in the Iberian Peninsula. Mr. Macdonald had discussed it with his wife only this morning, concerned as he was for his brother's safety and advancement.

Of a sudden, Rosamund's wish was granted. There was a thunder of approaching hooves, and there appeared, as if she had summoned them by magic, three officers from the Royal Northern cantering up on their great gray horses. These were Colonel Fitzgerald, his aide-de-camp, Captain Macdonald and Lieutenant Buchanan. The soldiers slowed their mounts and doffed their shakos to the ladies, and Colonel Fitzgerald called down to Hector Fleming, "See you at the summit," before galloping forward.

The Macdonald servants had been hard at work all morning, establishing a delightful picnic spot and laying out a sumptuous repast for the walkers. The young ones found the officers quaffing ale, their horses grazing idly by the carriages. The ladies were seated and brought lemonade, while Hector and Fraser were given tankards of ale also.

"How did you find the walk, Miss Lovelace?" inquired Captain Macdonald.

"Most spectacular. Colonel Fitzgerald will tell you that our part of the country is very pretty, but it is not so ruggedly beautiful as this. What a vista!"

"This is nothing compared with the Highlands, Miss Lovelace," interjected Lieutenant Buchanan. "You must go to Perthshire and northward. Will you have any chance to travel during this stay?"

"I do not know Aunt Lydia's plans or customs. Does she travel much, Captain Macdonald?"

"I am sure that she will be taking you to Stirling and the Trossachs, but I doubt that you will have time to see the real Highlands. The roads are very rough and it takes a matter of months to travel about."

"Is your home in the Highlands, Lieutenant Buchanan?"

"Yes, but I haven't returned since I joined up. My home now is my regiment, and we are promised much more excitement if we are indeed to go to Portugal. But the colonel plays his cards very close to his chest and will tell us nothing definite."

Captain Macdonald stood abruptly and offered his arm to Flora. "Come, speculation is idle. Let us go and look out for your parents and my brother, Miss Fleming. I am getting hungry, and we cannot start our luncheon without them."

Both Hector Fleming and Lieutenant Buchanan came forward, offering Rosamund a similar escort. She was immediately faced with a dilemma. She did not wish to insult or offend Hector Fleming but she wished for nothing more than to walk with the lieutenant. She smiled at Hector Fleming, but placed her hand in the crook of Rory Buchanan's arm and said, "Let us all walk together then."

From such small moments, such slight decisions, do our whole lives hang in the balance. Or so Rosamund was later to conclude. It was that point that signaled her interest in the lieutenant and drew his attention to her, so she came to think. And if she had not piqued his interest, her later troubles that summer would not have arisen at all.

TWO

To make amends to Hector Fleming for favoring Lieutenant Buchanan, Rosamund was most attentive toward the young man at lunch. She was seated beside him in any case, with Lieutenant Buchanan positioned midway between the youngsters and the adults. Hector was charming enough, but he had the slightly stooped air of the academic and lacked a ready, fluent tongue. Beside him, the lieutenant seemed to gleam with health and vivacity. Inexperienced and susceptible as she was, Rosamund could scarcely help being bowled over by the cavalry officer. He was clearly a great favorite of the whole company, keeping them in stitches with his mimicry and quick wit. But Rory Buchanan also pumped both Fraser Geesin and Hector Fleming for information about their studies and their professors, engaged them in debate, and expressed a wistful regret that he was not able to attend university and grapple with the deep questions of the day. He was not simply a soldier content to take orders and think of nothing but horses and the comfort of his billet.

After lunch, Mrs. Macdonald wished to take a turn about the summit and demanded the company of her niece. Colonel Fitzgerald stood and declared that it was time for his men to return to camp and their duty. They duly made their farewells. Lieutenant Buchanan came over to Rosamund and took her hand.

"I hope we shall meet up at the next assembly. I shall look for two dances from you—no more, for that would give rise to unseemly speculation."

"Is there any form of speculation which can be called seemly?"

"Oh, certainly, it is the speculation which attends Miss Fleming and Mr. Geesin. Here is a match which will suit all parties. The two young people are clearly exceptionally fond of each other and the only questions which arise regard the date of their marriage and the choice of wedding clothes and trinkets."

"But then must all other speculation regarding a lady and a gentleman be called unseemly?"

"Most of it must be, yes. That is why young ladies need to be so careful not to give rise to speculation: it is rarely seemly and never desirable to be an object of general discussion."

"You are strict in your notions, Lieutenant, like my uncles at home. The problem is that avoiding all activities that may give rise to speculation leads to an excessively dull life, and there are those who will speculate even if one's behavior would do justice to the cloister."

"Still it is best not to give them substance. So two dances only, Miss Lovelace." Rosamund smiled and consented, and watched as the three officers sprang into their saddles and cantered away. She became aware that the skies were clouding over and a breeze was rising. It was not long after that that the whole party climbed back into its carriages and headed back for the warmth of the comfortable houses of the New Town.

Mrs. Macdonald had been happy to see her niece sitting

beside Mr. Fleming. It was her dearest wish that one or other of her nieces might settle in Edinburgh. Both were well dowered and would bring significant capital to attract the canniest of families, but that was not her chief concern. Rather, it was the prospect of enticing one or other of her blood relatives to settle in the same city and to enjoy the same comforts as she herself experienced. She had had a London Season, as had all her sisters, but she had found London over-busy. Edinburgh was at once cosmopolitan and manageable, with a society less obsessed with rank and more interested in accomplishment.

The Flemings were a good family, by which Mrs. Macdonald meant a happy and productive family, fond of each other, with an abiding respect for education and the betterment of their fellow men. It was clear that Rosamund had won the confidence and affection of Miss Flora Fleming, which was a promising start to her time in Edinburgh. If only Master Fleming could equally effectively win Rosamund's attention, all would be well, felt Mrs. Macdonald. But there were plenty of other acceptable families and several months in hand. There was no need to push the child in any particular direction.

She would have been disappointed to read Rosamund's journal, which was already the recipient of entries extolling the charms of a certain cavalry officer and exploring the avenues a girl might use to engage his attention. Rosamund was in the full flush of her first crush and she almost wished for fewer social engagements so that she might reflect further on Rory Buchanan's many wonderful qualities. To impress the lieutenant was her first object and everything must be sacrificed in the achievement of that goal.

Rosamund was a systematic girl, and she made a list of

all the things she knew about Rory Buchanan, in an effort to identify the ways in which she could impress him. He was a good dancer and she knew that he esteemed her abilities in this area. He was a witty conversationalist, able always to find the right word to say to the right person. Here she must tread a fine line, for what was acceptable in a young man would be seen as pertness in a young girl. But in his company, she sought always to present herself as worldly and wise beyond her years in the ways of her fellow humans.

Clearly he was a fine horseman, but she had no access to a decent mount here in Edinburgh, for none of the ladies in her aunt's circle seemed to ride for pleasure while in the city. He played at cards, she knew, particularly enjoying quadrille, and she was able enough at that sort of thing, even if she did prefer whist. He cared for music: though she was an indifferent pianist, she was a passable singer and asked her aunt if it would be possible to engage a teacher, for then she might really make some progress. He did not seem to care much for art, or at least had no interest in sketching and amateur art, although he had expressed his admiration for Uncle James's latest acquisition, an interesting narrative painting by David Wilkie.

But an area of real interest to Rory Buchanan was the world of ideas. His was a military family, and there had been no question of wasting, as his father saw it, hard-amassed savings on a spell at university when there were commissions to be bought not only for Rory but also for two younger brothers. So when the young lieutenant met with fellows like young Geesin and Fleming, who were able to listen to lectures by men of learning such as Ferguson and Mill, who had the leisure to read the works of Hume and Smith and Reid, he could not resist grilling them and putting them through their paces. This Rosamund had discovered briefly at the picnic, and she witnessed with great interest his continued desire to expand his mind. She had never before met a man so curious and questioning, and his passion sparked an interest in these matters, which led to her locating in the library of her Uncle Macdonald's house Hume's *Enquiry Concerning Human Understanding*.

At first, Rosamund did not understand more than one word in five, then one in three, until finally Hume managed to exert an influence over her, and she began to realize the extent of her own ignorance. For although she was fascinated by Hume's arguments, she was not fully persuaded by them into a state of entire skepticism and then had to resort once again to the library to read those writers to whom Hume referred and those who sought to refute him. She also found in Hector Fleming a guide through the morass of ideas into which she had been plunged. It was all very well reading to discover the workings of a man's mind, but she did not wish to appear foolish before Lieutenant Buchanan, so she must test out her ideas and understanding before broaching such great matters with him.

So Rosamund's days were very full. She rose early to read and make notes before breakfasting with her aunt and entering into the business of making or receiving calls and shopping and keeping up with the latest fashions and fads. Then she would walk in the afternoons with Hector Fleming and discuss the reading she had done that morning, before returning home to dress for the evening's engagements.

Despite all her homework, Rosamund found it very difficult to use her information to good advantage, for the statutory two dances she was permitted by society and Lieutenant Buchanan's own standards did not allow her great scope for philosophical discussion, and every time she suggested to him that they might take a turn about the room, he always had her in fits of giggles with his dissections of the dress and manners of their fellow guests.

"There, look on Mrs. Oliphant, or should I say, Mrs. Elephant? Should we be kind and tell her that purple taffeta does not become a lady of her stature? It is most luxurious and cunningly draped, but I am reminded of howdahs and the sumptuous excess of maharajahs. I suppose all maharajahs must give way to sumptuous excess; it is in their nature, is it not, Miss Lovelace?"

He could talk indefinitely in this frivolous vein, fending off any attempt to steer the conversation in a more serious direction. There were few opportunities to encounter him outside the ballroom, for all the regimental officers were engaged in preparing for embarkation to Portugal.

The frequency of Rosamund's walks with him and the intelligent interest she showed in the subjects dearest to his own heart allowed Hector Fleming to hope. Rosamund behaved toward him with a friendly formality that he found most engaging. He was impressed with her devotion to her studies and her increasing understanding. He found her company more stimulating and interesting than any other young lady he had ever met. His estimation of his sister increased, for she had not only won the affections of his friend Fraser but also was the intimate of Rosamund. He had never previously thought much of his sister or any of her friends, for they had plagued him either with nonsensical conversations about nothing or by giggling helplessly in the company of the opposite sex. Rosamund was not only refreshingly free of such affectation, she was modest and respectful of his opinions.

Rosamund had arrived in Edinburgh at the beginning of April. It was the custom of the Macdonalds to leave the city in mid-July for a house near Loch Katrine, where they would spend six or eight weeks. Well into May, she was conscious that she must fix the interest of the lieutenant and deepen their acquaintance somehow. They had fallen into a pattern of behavior that seemed to lead nowhere. He would approach her at balls, at the assemblies, they would dance and exchange lighthearted banter, he would drop a kiss on her gloved hand and move on to other ladies. She saw him perhaps twice or thrice in a week. He certainly singled her out from all the other young girls, for his other partners at the dance were always the older ladies, married and safe. Apart from Rosamund, he eschewed females straight out of the schoolroom, for which sign of favor she should congratulate herself, she supposed.

Her dilemma was further complicated by lacking any kind of confidante from whom she could seek advice. Aunt Lydia had clearly warned her away from the lieutenant and Flora Fleming's interest lay in supporting her brother's deepening affection for Miss Lovelace. Perhaps if she had been able to consult with some sensible person, Rosamund might have been deterred from devoting herself to Rory Buchanan, or from encouraging Hector Fleming into developing an attachment to her. Instead, she hit on the idea of persuading the lieutenant to declare himself by making him jealous. Clearly, he would never be jealous of Hector Fleming. But there were other lieutenants. And ensigns and captains and majors.

So Rosamund embarked on a course that would see her made most unhappy during her remaining weeks in Edinburgh. She exerted herself to be charming to every officer to whom she was introduced, she never danced with the same officer twice, she smiled and giggled and fluttered her fan and her eyelashes. Every offer to squire her hither or thither was accepted until Rosamund's head was quite dizzy with the confusion of whom she was expected to meet and where. Of course, she was always properly accompanied by Flora or some other young lady, but she was clearly doing her best to cut a swath through the entire officer corps.

Flora was the first to comment, hesitantly, shyly. "Dear Rosamund, is it quite wise to dance with so varied a collection of officers? I saw Lady Glenister and Mrs. MacTavish glance at you in a most disapproving fashion, and though they are tabbies, they do talk."

"I do not know whether it is wise, Flora, but it is definitely most amusing. And what do you think! The new ensign, Mr. Macmillan, has invited us to go on a drive with him this afternoon." Rosamund's eyes sparkled with febrile excitement.

"What of your appointment to walk with Hector? I thought you met with him this afternoon?"

"Mr. Fleming comes here at half past two, and Mr. Macmillan at half past three. I am sure that Mr. Fleming and I will have entirely exhausted the possibilities of Plato and his cave by half past three. And if we have not, perhaps there will be room for him in the carriage, unless he must return to the office, of course. But he tells me that he is considering returning to the university for further study. Will your father permit such a thing? Or must Mr. Fleming remain forever in the office?"

Thus diverted, Flora forgot to press Rosamund to be more careful in the volume of her suitors. But it took only a day or two for Aunt Lydia to draw her niece aside one morning after breakfast. Mrs. Macdonald summoned

Rosamund to her parlor. She was on a love seat in the window embrasure, a table piled high with laces and ribbons and feathers pulled up beside the two-seater sofa. She patted the place beside her.

"Dearest, come sit beside me and tell me how I should trim this bonnet. I have had it for three years now, and it is beginning to show its age, but it is so comfortable that I hope to revive it a little, at least for one more summer."

Rosamund sorted through the mounds of haberdashery on the table. Her eye for color and shape was unerring, and she could bring to even the drabbest outfit a little touch of flair that lifted it from the commonplace. It was in Aunt Lydia's view one of Rosamund's greatest gifts.

"You are causing quite a stir in our little circle," said Mrs. Macdonald, holding up the bonnet to allow Rosamund to test the position of a brooch.

"Really, Aunt Lydia?" There was something about Mrs. Macdonald's tone that sent a shiver down Rosamund's spine.

"There is a balance to be achieved: it would be distressing to be ignored entirely, but to be discussed to the exclusion of other topics would be vulgar." Mrs. Macdonald laid the brooch to one side and picked up a feather dyed green. "What do you think of this? I suppose it will limit the range of outfits with which I can wear this particular hat."

"The green is too virulent." She paused. A little defensively she spoke. "I would not wish to draw excessive attention to myself."

"A stranger in town who comes gifted with looks, intelligence and a solid independence must always excite the interest of established citizens. But interest can swiftly become malice if the stranger, perhaps unfamiliar

with the ways of the town, seems to flout the accepted
way of going about one's business."

"Am I doing such a thing? I should hope not, Aunt Lydia."
Rosamund shifted a little in her seat. For some reason, the
room seemed over-hot.

"It is perhaps not the Edinburgh way to be seen in the
company of so many different officers. Normally, we
ladies try to limit our circle a little. I would not wish to
give the impression that you must refuse any introduction,
but perhaps you should not accept quite so extensive a
range of dance partners. And I am not sure that it is entirely wise to be seen out and about with such a variety of
officers. No one can take exception to seeing you in the
company of Captain Macdonald and one or two of his particular intimates, but I have heard comments suggesting
that you must be acquainted with every officer in the regiment. Of course you are not, but to hear such things
spoken of my niece does give me pain."

Rosamund swallowed a lump that seemed to stifle any
response to her aunt's words. The last thing she wished was
to cause her aunt any discomfort. But Aunt Lydia's next
words caused her even greater woe.

"And I believe it also gives Mr. Hector Fleming pain."

"I would not wish to bring him any unhappiness."
Rosamund could not disguise her increasing misery.

Aunt Lydia looked Rosamund in the eye. She shook her
head before she said, "I fear you are about to bring him a
great deal of unhappiness. He has formed a high regard of
your character and holds you in the highest esteem. He has
spoken of it to your uncle."

"He has said nothing to me. Nothing at all, Aunt Lydia."

"Would you welcome it if he did say anything to you?"

"I think you know I would not. I value Mr. Fleming's

friendship a good deal. He has been kind and most instructive to me, but my affection for him is that of a sister for her brother." A tear trickled down her cheek. She brushed it away, then continued sifting through her aunt's accessories.

"In that case, it would be a kindness to encourage him to spend more time at his work and less at this house. I had hoped that there was good cause for the frequency of his visits, but if there is no reason for them, then it would show some consideration if you were to make that clear to him at the first opportunity."

Rosamund bowed her head and bit her lip. Hard as Aunt Lydia tried to suppress it, she was clearly disappointed by Hector Fleming's lack of success. Worse, she was disappointed in her niece. Rosamund longed to run from the room and throw herself on her bed to have a good cry. Never before had she felt so mortified. Never before had her behavior been a cause for comment and gossip.

Aunt Lydia continued, "I am being too hard. You are only sixteen; you have not been out of the schoolroom before." She sighed. "The fault lies with me. I have been too easy a chaperone. Mr. Macdonald warned me that taking on that sort of duty was sure to bring me trouble."

"No, Aunt, it is I who should be censured. I have acted heedlessly. I never meant to bring you trouble, you must believe me."

"I do believe you." Lydia Macdonald patted her niece's hand. "Come, child, you will know better how to go on, and I shall know better how to manage a flighty miss. It will all blow over, provided you behave with a little more discretion."

"I'm sorry about Hector."

"So am I, Rosamund, but he will recover and you have learnt a valuable lesson, I hope. Speak to him kindly but firmly and all will be well."

***

It was the hardest conversation of Rosamund's brief life. First, she had to turn the conversation from the delights of Cicero, Plutarch and Marcus Aurelius to more personal matters. This took some time, for Mr. Hector Fleming admired the Roman stoics and waxed unusually eloquent on their virtues and their merits, pacing with great enthusiasm round the box hedging that graced the Macdonald garden.

"Your philosophers seem to value friendship far above love, would you not say, Mr. Fleming?"

"Friendship certainly was of great importance. When the slings and arrows of outrageous fortune fly, that is when one discovers who one's true friends are, and that is when their loyalty and encouragement are of most value."

Rosamund interjected before Hector could take flight once again. "You have been a dear friend to me, Mr. Fleming."

"Why do you speak in the past tense, Miss Lovelace?" Hector Fleming finally stood stock-still, his hands behind his back. Rosamund soldiered on.

"My aunt is making preparations for our sojourn in the Trossachs, and I believe we will then go to Glasgow and from there, my aunt will accompany me back home to England. I have only a short time remaining to me in Edinburgh."

"I hope that your return home will not mean the end of our friendship, Miss Lovelace." Hector remained stationary. Rosamund was the one to pace now.

"Of course not. I hope we will always be friends."

The young man bit his lip and scraped at the gravel path with the toe of his shoe. "Miss Lovelace, I did not mean to declare my hand so quickly, but circumstances force me to a point where I can conceal my affection for you no longer."

"Mr. Fleming, I am very fond of you, but I fear you have misunderstood me. I hope we will always be friends, but I can be nothing more to you than a friend."

"Nothing more?" Hector's expression of incredulity reminded Rosamund of a rabbit suffering a great affront.

"Nothing more. I never dreamt I had led you to believe there might be anything more." Rosamund hoped she did not sound shrill and self-justifying.

"Then there is no hope?"

Rosamund shook her head in response.

"Why not?" asked Hector. He shoved his hands into his pockets and looked Rosamund directly in the eye. "I had formed the impression that you found me to your liking. That you might feel, as I do for you, a bond deeper than mere friendship."

"I never meant you to think that. I admire you. I respect your learning, and your understanding is such as must please everyone who meets you. But my affection is not one that might deepen further."

"You are too young. You are just sixteen, younger even than my sister. I should have known better than to put my hopes in one so untried. But you seemed so thoughtful and so much older than your years."

Rosamund was stung into a thoughtless retort. "I'm not too young to love. I love another, if you must know, and no one in the world can measure up to him."

"Does your aunt know of this? Or is it the sort of clandestine tangle a girl might think more romantic than a good match with an acquaintance met in the normal course of events?"

"That is not your concern, Mr. Fleming. Just content

yourself, it is not that I am too silly and too girlish to love, it is simply that my affections lie elsewhere."

"I must thank you for being so unambiguous. I only wish you had been so lucid a little earlier in our acquaintance." Hector Fleming gave a little bow and marched smartly out of the garden at a considerable clip.

Rosamund pouted and kicked at a branch that lay on the lawn, shamed confessions and self-justifying rants vying for supremacy as she put off the evil hour when she must go inside and face her aunt. She did not realize that Hector Fleming had visited her aunt's parlor before leaving the house and there had revealed the secret she had let slip.

As soon as she managed to send the young man on his way, somewhat placated by a mutual agreement that Rosamund was a singularly silly young woman who could scarcely be expected to know her own mind, indulged as she had been by her uncles in Yorkshire, Lydia Macdonald hastened to her garden to confront her niece and discover the exact identity of her niece's lover.

THREE

Three quarters of an hour was the length of time it took Lydia Macdonald to winkle out of her niece the name of the young man for whom the child had developed a tendre.

"Rory Buchanan! You have been sent to try me. Rory Buchanan! Just the person I advise you against and you must fancy yourself in love with him. Was there ever anything so perverse as a girl of sixteen?"

At this, Rosamund did dissolve into tears. "I don't fancy myself in love with him," she sobbed. "I do love him. I cannot help it. I did not deliberately disregard your advice, Aunt Lydia, but I could not help myself from finding him the most fascinating man I have ever encountered."

Aunt Lydia rolled her eyes and reached toward her niece. Pressing a handkerchief into Rosamund's hand, she embraced the girl and held her until the sobs subsided.

"I shall advise Mr. Macdonald that we will leave for Loch Katrine early. If we remove you from Lieutenant Buchanan's aegis, perhaps you will discover that this grand passion is less magnificent than you think." She paused. Another paroxysm seized Rosamund. Lydia Macdonald waited until it subsided before continuing. "Has the lieutenant given you any indication that your affection is returned?"

Rosamund was swift to reply. "None at all. He has given me no reason to believe that he thinks of me as anything other than a pleasant acquaintance."

"Well, I suppose I must be thankful that you have not deluded yourself into hoping that your fondness might be requited."

Lydia Macdonald stood up and held out a hand to her unfortunate niece. "Come, child, come inside and I shall speak to Mr. Macdonald about our departure for the Trossachs. It is a most picturesque spot, and you will either indulge your romantical notions to the full or forget them entirely once we are there. Either way, your heart should be mended by the time you must return to my dear brother's house."

Rosamund did not protest. Of course, she was certain that her feelings for Lieutenant Buchanan would never, ever alter, that her heart would never recover and that her life was quite ruined by the prospect of being removed from Edinburgh even a day before it was strictly necessary. There was always a chance, however slight, that the lieutenant would confess that all this time, he had not been flirting with her simply because she was a pretty girl with a way with words—that in fact, he was as passionately in love with her as she was with him.

In her room, the elegant guest room to which she had been appointed as an important visitor to the Macdonald household, she paced and paced, pulling and wringing the lawn handkerchief her aunt had pressed into her hands, her agitation unabated. This early removal from Edinburgh was the worst possible outcome. Try as she might, she had never been able to persuade the lieutenant into anything more than the most superficial of conversations. She was not even sure whether he felt anything more than the vaguest stirring of pleasure at encountering her in a ballroom. Perhaps all her flirtations had simply served to disgust him as they had clearly repelled most of Edinburgh society.

A distinctly nauseous sensation overcame Rosamund. She sat in the wing chair by the fireplace and rocked a little, holding her stomach, and the reaction passed but left her feeling weakened and heady. There must be some way of finding out how Lieutenant Buchanan felt. Rubbing her temples, she rose and started pacing once again. Her steps led her to the writing desk and sat there for some minutes. The ivory and silver quill-holder Aunt Lydia had bought for her from Macniven & Cameron lay there, and she rolled it to and fro before picking it up and fixing a new quill there.

She reached for a piece of paper and flicked open the lid of the silver and crystal inkwell. She dipped the quill in the ink, raked off the excess, breathed in sharply, and started to write.

Sir,

Now that I am to leave Edinburgh and will see you no more, I can keep silent no longer. Since our first encounter, you have impressed me as a man of honour, of wit and of excellence in all things at which a man should excel. Wonder not that I love you, wonder rather that I have kept my counsel even so long as the six weeks that we have known one another.

It may be said that I am a foolish child, scarce old enough to know my own mind, but you have said on more than one occasion that my percipience and my sensitivities were greater by far than any of the fine ladies you have known. Believe me when I say that my course is decided, my choice is set on you, even if I may not have you. There will never be another who pleases me half so well, for there can never be any gentleman at once so amusing and so wise, at once so lighthearted and so profound. I have struggled to overcome these feelings, uncertain as I am that you could ever return my sentiments. But in the lengthy passage of many a dark night, I have lain awake thinking only of you, dreaming only of you, not sure whether you were an angel sent to soothe me or a devil intent on tormenting me.

Never have I met a being who understood me so well, who saw the inner workings of my soul and could explain these better to me than I could to myself. When I see you enter a room or round a corner, my whole world seems to lighten even if the day is dark with cloud and dank with rain.

In vain have I fought to suppress the urgent workings of my heart, warned by my acquaintance that you could have no interest in any girl fresh from the schoolroom, sensing myself that any sign of an untoward and unexpected affection on my part would be unwelcome to you. I can contain myself no more but throw myself on your mercy. The very act of writing this places me in your power entirely. The anguish I feel at the prospect of parting from the place where you are seems only to increase with every passing moment that I am forced to think of it, and nothing can assuage it. Long have I tussled with my conscience, for exposing myself to you thus is indelicate and no doubt unwelcome, but in truth, I cannot depart without confessing all.

I do not expect you to act on this letter. If I were wise,

I would ask you to destroy it. It would be wiser still on my part to destroy it myself rather than send it to you, but since I have known you, the sense for which I have hitherto prided myself has been overcome only by sensibility. Know only that my devotion to you is as regular as the rising of the sun and as dependable as its setting. If ever there is anything that I can do for you, it will be done, you have only to ask, although what a poor weak vessel such as myself can offer is as nothing to one so strong, so mighty as you.

There is one here who will deliver this to you. If you feel anything for me, I beg of you, respond by return and let me know my destiny, whether it is to wait for you as long as you desire or to love you from afar, forever hopeless.

Then she signed it with a flourish and in agitation, threw sand over the letter, shaking off the excess before folding it without rereading it. She scrabbled for a stick of wax, struck at a tinderbox, melted a few drops onto the paper and slammed her seal into the warm green liquid. She went to the bell and tugged at it, hoping that young Moira, a sweet maid, would answer as she usually did. By the time she returned to the desk, the wax had set. She turned the letter over and dashed down Lieutenant Buchanan's direction before sanding that.

The door opened and Moira slipped into the room, curtseying to the mistress's niece and waiting expectantly.

"Do you run any errands this afternoon, Moira?"

"Aye, miss, I'm going to the Grassmarket this afternoon."

"You told me that you had a sweetheart in the Royal Northern regiment?"

Moira looked nervous. If the mistress ever heard she had

a sweetheart, she'd be dismissed. But Miss Lovelace looked so very distressed, and she'd been a kind girl so far. Moira nodded to confirm the existence of the young lover.

"I need to get a message to an officer in the regiment. An urgent message, but of course, Aunt Lydia must know nothing about it. Can you pass the letter to your man and ask him to give it to Lieutenant Buchanan?"

Moira almost laughed in relief. She'd be safe as houses, for Miss Lovelace would want Mrs. Macdonald to know as little of her own intrigue as possible.

"Aye, Miss, Lieutenant Buchanan." She held out her hand. Rosamund pressed the letter into the girl's fingers, along with half a crown. Moira looked down in surprise; she'd not expected any reward, but she wasn't about to turn it down now it had been offered.

"It must be delivered direct into his hands, no other. Go quickly."

Moira removed herself and the letter without further telling, and Rosamund began a vigil during which she imagined all sorts of wonderful scenarios, each one more farfetched than the previous, in which Lieutenant Buchanan would gallop round George Square and up Charlotte Street, hurl himself down from his mount and demand to take her with him to Portugal or wherever else he might be posted. Or break into the house and swing her into his arms and sweep her out of the doorway, proclaiming that she was his and need never be parted again from him. Then she tried to imagine her life following the drum, indulging in chitchat with generals, hobnobbing with colonels and dancing at regimental gatherings.

Years later, Rosamund was well aware that she had at sixteen been a peculiarly foolish young woman. But she had also been unusually unlucky, for in addition to the shame of having written so nakedly naive and exaggerated a letter, it had fallen into the wrong hands.

Moira had met her young man, an enlisted man in the cavalry, James Ferguson. As always, their time together was too short, but she did remember to give him the letter. She couldn't remember the officer's name, though, so together, she and Jamie tried to make it out from Rosamund's hasty scrawl.

"There's a *b* and a *u,* then a *ch* and then it all tails off." Moira squinted at the rough hand on the paper.

"There's two lieutenants it could be, either Buchan or Buchanan. Which do you think is the more likely?"

"Heavens, I don't know. She'll have met him at some dance, I daresay. It'll be whichever is closer to Captain Macdonald, I should think."

"They both hang about with him, and with Fitzgerald. Buchanan is large and fair and a touch disheveled, but Buchan is a neat, dark fellow. They're both popular, if you take my meaning. Hang it, Moira, what should I do?"

"Give it to whichever you meet first. If it's for the other, well, they're both gentlemen; it'll reach the right one eventually. I've done my part, and I shall put the half crown back on her dresser, for I don't feel as though I've earnt it."

So Jamie Ferguson headed back for camp and bumped into the small, dark, neat one first. "Sir, I've been passed a letter from a lady. It's either for you or for Lieutenant Buchanan, but I couldn't make out the hand."

Buchan held out a languid hand for the missive. He inspected the address and raised his eyebrows, apparently recognizing the lady's hand. "Intriguing, I must say, Ferguson. Thank you."

Scarcely looking at the direction, he slipped his thumb

beneath the seal and flicked the letter open. He shook it out as neatly as a lady opens out a fan and looked up at Ferguson. "That will be all. You are dismissed."

So Lieutenant Buchan read the letter and grinned. Strong and mighty! Wise and witty! Oh, the encomiums and exaggerations of a girl in love. Poor Miss Lovelace, if only she knew how very little she had ever figured in Buchanan's world, for he was quite absorbed by the charms of his current inamorata, a high-colored, high-tempered ladybird by the name of Gillespie. Poor Miss Lovelace, if only she knew how very useful her letter would prove to discredit Buchanan in Fitzgerald's eyes, an aim long held by Buchan. Although he came from a grander family and possessed a significant fortune, Buchan had always envied Buchanan, ever since their school days at the Academy. Their paths had crossed continuously since the boys had reached the age of eight, and with every encounter, Buchan's detestation of Buchanan had increased. Rory Buchanan had always been magnetic and attractive, he had always approached challenges with a calm insouciance, he had always succeeded where Buchan struggled and occasionally failed.

Buchan took the letter to his quarters and read it through once more. He sat back in his armchair and gazed at the ceiling, contemplating the possible courses of action open to him. He could not spread the contents of the letter directly, for that would lead immediately to his exposure as a man sufficiently dishonorable to open a fellow officer's letter. But if he could come up with a way of accidentally "losing" the letter at the soiree to be held by Miss Emily Gillespie for the officers, the little harridan would be sure to cause a scene. And he could anonymously circulate a riddle, for Miss Lovelace's name lent itself to such games.

It was an easy enough matter to drop the letter on the hall table at Miss Gillespie's welcoming home. The riddle took a day or two longer to circulate. But it was most satisfying to arrive at one of Mrs. MacTavish's homes and find the tabby along with the last of her string-bean daughters poring over a copy of the riddle and working out the puzzle.

"Have you seen this, Lieutenant Buchan?" enquired Miss Sarah MacTavish. "Allow me to read it to you:

My first is in madder and in your garden may grow,
my second is the world, as any Frenchman knows,
my third is a passion tender and true,
my fourth is essential for a boot or a shoe.
Unfortunate am I, as my name indicates,
for the lieutenant I adore when he sees me only hates."

Miss MacTavish ended with a dramatic swoop to her rendition. "It must be Rosamund Lovelace, don't you think?"

"I do not know the young lady well enough to tell. It seems very likely. But who is the lieutenant she adores?" Buchan strove for a noncommittal and only mildly interested tone.

"There's the question," said Mrs. MacTavish. "She's flung herself at such a variety of our military men, one is hard-pressed to determine whether she loves one man or twenty-one."

"I believe it is Ross Macintyre. I have seen her dance with him so often, why, even three times in a night." Miss

MacTavish simpered. "Three times in one night. She is brazen. So forward."

"I am not so sure," responded Buchan. "Mcintyre was, I think, simply striving to pique the interest of Miss Abercrombie. He has spoken often about his admiration for that lady."

"Then it must be Buchanan," stated Mrs. MacTavish. "She was making sheep's eyes at him weeks ago. Well, Lydia Macdonald will be regretting sponsoring a southern miss now, mark my words."

Mrs. MacTavish was not the only one to have reached this conclusion. Miss Emily Gillespie gave her lover an extremely penetrating and difficult time of it when he came next to visit her. She received him in her front parlor, rather than leading him upstairs to her boudoir as was her usual practice. He shifted somewhat uneasily in the delicate rosewood chair in which she had indicated he should sit. She lounged in a wing chair, her legs tucked under her, her fingers plucking at a shawl.

"I've heard about you and this girl, this Lovelace child. You're making a laughingstock of me, and I don't like it." Her green eyes were hard, her tone clipped.

"What are you talking about, Emily? I've danced with the girl every now and then. She's amusing enough for a child hardly out of the nursery, but there's nothing more."

Emily pondered this. She reached for a book on the side table beside her and tossed it across to the lieutenant. "Read the letter I've tucked in there."

Rory opened up the book and unfolded the letter. He did not know the writing, but the sentiments were unmistakable. He could feel the blood rising up his cheeks and a prickle of discomfort making its way down his spine. The missive was so excessive in its sentiments, so pathetic in its demands.

"I've never seen this before. How do you come to have it, Emily?"

"Well might you ask. It was on my hall table two nights ago."

"I haven't seen you for nearly a week."

"I am well aware of that, Lieutenant. I wondered whether this might not be some explanation for your absence. I wondered whether one of your charming fellow officers deposited this here for me to find and understand that I was no longer first in your affections. Do you think that is possible?"

At that Rory stood, incensed. "What sort of a man can you think me, Emily, first that I would allow a letter of this nature to circulate so freely, second that I would be so cowardly as to give you your congé in so distant and dishonorable a fashion, a way which I agree would make a mockery of all we had shared?"

Miss Gillespie was convinced by Buchanan's outburst that there was nothing to the letter, that he had had as little idea as she that Miss Lovelace nurtured so burning a passion for him. But that did not explain his absence from her soiree.

"You speak in the past tense. As though we have no more to share." Buchanan sighed. This was always the tricky bit with women. The truth was, the regiment was almost ready to set sail for Portugal, and his interlude with Emily Gillespie was drawing to its natural conclusion. He had been away this past week on regimental business.

"The Northern is to ship for the peninsula in a few days' time. I do not imagine that you will wish to follow the drum, so we must part."

Emily uncurled herself and sat straight in her chair. She looked up at him. "I would follow, Rory, if you were prepared to marry me."

"You know that is not possible, Emily, for either of us. You have always known it. Nothing has changed. I have insufficient funds, you have no inclination for the life of a poverty-stricken cavalryman, and we may be fond enough of one another, but there's no real love between us."

"So this is the last I'll see of you." It was a statement rather than a question. They neither of them had time for the other. She must look for her next protector and he must fulfill his regimental obligations.

"It seems to me that that is the case." Rory took her hand and kissed it. "It has been a good deal of fun, Em, and I wish you well. I'll send you a present before I go."

She smiled up at him. "Thank you, Rory. You've been as generous as you could be. But watch your back; you've clearly got an enemy if there's someone willing to interfere with your post and spread this letter about the place. There's a riddle doing the rounds, I believe. This poor girl has been undone, and you are being made to look like an unprincipled trifler."

"Who was here that night, Emily?"

"Lord, half the regiment, and half the university too. It was a wonderful evening, I must say. I don't know where you should look. Perhaps the young lady has other suitors who have been spurned as a result of her feelings for you?"

Rory winced. He knew as well as anyone else that Hector Fleming had been wearing the willow for Miss Lovelace this six weeks. But it wouldn't have been he who'd use his love's folly so cruelly.

"She does, but none who'd deliberately bandy her name

about in public or who'd seek to cause trouble between you and me."

"In any case, you'd better take the letter, since it is rightfully yours. Poor girl, she'll be suffering over this."

Rory had not thought of the matter in that light. He suddenly felt very weary. He had hoped for a final night with Emily before parting with her amicably, and here he was faced with an almighty scandalbroth to sort out.

As he left Emily Gillespie's home for the last time, Rory turned over and over in his mind the conundrum he had been presented with. He could not work out the identity of his enemy, nor could he think of any sensible way of helping Miss Lovelace overcome the consequences of her unguarded pen. In fact, he began to consider the girl positively tiresome in her infatuation. He had warned her quite explicitly against compromising her reputation. Then he thought back the five years to his own sixteen-year-old self and remembered how little anyone of that age liked to heed others. He supposed he had better face the music and visit the Macdonalds. He was not entirely sure what he hoped to achieve there, but he did not feel that it would be the behavior of a gentleman to ignore the plight of a girl in Miss Lovelace's situation, however much she had brought that on herself.

It was unfortunate that he met Lieutenant Buchan on his way to George Square. He had never much cared for the fellow, but they had always managed to preserve a civilized surface acquaintanceship. But Rory found himself sorely tested when Buchan shared the riddle about Miss Lovelace with his fellow officer as they sauntered along the street.

"I've no notion who the lucky dog is that she's meant to

be pining after, have you?" Buchan's mischievous question roused Rory's suspicions.

"None," he replied brusquely, the letter that Emily Gillespie had given him burning itself against his breast. "It seems to me very poor sport to pass on riddles about this young woman. She's a foolish thing, certainly, but that is no reason to bandy her name about and make her seem ridiculous."

"These young girls, they think to make us their lapdogs. She has behaved in so public a fashion, I am astonished that you are not more delighted that she should have received her comeuppance."

"I am heartily sorry for the Macdonalds, who have offered her their home and their hospitality. It does not become anyone to succumb to the inclination to mock their guest."

This exasperated Buchan, conscious that with every utterance, Buchanan despised him more for giving way to gossip and sympathized more strongly with the girl whom he should more justly have blamed.

"If you rally to her side with so spirited a defense, the talk will be of how you are the young blade that she adores."

"Utter nonsense. She scarcely knows me. We've danced occasionally, nothing more. Are you being deliberately provoking, Buchan?"

"By no means. Of course, I take your word for it. She means nothing to you and you nothing to her. I suppose you had better go straight to the Macdonalds to console them in their hour of need."

Buchanan realized that they were by this time standing outside the Macdonalds' house. He bowed to his brother officer and made his way up the steps, wondering if they would be receiving, and if Lydia Macdonald knew of this latest on-dit circulating about her pretty but improvidential niece.

FOUR

It was an apprehensive lieutenant who stood on the doorstep of the Macdonalds' house, listening to the clanging of the bell as it rang indoors. All too soon, the cheerful face of a footman inspected Mr. Buchanan and announced that Mrs. Macdonald particularly wished to see him. He was ushered immediately to her private parlor. She was alone.

"Good day to you." Her tone suggested that the day was considerably worsened with his appearance. Then she relented and held out her hand. He bowed over it and waited for her to indicate that he should be seated. She looked on him sorrowfully, shaking her head and sighing before signaling that he should sit in a rather uncomfortable-looking chair.

"My apologies. I have been out of town on regimental business. I came as soon as I heard of this lamentable affair."

"Heaven knows, it is hardly your fault, Mr. Buchanan. My silly niece has dished herself, and there is little I can do to assist her. It is just as well that we depart for the Trossachs in a day or two." Mrs. Macdonald huffed like a ruffled hen, then resettled in her own chair, feeling quite as uncomfortable as the lieutenant and not entirely sure what reason he had for calling on her at all unless it was to offer for Rosamund, a prospect that might have the merit of trumping the effects of the riddle but would have no real benefits.

Rosamund was much too young to accept an offer from a soldier on his way to serve in a foreign country.

"You understand that I cannot offer for her. It would not be right. We leave for Portugal imminently, and if, as I suspect, this is some infatuation, for us to enter into a betrothal only for her to have to break that when she meets a genuinely eligible prospect would do even greater damage."

Her faint hope now extinguished, Mrs. Macdonald snapped back, "Of course you cannot offer for her. The notion is preposterous. You have stood up with her for a few country dances and she must fancy herself madly in love with you. This is bad enough, but any suggestion of taking it any further is quite impossible. The whole business will die down in a few days, I am sure."

"Have you any idea of who might have penned the riddle? If I could identify the author, at least I might take some action in that quarter."

"How? By fighting a duel, I suppose you mean. Well, you might, and she'd find her name even more blackened. If, of course, it *is* a man who wrote the nonsense. The only people who have passed it my way have been ladies, of course, most notably that poisonous witch Isobel MacTavish."

This gave Rory Buchanan a fairly clear idea of the identity of the author, for the MacTavish ladies were singularly unimaginative and consequently unlikely progenitors of the rhyme. But Buchan did spend a good deal of time with them. It all began to make sense. Buchan's reasons for drawing Miss Lovelace into the vendetta he was intent on waging against Buchanan was a mystery, but it seemed to be the most likely explanation for this unpleasant exposure of the poor girl.

"You may think it unwise, but I would like to take my leave of Miss Lovelace in person. Since I have brought so great a trouble to her, I feel that the least I can do is bid her a proper farewell."

Lydia Macdonald tightened her lips a little. Then her eyes filled and she nodded. She went over to the bell pull and summoned a maid, who was sent to bring Miss Rosamund down immediately. Both Rory and Mrs. Macdonald waited uneasily for the girl to appear. Finally, after a long silence, they both jumped as the handle turned and she slipped in, her eyes very blue, her hair thick and lustrous, her face unusually somber. Her creamy skin was slightly blotched, showing distinct signs of tears only recently rinsed away. Her shoulders were squared and for the first time, Rory Buchanan was struck by what a beauty she was likely to become as she emerged from girlhood. But now she was still a child. Lovely, defiant and spoiled.

"Mr. Buchanan has come to bid us farewell. He is leaving Edinburgh very soon, just as we are, but for a far less comfortable billet."

Rosamund closed the door behind her and went over to stand beside her aunt. She did not meet the lieutenant's eye as she spoke haltingly.

"I must apologize, for I feel sure that I have caused you to listen to a great deal of unwelcome comment. If my foolishness has given you any discomfort, I am heartily sorry for it." An unmistakable sob escaped her.

"Come, Miss Lovelace, sit down and compose yourself." As Rory approached, she skittered off and went to the window seat overlooking the square. Mrs. Macdonald shook her head as Rory made to follow, then went over to the pianoforte, where she sat and began picking out a tune.

"Mr. Buchanan, have you heard this tune? It is new from Germany, a charming piece. Come, turn my pages for me.

I haven't yet found the trick of the piece; you may be able to advise me."

Mrs. Macdonald was striving to play Weber's *Momento Capriccioso,* perhaps not the most sympathetic of choices while her niece was swallowing back another bout of tears, but on the other hand, playing a more lugubrious piece might simply have aroused another flood. Rory had not come across the piece before, but as with most of Mrs. Macdonald's choices, it was a pretty enough work. She played away, really not needing any assistance and clearly watching the reflection of her niece in the mirror that hung on the wall opposite. She caught Buchanan's eye and nodded in Rosamund's direction as she continued playing the little melody.

The lieutenant went over to Miss Lovelace. She twisted round and looked up at him, apprehension oozing from her.

"I'm not here to scold," he said in a low voice.

"Then what can you have to say to me?" Rosamund turned, genuinely baffled, and a little hopeful. Perhaps her wildest dreams might come true and she might find herself engaged to the lieutenant and then let the Edinburgh tabbies swallow that.

"Simply that I am touched by your sentiments. But I cannot reciprocate them. I thought I had dealt straightforwardly with you, made it clear that there could be nothing more than a civil friendship between us."

Rosamund had never encountered the least violence. The worst hurt she had ever sustained had been a fall from a horse that had left her winded, and this utterance from the lieutenant acted much as that sudden tumble on her constitution. It felt as though all the breath had been knocked out of her by a considerable thump to the back. But she strove to conceal this with as much dignity as she could summon. She knew she should not have expected anything more from the lieutenant, that indeed he was acting as kindly as he knew how, but nothing could alter his definite tone, his emphatic words.

"Then in the name of civil friendship, might we at least be allowed to correspond?"

"That is unwise, as I think you know. It must get out, and if it does, the only acceptable construction that one could place on such a correspondence would be that we were betrothed."

Finally, she looked up into his eyes, gazing at him intently, as though he were a message she might decipher if she only understood the code in which he was written.

"I understand. Good-bye then, Lieutenant Buchanan, and Godspeed."

"Thank you, Miss Lovelace. You are kinder than I have a right to expect. But I hope that I can be kind to you too." He glanced round at Mrs. Macdonald, who appeared to be engrossed in her music. Surreptitiously the lieutenant withdrew from his sleeve a much-folded piece of paper. "I feel I must return this to you. Perhaps I should have burnt it without further ado, but since it is your letter, it seemed to me that you were the only one with the right to dispose of it entirely."

Rosamund's fingers clenched automatically about the paper, crushing it. If there had been a fire burning in the grate, she immediately would have hurled the letter into it, but since it was June and even in Scotland far too warm for a fire, she simply clung to it, as if it had frozen to her skin.

"Goodbye, Miss Lovelace." Rory lifted her other hand and carried it up to his lips. She was not wearing gloves, and he did not observe the proprieties, for she felt quite distinctly the imprint of his mouth against her skin. She pulled her hand away and he stood, took his leave of Mrs. Macdonald and withdrew.

"Go, child, go upstairs and rinse your face again. We are expecting guests imminently and I cannot have you drooping about like one of Don Giovanni's castoffs. I shall expect you downstairs in an hour's time."

Up ran Rosamund to her room and there looked over the letter she had so foolishly written to Rory Buchanan. What a stupid, stupid creature she was, and what a hard-hearted, granite creature he must be to resist such passion. What a block! What a villain! The seeds of hatred were sown as she took with trembling hand her tinderbox and scraped up a flame in which she placed a corner of the letter, watching the paper blacken and shrivel.

Rosamund spent only three more days in Edinburgh, but they were to be the three most uncomfortable days she had ever spent in her life. She ran the gamut of sly smiles, muttered asides, stifled giggles and contemptuous glances, which seemed only to increase once a certain small, dark cavalryman was seen about the town with his arm in a sling. While all those who called themselves her friends were stalwart, there were many people, Rosamund found, who were all too ready to disassociate themselves from a young woman who was widely regarded as having flouted the common decencies.

Mrs. Macdonald kept her niece close by her as she made her final calls about town, going from one house to another for cups of tea and discussion of the pleasures of the Scottish landscape, the choice of reading materials necessary to occupy one's brain while away, the quality of paints and drawing materials from the competing stationers of

Edinburgh and whether the pianoforte should have been boxed up and sent in advance. Previously, Rosamund would have hurried off with the younger ladies of the house, eager to enter into a postmortem of the events of whatever social gatherings had taken place the night before, who had danced with whom, who had smiled favorably on whom, who had spurned whom, but now she stuck close by her aunt. The young ladies were careful not to address the southerner directly and somehow managed to melt away to their own quarters without including Rosamund in their deliberations. In what seemed like an instant, she had become a pariah, and she realized what it must be like for the newly rich tradesmen and their families, attempting to enter Edinburgh society, encroaching, enduring direct cuts, forever attending social events yet forever on their fringes, never at the heart of things. It was a miserable end to her sojourn in the Scottish capital, and a time that later always elicited a shrinking sensation within her, an uncomfortable blend of repugnance for her own behavior and resentment over the behavior of others.

Lydia Macdonald was wise enough neither to shelter her niece from the disapprobation of Edinburgh's social elite nor to comment on her niece's travails. There was no point in berating the girl for her unfortunate passion, for its public unveiling and denouement were punishment enough. She reasoned that her niece's understanding (never the strongest attribute of a sixteen-year-old girl) had been dazzled by passion but that the adverse results of this foray would be sufficient to deter Rosamund from repeating such a mistake. Perhaps Hector Fleming might be prevailed upon to stay at Cheveley on his way to London in a year or two and Miss Rosamund might then appreciate his true worth and the quieter satisfactions of an affection born of common interest and familial connections.

Sadly, if Mrs. Macdonald had been privy to the contents of Rosamund's journal, any expectation that the chit would calmly marry the sort of man with whom her family would wish her to form an alliance would have died. There, in the pages of her diary, Rosamund gave way to the torments and travails that she suffered. She railed against her aunt, her uncles for their folly in allowing her to travel to Scotland, herself for her own naivete and arrogant folly, against the jaundiced eyes of Edinburgh society and finally, against her beloved lieutenant, who had in an instant converted himself into a predatory libertine with his refusal to propose to her.

In later years, Rosamund did reread her journal from this time, cringing all the while at the intemperate language, the willful blindness and the searing shame that it revealed. But she could not in her heart of hearts entirely blame a romantically inclined child for the debacle, and she could not wholly absolve the lieutenant of all culpability and so, even though her burning hatred for him had waned, she could not help but remember him with disgust and distaste. What sort of young man, after all, raises the hopes of a girl so wantonly? Certainly, while she could be polite, she could never again be favorably disposed to so careless a fellow.

At least her uncles had never heard of the whole miserable debacle. Aunt Lydia had discussed with her own husband whether she should inform her brothers of the business, but he counseled against it. "It is a five days' wonder and will be forgotten as soon as you are gone from Edinburgh."

By the time they had spent a happy six weeks on Loch

Katrine, Mrs. Macdonald was entirely in charity with her niece and had no wish to dredge up an experience that had been deeply unpleasant, albeit salutary.

Initially, of course, Rosamund had no reason to believe that she would even be called upon to be polite to Mr. Buchanan ever again. She never thought to see him after their parting in Edinburgh. But she had not counted on Colonel Fitzgerald's inheriting Brackenbury Park, the estate lying to the east of Cheveley, which passed to him through a cousin on his mother's side quite unexpectedly. Naturally, the colonel, on leave from the wars in Spain and Portugal, came to inspect his new property, a property that offered him the prospect of giving up soldiering altogether. And naturally enough, he was accompanied by two of his subordinates also on leave and heading northward, namely Captain Macdonald and the recently promoted Captain Buchanan, who had distinguished himself on the field.

Brackenbury Park had been neglected by the colonel's distant cousin. While Captain Buchanan was quite happy to bivouac in the somewhat uncomfortable surroundings despite the chill of the January nights, Captain Macdonald, knowing he could presume on the relationship with his sister-in-law's brothers, sent a note over to Cheveley soon after arriving in Yorkshire, conscious that even the simple task of caring for Colonel Fitzgerald was straining the resources of Brackenbury Park to breaking point.

The captain was welcomed with great warmth by Leonard and Anthony Veasey, for their business interests all over Europe were in jeopardy with every expansion of the empire built by the Corsican Brigand. They regarded with gratitude and admiration all members of the army that Wellesley was building in the Iberian Peninsula and were delighted to be given the opportunity to demonstrate that gratitude at first hand. Naturally, they were swift to invite the colonel and his fellow officer to take their dinners at Cheveley, since the kitchens at Brackenbury were in a rackety condition.

As an aide to the regimental quartermaster, Captain Macdonald had been away from Edinburgh at the time of Rosamund's great shame, and though he had heard a little of the affair of honor between the lieutenants Buchan and Buchanan, had never been a man interested by what he regarded as petty gossip and the trifling matters of young cubs. He had greeted Rosamund with a bluff comment that Hector Fleming had been a fool not to snap her up and entirely neglected to mention Buchanan's name when requesting two seats at the Cheveley dining table. Similarly, he simply mentioned to Fitzgerald that his sister-in-law's brother would be delighted to make the acquaintance of a new neighbor without any mention of the girl who had graced Edinburgh society two years previously.

Rosamund was late down, unusually, when Colonel Fitzgerald and Captain Buchanan were announced and shown into Leonard Veasey's comfortable library. The fire crackled and spat in the grate, the lamps were lit and Captain Macdonald was nursing a glass of claret while conversing with Mr. Anthony Veasey about a certain prospect in the steeplechase meet taking place that very week. Hero was seated beside her father, looking about rather anxiously for Rosamund, who was normally most prompt especially when there were visitors. Both gentlemen were very tall and very smart in their uniforms to be sure, and at least they had come without their sabers, which did tend to make Hero feel a little uncomfortable, and Uncle Anthony was very prompt to engage them in his discussion about some sweet-goer or other while Papa poured out more wine. Uncle Anthony had talked Papa into allowing her to join the adults at supper, for Miss Forster, who normally served as Rosamund's chaperone on such occasions, was confined to her bed with a chill, and it would not be right to have Rosamund dining alone with the menfolk, nor would it be right to send them away without any supper. Rosamund had offered to eat on a tray upstairs with Hero, allowing the gentlemen the dinner table to themselves, but such a prospect made Leonard Veasey feel uncomfortable, for he relied on Rosamund to direct the household and it would have been far more tiresome to be required to take on that role than to allow Hero a little foray into society, even if she was a mere fourteen years of age.

Captain Buchanan was quite at home by the time the library door opened again and Rosamund stepped into the room. Of course, the gentlemen all looked up at the sound of the latch. Her smile was warm and her eyes sparkled with mirth as she bounced up to her Uncle Anthony and greeted him.

"My apologies, I have been calming down Cook, who is all of aflutter tonight. I am not entirely sure why, except that it has something to do with morels and chanterelles, which I believe are varieties of mushroom. She was being very scathing about that book of receipts you brought for us, dear Uncle."

"There's no pleasing the woman. She asks for books to extend her repertoire, then flies up into the boughs at the insult offered if you present her with such articles." Anthony turned to his brother. "If she weren't such a genius, I'd advise you to send her packing, but you cannot, of course."

"Rosamund, you know Colonel Fitzgerald, I believe." Leonard paid no mind to his brother, intent as he was on the formalities. Rosamund held out her hand to the colonel and curtsied. "How delightful . . ." She faltered as she bobbed up and his companion caught her eye. "To see you again, sir. And how lovely to have you as our neighbor."

"Miss Lovelace. I believe you also know Captain Buchanan."

"I do indeed. Congratulations, sir, you have risen in the ranks since we last met." She bobbed at him and then turned to Captain Macdonald. "You might have explained that it was Captain Buchanan sharing such uncomfortable quarters with the colonel. He was kind enough to dance with me on more than one occasion when I was in Edinburgh."

"I had forgotten entirely that you were acquainted. My apologies." The captain bowed toward both parties, giving Rory time to recover from the shock of seeing Miss Lovelace so unexpectedly. Except that the shock was not entirely wearing off. In fact, it was not wearing off at all. He felt as though he'd taken a bullet in the shoulder. She had struck him as a fine-looking girl, certainly, with the promise of real beauty. But he had never expected to encounter such beauty. Her hair was a rich toffee color, her skin creamy and flawless, her nose straight, her figure elegant and neat. She wore blue, a vivid ultramarine the color of a sky by Titian, and she glowed with warmth and health and vivacity.

He was so caught up in her appearance that he forgot entirely to respond to her congratulations. The colonel laughed. "It looks as though Buchanan too has forgotten he was acquainted with you, though how he could forget so charming an acquaintance, I am not sure. It makes me question my judgment in advancing his promotion."

"Fortunately, forgetfulness where women are concerned cannot be held a fault on the battlefield. I am sure that the captain has many qualities which merit his promotion, even if he has lapsed so far as to forget me."

"I could never forget so charming and so lively a lady as Miss Lovelace. She was the belle of the season in Edinburgh."

Rosamund had hoped that he would not mention her time in Edinburgh. There was something in the tone of his voice as he spoke the word *belle* that aroused her darkest fear, that somehow her uncles would hear that she had behaved with deep impropriety while away. For if they heard of her conduct, they would surely bar poor Hero from visiting Aunt Lydia, and that would dash her hope of meeting anyone out of the ordinary. Cheveley might well be the loveliest spot in Yorkshire, but it was sparsely furnished with suitors for a shy child like Hero.

Perhaps she might at some point draw the captain aside and point out that her uncles were unaware of her disgrace and that it could only bring them sorrow to discover it now, nearly two years, well then, eighteen months, after the event.

"How long is it until we sit down, Rosamund?" asked Leonard.

"We may go through as soon as you are ready, Uncle." Rosamund went over to the colonel. "Will you escort me in, sir? And Captain Macdonald, if you will lead Hero, and then Captain Buchanan may follow." Neatly, she satisfied Leonard Veasey's longing for fine manners and proper address while still conveying an elegant but comfortable informality with the guests.

The party moved through to the dining room, Rory Buchanan bringing up the rear and wondering what this evening would bring. He had been ready to desert Colonel Fitzgerald for a foray north to visit his own family. But now he had seen Miss Lovelace again, the attractions of remaining in Yorkshire to assist his senior officer in setting Brackenbury Park to rights had amplified considerably.

FIVE

The dining room was Rosamund's favorite room at Cheveley. The house was commodious but not stately, and the dining room seemed to epitomize the heart of the house. The table there was a round one that could be extended with leaves to seat up to twenty, but more usually allowed six or eight people to sit down in friendly proximity. There was a magnificent sideboard of oak, on which sat a great silver epergne and other finery, but Leonard Veasey preferred a setting with as little frippery, as he called it, as possible. Captain Buchanan was struck by the elegant simplicity of the crystal and chinaware, by the high polish of the chairs and table, by the warmth imparted to the room by its red walls, on which hung cheerful paintings of Bacchus at his frolics and happy Dutchfolk swigging from tankards, singing and playing at cards. The air was pleasantly warm too, kept so by the neat fire burning in a fireplace graced with a delightful mantel of white marble with a Grecian frieze displaying dancing ladies carved into it. It was a hospitable room, suggesting a hospitable family.

The guests were evenly spaced between the two brothers, with Colonel Fitzgerald seated between Leonard Veasey and Rosamund, at whose right was seated Captain

Macdonald, then Anthony Veasey, Hero next to her uncle and Captain Buchanan between the girl and her father.

Ebullient as ever, it was Anthony Veasey who led the conversation, demanding to know all about the hunting in Portugal, which he had heard was as good as one of the Leicestershire runs, scoffing at the Scots' insistence that deer-stalking was a far superior sport to chasing foxes and waxing enthusiastic about the shooting to be had at Cheveley.

Leonard spoke up. "Gentlemen, come tomorrow! We'll take you out and you shall see that our coverts are second to none."

"An excellent notion, Uncle," said Rosamund, "for we're eating the last of the partridge now and if you can bag eight or nine birds, the colonel may take some over to Brackenbury."

"I hope one day to return the favor, once I have sorted out my own coverts," said Fitzgerald. "This is one area in which I hope to put Captain Buchanan to work. His family has the finest shoot in Scotland. I must say, there is a great deal to do."

"Your cousin lived most retired. He scarcely came out from one year's end to the next, and when he did, he demanded nothing and accepted nothing from his neighbors." Anthony looked down at his plate, unsure whether his tone had given away too much.

"My cousin was a cantankerous old fellow, as I understand it, although I never knew him myself. My family confesses itself quite astounded that he should have left me the property, and predict that it must be a poisoned chalice. But if you will lend me your assistance by recommending a good steward and keeping a neighborly eye on matters on the estate while I am back in Portugal, perhaps the estate will come round."

"You are returning to your regiment then?"

"He cannot resign his commission now," interjected Buchanan. "There are too few good men about; Wellesley cannot afford to lose such men as Colonel Fitzgerald, not while we remain in so defensive a position as we are now. The action we have seen has been inconclusive, and we must be ready to fight the French a good deal longer, I fear."

The gentlemen shook their heads but remembered the presence of the ladies and turned the conversation to less pressing matters, such as the entertainments to be had in the nearest local town, the frequency of assemblies and parties in private homes in the area, the best shopping and a source of servants.

"There you must inquire of Rosamund," said Leonard Veasey. "She's had the management of our household for over a year now, and a most creditable job she's done of it."

"Thank you, Uncle, but I couldn't have done it without the assistance of Mrs. Sowersby and Uncle Anthony, who have been my guides throughout. I defer to them when it comes to offering employment to reliable people."

"It must be a daunting prospect to take on a house like Cheveley at so young an age," said Captain Macdonald. "Mrs. Macdonald will be very impressed to hear this."

"I think it is less daunting because it has been my home for so long. I am simply learning how things go on, rather than having to initiate any new habits and practices."

"Still, it will be a good training for taking on your own residence. There's many a girl hasn't the first idea of how to bring order and comfort to a house, and many a marriage that suffers as a result." Having spoken, Anthony Veasey tucked into a dish of stuffed cabbage with veal.

"Mmmm. Delicious. Any man would be glad to have a wife able to offer a table as good as this. I hope you're learning from your cousin's example, Hero."

"Of course, Uncle," whispered the girl, overwhelmed by the eyes that were turned toward her. Rosamund came to her cousin's rescue.

"In all fairness, Uncle, Hero is more inclined to spend time on household management than I am."

"What is your preferred occupation, Miss Lovelace?"

"I'd have thought you would remember, Captain Buchanan, that I'm a flighty creature, more interested in dancing and novels than in pickling vegetables and making jam. I have learnt the ways of a competent housekeeper because I know that it will make my life more pleasant in the long run if I am not forever wondering whether I am being choused by my staff."

Buchanan surmised that Rosamund's sally was intended to ward off any adverse comment he might make about her. He was about to rebuff it but Captain Macdonald was refuting it with vigor. "Flighty! Novels! Why, my brother was astounded at the gaps that appeared in his library while you were staying with him in Edinburgh." He spoke across the table to Leonard Veasey. "Your niece was intent on discovering exactly why we like to call our city the Athens of the North. She waded her way through philosophers natural and moral, through tomes concerned with matters of national economy and governance, through the works of the great Greeks and I know not what else. I was sworn to secrecy when I was told this, in case the lass should be mistaken for one of those Bas-Bleu types of forty years past."

"Now my dark secret is out, Captain Macdonald, and you must pay a forfeit. I happen to know you've the finest tenor in Scotland and I must beg you will share it with us in a ballad or two after dinner."

Having turned the conversation immediately, Rosamund engaged the company in a fervent discussion about the best new songs, but Buchanan was intrigued by Macdonald's revelation and determined that he would test the intriguing Miss Lovelace's interest in intellectual matters.

Rory Buchanan's penetrating gaze made Rosamund feel decidedly uncomfortable. It was bad enough that he should have fetched up on her doorstep; the last thing she wished was to excite his notice. While she no longer felt the resentment that had tolled the death knell for her affection toward Buchanan, the possibility of arousing his attention was not one she could face with any equanimity. Still, he would shortly leave the area, she was sure.

The evening passed off calmly enough, the gentlemen forgoing their port for the chance to hear some fine singing from Captain Macdonald and, it turned out, Miss Hero Veasey, whose singing voice was far stronger than her speaking one. Singing was Hero's real passion, and when fully absorbed by a song, her eyes sparkled with enthusiasm and her sometimes bland features took on great animation, to the delight of all those who cared for her. Rosamund was happy to provide accompaniment on the pianoforte and displayed a real gift in allowing the singer to shine at his or her own pace. Her repertoire was extensive and she cajoled the entire company into singing together, to their mutual delight and entertainment.

After a final bite of supper, Colonel Fitzgerald and his companion set off for Brackenbury Park. It was a cold night, and their lack of familiarity with the road forced them to ride slowly. They were both weary and chilled to the bone by the time they reached the Park and bade each other goodnight as soon as they got in.

"I ordered fires for both of our rooms. Seek me out if none has been lit," commanded the colonel. "This confounded place is at sixes and sevens, but there may be hope if they can follow a simple order to keep our chambers warm."

Rory retired to his chamber, where he found, to his relief, that a fire had been burning all evening. The room could not be said to be warm, but it was not freezing. He unbuttoned his tunic, kicked off his boots and looked longingly at the bottle on the mantelpiece, beside which sat a crystal tumbler he had lovingly carried around Portugal. The amber liquid in the bottle beckoned him, a potent reminder of home and his irascible father. He went to the table, uncorked the bottle and poured himself a scant finger into the glass. Then he went to the wing chair by the fire and sat, holding the glass and gazing into the flames. Finally, he raised the glass to his nostrils and inhaled the scent of the whiskey. A smile softened his features. The soft, oaky smell transported him straight to the whitewashed outhouses where his father supervised the distilling of the barley from their fields. Then he sipped and allowed the flavors of smoke and peat to roll round his mouth and the sting of the spirit to numb his taste buds. He wished that more could be numbed too. If he had been a less scrupulous man, he could be embracing an armful of Rosamund Lovelace at this very moment instead of wishing that he had her in his bed. But children fresh out of the nursery had never been to his taste. Now it looked as though he had missed his chance with a woman who promised to be all that a man might desire. She had thrown veiled, pointed glances his way all evening long, making it abundantly clear that she regarded him as negligible, untrustworthy, unsafe. A trifler.

It was unjust. Since Emily Gillespie, he had been too busy for dalliance and too fastidious to join his fellow officers in the stews of Lisbon. If the truth were known, his stomach had been turned by the casual looting and rapine that seemed to be part and parcel of soldiering. It was scant comfort to know that his revulsion was shared by Wellesley, for few enough seemed prepared to control their men and all too many of the British officers appeared quite ready to condone it. He had never considered himself straitlaced, but he balked at the outright theft and pillage that was conducted by enlisted men and officers alike.

It was strange to be back in Britain, to be in civilized territory again, untouched by the terrors of war. Fitzgerald had every reason to resign his commission and concern himself only with the estate he had unexpectedly received. But to Rory's relief, his colonel had stated quite clearly that while Brackenbury Park and its lands needed some stewardship, he himself was not prepared to renounce the fight against Bonaparte and his generals. Inheriting the estate seemed to have firmed the colonel's resolve. It was for the peace and tranquility of such oases as Brackenbury that they were fighting. It was for solid men of business such as the Veasey brothers and innocent children like Hero Veasey and maidens of Rosamund's age. It was for the survival of Britain.

Like many Scots, Rory's family had had close ties with France, but the Auld Alliance had been whittled away by the opportunities offered by the growing ties between

England and Scotland, by the wilder excesses of the
French Revolution, by the power-crazed landgrab that
Bonaparte and all his hangers-on had indulged in throughout Europe. Whether there was any hope of defeating him,
Rory was not so sure. But the French were making mis-
takes enough in Spain and Portugal. Rory looked at his
tumbler, now drained. He could fill it again and drink
again, but it would alter nothing. He had temporarily
cleared his brain of the charm placed on it by Miss
Lovelace, only to replace it with the specter of a prolonged
war that would consume resources and men with a relent-
less hunger. Well, tomorrow he would enjoy shooting at
the Veaseys' birds, and thereafter he would take whatever
pleasure he could until it was time to return to his post, his
duty and a life that seemed strangely remote but was full
of purpose.

Colonel Fitzgerald and Rory Buchanan rose early. It was
still dark as they rode to Cheveley, but by the time they had
breakfasted there, the sky had lightened and the first birds
were singing in the walled garden to the south of the house.
The beaters and gun carriers had gone ahead with the game-
keeper and were waiting for the Veasey brothers and their
guests on the edge of the moorland, past the woods to the
southeast of the house. It took twenty minutes to walk there
across the frost-encrusted lawn that crackled underfoot and
through the stands of beech, sycamore and birch, the trees'
branches glinting in the sunlight, occasional autumnal leaves
captured, shimmering with crystals. The sun was watery behind a thin layer of mist and the air was fresh and crisp, a
glorious morning. Finally, the wood thinned and the party
swished through brown curled fronds of bracken until they
were treading on springy heather and brushing aside dense
gorse. The Veaseys were sensibly togged out in heavy jackets

and moleskin trousers, and the military men were in their regular uniforms, layered with undershirts and woolens. The chill of the February morning nevertheless seeped through the cloth to the skin and bone beneath, encouraging the men to keep up a good pace until they reached the clearing where eleven or twelve men awaited, accompanied by two springer spaniels and a pointer.

Fine weather, congenial company and the excellence of the dogs combined to make the morning's shooting truly memorable for all the gentlemen. They returned to the clearing where they had started the day's work to find a dog cart had been sent from the house with food and ale for all the company, with a couple of bottles of an excellent burgundy for those who preferred wine. As the hampers were being unpacked, there was a distant thunder of hooves. Leonard Veasey looked up and turned to his brother.

"Sounds like Rosamund's mount. She'll want to see what we've bagged and check that our lunch is sufficient."

Sure enough, Miss Lovelace appeared in the distance, keeping her mount at a steady canter, then slowing down the bay gelding gently as she neared the clump of men. She was accompanied by a groom, to the Veasey brothers' satisfaction, and wore a stunning habit of bottle green, to Rory Buchanan's pleasure. She had a sure seat, a steady pair of hands, and a delicate little hat with a shimmering green feather and a little veil. One of the men took the reins of her horse, and she held out her hands to her Uncle Anthony and delicately dismounted from her sidesaddle with an elegant swish of petticoat and redingote. Her cheeks were pink, her eyes danced with relish for the day and there was a delightful spring to her step. Again, she caused in Rory Buchanan a sudden, unaccountable loss of breath, a distinct thump of sensation in the pit of his stomach. Quite out of nowhere came the desire to place a hand at her waist and feel the warmth of her close to him, a wish for the right to drop a kiss on that smooth patch of skin just under her left ear, a longing to feel the warmth of her breath against his skin. He stepped back and shook his head to clear the dizziness that had overcome him so unexpectedly at the sight of her. He turned away and missed her glance, the glance that took in his withdrawal and dimmed the pleasure that had animated her features.

"Did you have a good morning?"

"We certainly did," replied Colonel Fitzgerald, going forward to kiss Rosamund's hand in greeting. Then he tucked her gloved hand in the crook of his elbow and led her over to the mound of feathers and flesh they had amassed. Rosamund nodded and turned away swiftly.

"It is silly, being born and bred in the country, but the sight of the corpses always makes me feel a melancholy. I know we shall have good eating from this morning's work, and we shall use the down for stuffing quilts, but they do look mournful."

"It is true, an excess of sensibility serves one ill in a rural setting. One needs to be both pragmatic and phlegmatic." Rory was aware that he sounded as though he were offering censure, but that was not his intention.

"You must think me ridiculous. It may not be delicate to speak of it, but I am sure that you will have seen sights that make this poor mound of fowl seem very mild."

"Not remotely ridiculous, Miss Lovelace." But Rory could see that he had not convinced her of his sincerity. She remained only long enough to establish that the gentlemen proposed to walk back to the house the long way round, taking them past the pond occupied by numerous waterfowl.

"I do not promise that we will bag you a brace of duck, but we shall try. Then we shall have a fine meal. Our cook is particularly good with duck," promised Leonard Veasey, rubbing his hands in anticipation. He led his niece back to her neat bay horse and helped her mount.

The Veaseys were deep in consultation with their game-keeper about the likelihood of shooting duck. Captain Macdonald came over to Buchanan and watched with him as Rosamund disappeared over the horizon.

"She's a fine catch. Quite the heiress, some wit beneath the hair and a welcoming air about her."

"Do you think to try your luck with her?"

"Not me. I still have hopes of my Catriona. Another year or two of savings, some decent booty and some success on the part of my brother's company and I shall finally be able to offer her something worth having."

"A good Scottish girl, with patience and fiery red hair."

"Aye. But Miss Lovelace is a fine-looking creature. And my brother was very keen to see Hector Fleming bring her money into the firm. Still, Fleming's found another prospect, and a less flashy piece, a girl who'll suit him and his quiet ways far better."

"Flashy? What makes you think I have any desire for a 'flashy' heiress, Macdonald?" Macdonald's comment somewhat baffled Rory.

"Oh, I don't mean vulgar or loud. But she's a fetch-ing figure of a woman, bound to catch the eye of other men. Well, my taste is questionable, I am told. The women I admire never seem to hold much appeal for my fellow men. Take Catriona—she is not widely regarded as a beauty, yet I have never seen the woman who could hold a candle to her. People tell me her face is too round and her eyes too long or her nose too short. She does not conform to a general standard of beauty, where Miss Lovelace is at the pinnacle of those standards."

"Beauty is not merely a matter of appearance, though, Macdonald. I believe that Miss Lovelace would be far less lovely if she were less vivacious and intelligent. She is animated and engaged with the world."

"Exactly my point, Buchanan. This is where your opportunity lies. Miss Lovelace's intelligence and liveliness will seem excessive to many. She will never be a complaisant, calm creature, content to remain quietly at home producing heirs. She is the sort of woman who must be out and about in the world, who will wish to cut a dash and take her place in society."

While this statement did not ring true to Rory, he was not able to pursue the discussion further as the Veasey brothers approached and led them toward the pond where the ducks might be found. The men were successful in their aim and returned to the house laden with two brace of ducks in addition to all the pheasant and partridge they had bagged.

It was inevitable that the Veaseys should invite Colonel Fitzgerald to join in the feast that he and his subordinate had helped to create. As they were walking back toward the house, Anthony Veasey was extolling his elder niece's qualities.

"Without Rosamund, we should never have had so fine a table, you know. She has fostered our cook as a farmer might foster a lamb, ensuring that the woman gets the finest ingredients and uses them well. She has found French recipes and translated them into English, sat in the kitchen with the staff supervising the outcome, and now I believe I can say that here at Cheveley, we have the most delicious table the length and breadth of our isles. Of course, I don't know how it is in the fine houses of London, but I hear there is a fashion for importing cooks from the Continent, which I can only deplore."

"I believe that however much we war with the French, sir, we shall always follow their lead in food, fashion and folly, sir, for we always seem to believe that everything good comes out of Paris."

Colonel Fitzgerald caught up with the two men in time to overhear Rory's comment. "True enough. You remember how it was six or seven years ago now, as soon as peace had been declared, we were all rushing to cut a dash in France, and I daresay it will be the same the next time the fighting finally stops." Then Fitzgerald drew aside his subordinate officer, allowing Macdonald and the Veasey brothers to walk on ahead.

"Hold back a little, Buchanan."

The two soldiers dawdled a little, seeming to admire the prospect of the moorland and the high, clear sky, streaked only with herringbone clouds.

"What's your opinion of Miss Lovelace, Buchanan?"

"When Macdonald asked me the same thing, I told him I thought she was a very fine young lady. He tells me she comes with a tidy fortune."

"So I hear. I wonder whether she'd look at a grizzled old campaigner like myself."

Rory looked in disbelief at his superior officer. The colonel was renowned for his dapper appearance. His hair was still abundant and dark; his face was largely unlined apart from a few creases about his eyes. All in all, he presented a most attractive prospect, a prospect considerably more enticing what with two fortunes, the one acquired as part of the spoils of war, the other inherited and in the form of that most acceptable indicator of status, land. But the other cause for astonishment was the idea of anyone else having an interest in Miss Lovelace. Fitzgerald's words brought home to Rory just how proprietorially he had come to regard her.

"Well, Buchanan? What do you say?"

"Any lady who attracted your attention would be fortunate, sir."

"Flattery is no substitute for a straight answer. Do you think I have a chance with Miss Lovelace?"

"You are so taken with her?" Rory strove to buy himself some time. He could not answer for Miss Lovelace, but he was certain that he did not want the colonel to pursue this line of questioning.

"I am. She's a lovely girl, charming to the eye and the ear, endowed with fortune, breeding and intelligence. What man would not want her?"

"I'm surprised you should trust me to answer you honestly, sir. What if I wanted her for myself? I should be sure to discourage your interest in her."

Fitzgerald glanced at Rory, then laughed. "You are a serving officer under my command. I should be able to trust you implicitly."

Rory was not sure that this was entirely true. He pondered for a moment, biting at his lip, his gaze lowered toward the ground.

"Speak, Buchanan. Why do you pause?"

Rory inhaled deeply and stopped walking. His decision was made. "Sir, I have a story to relate about Miss Lovelace which perhaps you should know before you express any further interest in her. I cannot say whether she has altered in her affections or her character since the events which I shall relate to you."

The colonel listened, impassive and intent, as Rory told

in a few succinct sentences his dealings with Miss Lovelace two summers previously. At first, the colonel was incredulous.

"Miss Lovelace! Such a flirt! Impossible." But as the tale unfolded, Fitzgerald shook his head and hemmed and hawed. "I suppose she was only a child. Sixteen summers or so. Finally, I get to the bottom of the ill feeling between you and Buchan. I knew there was a jade in it, but Miss Lovelace! Well!"

The two men stirred themselves, realizing that they had been left behind by their companions. Pacing sturdily on, they made their way back to Cheveley, the colonel relieved at his narrow escape, Rory Buchanan feeling at once ashamed and delighted that his story had acted as sufficient deterrent for the colonel to abandon any notion of wooing Miss Lovelace.

SIX

Back in the housekeeper's study, Rosamund was discussing with Mrs. Sowersby the possibility that the military gentlemen would be visiting Cheveley at regular intervals for at least another month. As she left Mrs. Sowersby, Rosamund recognized that apprehension was her predominant reaction to the arrival in the neighborhood of Colonel Fitzgerald and his satraps. She found Rory Buchanan as enticing as ever. His fair, unruly hair, his direct blue eyes, his upright carriage and perpetually amused expression were as compelling as they had been two summers since. But he had made it clear then and he continued to make it clear now that he had no interest or time for dalliance, let alone anything more serious. In addition, his presence was a constant menace, threatening her with the exposure of her immoderate conduct in Edinburgh.

Of course, no gentleman would ever expose a lady who had written so compromising and ill-considered a letter. He had done as a gentleman should and returned the letter to her. She had destroyed the letter. There was no proof of her misdemeanor. But still, Rosamund could not quell a sense of unease and discomfort. She would do her best to make the colonel and his two captains welcome, but the sooner they were on the way north or overseas, the better.

It did not cross Rosamund's mind to entertain the colonel or Captain Macdonald as prospective suitors. She was not the sort to view every single male who came into her orbit as a potential spouse. Since her season in Edinburgh, she had calmed down a good deal, as one would have expected, but she had also had the opportunity to observe young couples in the locality of Cheveley, to weigh up whether marriage was truly the only ambition a young lady should entertain. If asked directly, she would have identified Hero immediately as a girl intended to be a wife, simple, pure, loving and good. But when she considered herself in all honesty, Rosamund would have described herself as having an odd kick to her gallop. Otherwise, what could have prevailed upon her to write to Rory Buchanan in the first place? She was not wise, warm or affectionate. She would admit to wit, learning and loyalty, but she had little tolerance for the foibles of others and gave short shrift to fools. So far, most men she had encountered had been either fools or fribbles.

Sometimes even the Veaseys wore Rosamund down. Her uncles and her cousin were her only family, but every now and then, in the depths of winter in particular, when she saw no one else for ten days or a fortnight, her patience was strained to breaking point by Uncle Leonard's fussiness, Hero's vacillations and Uncle Anthony's blunt manner. Her only escape had been books, sent to her in great mounds by Hatchard's of Piccadilly. Leonard and Anthony might tut and fuss about her desire to fill her head with ideas, but she spent her own money on this indulgence and of all the things she might have chosen to spend her money on, it was the least easily criticized.

Rosamund wondered from time to time about the future. She could not in all honesty imagine accepting an offer of marriage. It was after all quite comfortable to care for her Uncle Leonard, and it was certain that Hero would be wooed and won by someone suitable within four or five years, leaving Rosamund in sole charge of Cheveley. While Cheveley would eventually go to Hero on Uncle Leonard's death, Rosamund was sure that as a maiden aunt with a substantial fortune to confer unencumbered on nieces and nephews, she would be encouraged to make her home there so long as she found convenient.

There were alternatives. A competence of three thousand a year would allow her to cut a considerable dash in the capital if she so wished. Her real desire was to find a traveling companion and take herself abroad. How delightful it would be to see the remains of the Roman Empire and Republic, or the oracle at Delphi, or the place where Alexander of Macedonia had tamed Bucephalus and learned his lessons from Demosthenes. But even if she had not been encumbered with tiresome relations who would strenuously object to such gallivanting, there was Napoleon to consider and his stranglehold on the Continent.

Which brought her thoughts neatly back to Colonel Fitzgerald and his two officers. As she entered the music room, where Hero was rounding off her daily practice, Rosamund readied herself for a thorough dissection of the gentlemen's visit, for Hero, unlike her cousin, always thought of the romantic potential of those she met, whatever their sex. Her great object in life was to find herself a mate and to see those around her suitably paired off, for she thought that only through marriage could her fellow humans achieve true happiness. She weighed every prospect, considering suitable ladies to attract Uncle Anthony or her own father, evaluating the local youths and their worthiness of the serving maids at Cheveley, building great character studies of the sort of man who might entice Rosamund out of her devotion to spinsterhood and dreaming of her own beau idéal. She ceased her singing as soon as Rosamund came in, leaped up and hauled her cousin across to a love seat beside the window.

"Aren't they charming? Captain Macdonald is very charming, and the colonel had eyes for no one but you, dear Rosamund."

"The colonel!" Rosamund was taken aback, having expected to fend off questions about Captain Buchanan.

"Did you not notice how he watched you throughout dinner? He is a little older and must be wiser than the normal run of men, and he told such jolly tales. Why, what a delightful neighbor he must make."

"Hold fire, Hero. According to Captain Buchanan, he must return to Portugal in weeks. He will not take up his residence at Brackenbury before Napoleon is routed."

"Nonsense. Papa must ensure that he is invited to all the assemblies before he's due to leave, and you must get him to dance with you and take you into supper and it will be settled before the spring. He *should* resign his commission and care for his land. He would do just as much good as ever he could in the army."

"But I should not care for a man who deserted his post for a pretty face."

Hero sighed. "You are so difficult to please, Ros. How shall we ever find a decent husband for you when you pass up every opportunity to secure a man who would suit you?" She took her cousin's hand and played with it sulkily. "I cannot begin to seek out a suitor for myself until you are safely stowed."

Rosamund rolled her eyes at her cousin. "You are fourteen, Hero, not yet out, still less left on the shelf. Besides,

I am hardly at my last prayers." She suppressed the urge to
shake Hero. "I am certainly not hanging out for a man
twenty years my senior."

"He's not grave at all, Ros. But I suppose if you cannot
like him there is no point in nagging at you. You always do
exactly the opposite of what one wants when you are
nagged."

Rosamund laughed, surprised that her cousin was so observant, and a little amused to be found out. "I don't strive
to be contrary. It just seems to happen. Do you forgive me?"

Hero leaned her head against Rosamund's shoulder.
"You know I do. And I know you are right, really. You are
still quite young, and I don't suppose it really matters if I
am married before you."

"Of course it doesn't matter. Even if we were sisters, it
wouldn't make the slightest difference. Uncle Leonard is
not like that fellow in *The Taming of the Shrew* who would
not allow poor Bianca to marry before he'd disposed of the
tempestuous Katarina. I am not sure he wishes either of us
to marry in any case. It might suit him best to have us all
about him forever."

"Not if we could find a suitable wife for him. They say
a lady of older years is moving into Greenbriar. Perhaps
she will prove just the one to entice him."

Rosamund shook her head at how easily her cousin had
taken the bait and was now busily scheming to visit the
newly arrived widow and introduce her to Leonard Veasey
as soon as it could be decently achieved. Rosamund was
to take them both in the dogcart the very next day, and if
the lady proved suitable and amenable, why, the nuptials
might be celebrated before Easter.

That evening, Rosamund watched the colonel carefully,
but he seemed if anything a little withdrawn and not in the

least inclined to watch her every move with any appearance of interest. She thought that Hero must have mistaken Fitzgerald's pleasure in a decent table and supportive neighbors for a more concentrated form of attention. In addition, she had to suppress a degree of disappointment that Captain Buchanan had chosen not to join them at Cheveley. He appeared to have caught a chill and preferred to remain in the warmth of his room at Brackenbury, even with a somewhat unpromising supper of cold mutton and potatoes instead of the famous duck. It was ridiculous to miss him; she was safer by far in his absence.

The next day, though, she encountered him while out riding. She had heard that the wife of one of Veasey's tenants was ailing after the birth of her fourth child, and wished to check that it would be acceptable before offering assistance. The local people were proud and independent, requiring a tactful approach when aid or what might be interpreted as charity were suggested. Accompanied by her groom, she had ridden over to the farm, noticing for the first time a distinct warmth in the sunshine and clumps of snowdrops and purple crocus beneath the trees, heralding the first inklings of spring. It was on her way back that she met Captain Buchanan, exercising his horse, a sturdy gray gelding that dwarfed her own neat bay.

"Take pity on a stranger to your area and show me a track where I may give Trojan a good gallop, Miss Lovelace."

Rosamund looked round at her groom, who she knew was anxious to return to his special charge, Hero's mount, who had a dodgy knee and required regular poultices.

"Jim, you may return home. Captain Buchanan will see me safely back to Cheveley. Send one of the boys up to the house to let them know I shall be a little delayed and ask Miss Hero to see about sending one of the scullery maids

over to Mrs. Allerton at North Farm." The groom nodded
and continued down the path toward the house, a couple of
miles distant.

Rosamund turned her mount down another track and
said, "This way, Captain Buchanan. I shall guide you onto
the ridge and then return home, for I have a good deal to
do this morning."

He followed her at once, delighting in the prospect of
watching her freely, admiring her firm seat and light
hands, remembering guiltily that he had broken a confidence in telling the colonel of her indiscretion. The track
widened until they could ride two abreast and he brought
his gray up to her mount.

"It is most spectacular country hereabouts." The scenery
must be an innocuous enough subject, thought Rory.

Rosamund smiled at him. "It is kind of you to say so, for
coming from Scotland, you are accustomed to perhaps the
most lovely countryside in Britain."

"It is true there are no great mountains, but the hills and
dales are charming and the moorland is handsome."

"Is it very different from Portugal? I cannot imagine
what that country must be like."

"I find it very bleak. Perhaps it is because we are in
search of the enemy and the local people have been looted
by the French. But it seems thoroughly impoverished. The
villages and towns are poor little whitewashed affairs hud-
dled on hilltops, and there are far fewer decent houses.
There seem to be palaces and hovels only, with little in between." Rory's mouth hardened as he recalled some of the
more vicious sights he had seen, the brutalities visited on
the Portuguese and Spanish by soldiers who theoretically
were civilized. Then, remembering he was addressing a
lady, he strove to make light of his time there. "But the

hunting is good and the wine is excellent. I shall suggest to Colonel Fitzgerald that he send over some of the white port. It is a most delicate and pleasant drink."

Rosamund was not deceived. "This war is like nothing else you have experienced. Aunt Lydia is most concerned for Captain Macdonald, for all the men fighting there. It seems likely that it will be a campaign which will last for years to come."

"We must defeat the French and that will indeed take time. There are few here who understand that, for so much seems to carry on as it did before."

"But it will be done?"

"It will be done, but at what cost, I cannot tell."

Both riders preserved a somber silence as Rosamund continued to lead Rory up to the moor and the stretches of land where he might give Trojan a decent run. Rory was feeling particularly glum. He knew now that he had been wrong in speaking to the colonel. Rosamund was no longer a thoughtless, flirtatious child and he had over-stepped the bounds of gentlemanly conduct in painting her as such to his commanding officer. But he could hardly confess his misdemeanor to her. Her next words made his position still more uncomfortable.

"I must thank you, Captain Buchanan, for keeping to yourself my foolish behavior in Edinburgh. I was a very silly child, and I fear my head was quite turned by my first visit to a substantial city. And perhaps," continued Rosamund, "by your bonny uniform."

"Older and wiser heads than yours have been swayed by a fellow in a smart red coat. But I think the whole business must have blown over before any of us were five leagues out of the city."

"I hope that may be the case. Hero is to go to Edinburgh

when she is sixteen, and I fear that society there may assume that she is as flighty and idiotic as her cousin was. I am sure that those MacTavish ladies will have long memories, or long enough."

"You need not fear. Miss MacTavish has left Edinburgh for a parsonage in Ayr, and her mother now travels between her three daughters, I daresay making each one thoroughly miserable for a space until it is time to move on again."

Rosamund smiled at the vision this conjured up. "It is kind of you to try to set my mind at rest. And I am quite sure that I will have been entirely forgotten by the time Hero visits Aunt Lydia. Still, the memory of my own idiocy is a mortification."

"I am surprised then that you have managed to welcome me at Cheveley with such equanimity."

"It has been hard, Captain Buchanan." Rosamund's mournful tone was belied by the twinkle in her eyes. "It has been difficult, but such are the trials that are sent to beset us. I am simply relieved to see that Hero does not find you quite so compelling as I did."

"Oh, Miss Lovelace, you wound me. Are you suggesting my charms have worn off?" These flirtatious words escaped Rory before he could master himself.

"Entirely, Captain Buchanan. I am impervious to your attractions. I have grown out of the notion that every man I meet in a red coat must be a pillar of chivalry. My heart no longer flutters at the sight of a shako or a little gold braiding. Of course, you still look very fine, but I believe I am immune to the military." By this time, they had climbed a considerable way, and now they were on the edge of a ridge of land below which it seemed that all of Yorkshire was spread for their delight.

"Oh, this is magnificent, Miss Lovelace. But once I've taken Trojan to the end, how do I return to Brackenbury?"

"Here the bridleway widens, but as you near the end of the ridge, it narrows and leads you back down the hillside. You will come to a stone wall, and you must head west from there. You descend into the valley and come to a mill. You cross the stream and then continue following it south-westward and eventually you will come to the eastern gates of Brackenbury Park. They have not been opened for many years now, but if you follow the walls round another hundred yards or so, you can take Trojan through a break in the wall and so find yourself in the parklands."

"It sounds fearfully complicated. Can I not prevail upon you to accompany me? It would set my mind at rest. I must confess that although it is not soldierly, I have no real sense of direction at all."

"Surely you can tell east from west?" Rosamund looked wistfully at the path along the top of the hill, conscious that her duties called her home but very tempted by the prospect of a good gallop.

Rory shook his head sorrowfully. "I find it very difficult." He hoped she would accompany him and was only slightly exaggerating his inability to find his way in strange places. Generally, he relied on his batman to guide him, for Easter-house was like a pointer when it came to tracking the way forward. Just as well he had never been a scout.

Rosamund made up her mind. "I should leave you to your own devices, but I shan't. It is the most glorious morning and I can tell my own Arcturus is as keen for a thorough run as I am."

"He's a fine fellow, but I daresay he will find it hard to keep up with Trojan." Rory's sally was deliberate. If he read Miss Lovelace right, she would never allow such a slight to her horseflesh to go unchallenged. Almost immediately, she bridled and responded.

"We shall see. Arcturus is nimble and carrying less weight. Shall we race?"

Accepting this challenge was indecorous, but she did not care. And nor did Captain Buchanan, content with his victory in keeping her by him. They each steadied their horses, glanced at each other and counted down from three. Trojan's initial start was certainly stronger than Arcturus's, but Miss Lovelace had spoken truly when she described him as nimble, and their knowledge of the terrain combined with the little bay's fleetness of foot had them steadily gaining ground on the large cavalry horse until they were riding neck and neck, Miss Lovelace's face buried in the mane of her mount, urging him forward with yells of encouragement. Slowly, steadily, Arcturus inched past Trojan until all Rory could see was the bay's tail streaming behind his pounding flanks.

Rosamund steered her horse round a gorse bush and began the incline down to the wall and the mill stream, the thunder of Trojan's hooves fading behind her. She slowed down Arcturus—there was no need for him to become windblown; the race was well and truly won by now, a Captain Buchanan would have to slow down to get his bearings and prevent his gelding from hurtling into the wall before them. She straightened in the saddle and laughed with exhilaration and excitement. She had not been ladylike, but what glorious fun! Arcturus's stride dwindled into a canter and then into a steady trot until horse and rider arrived at the millhouse, thoroughly stretched and relaxed from their exercise.

Unhooking her leg from the pommel, Rosamund slid down to the ground, pulled the reins over Arcturus's head and led him to the stream to drink a little water and crop idly at the grass. From the millhouse, a round-cheeked woman appeared with two small children hidden in her skirts.

"Miss Lovelace? Where's young Jim? Are you riding without a groom today? What will Mr. Veasey say?"

"I sent Jim home, Mrs. Jephcott. But I do have a companion; he will be here directly and if you have drinking vessels, he'll be in need of some water, as am I."

"Water! What nonsense. You'll have some of my tea and a bite of my moggie cake, sitting down in comfort in the parlor as befits a young lady. Who's this companion you talk of?"

Just then, Trojan came loping down the path, Captain Buchanan steady in his saddle. The captain patted the horse and climbed out of the saddle, leading him to the stream where Arcturus was still drinking.

"Here, let my two boys do that and the two of you come into the parlor and warm yourselves." Mrs. Jephcott gave a bellow. "Christopher! Timothy! Stir yourselves this instant." Obligingly, a pair of lanky boys emerged from an outbuilding and came to their mother. "See to these horses, boys; don't let 'em drink theirselves stupid."

Then Mrs. Jephcott bustled her two guests indoors, setting another child to lay a fire in the parlor and installing the lady and gentleman there. The girl, Sarah, struggled with the kindling and the tinderbox, so Rory dismissed her and took the task in hand himself. Soon, Rosamund was able to draw off her gloves and warm her hands at a tidy blaze in the grate while they heard Mrs. Jephcott in the distance harassing her children into assisting her and delivering judgments all the while on their competence, their attitude and their general usefulness.

Rory could not take his eyes off Rosamund. She stood, slim, straight and full of vitality by the fire, the flush of victory and the hard gallop still on her. He wanted to take her by the waist and hold her close and kiss her very hard. He stood by the window, feeling too large for the parlor, his arms crossed to prevent him from going over and touching her. She glanced toward him.

"You have led me quite astray, Captain. I was meant to return home immediately and perform innumerable tasks, but here I am, trapped into tea and cake."

"What forfeit will you demand of me?" He could not quell his desire to flirt with her. "Demand what you like; I am at your service."

"If only that were true, Captain Buchanan. But you are the sort who will say he is at another's service and do only what suits yourself."

"What a low opinion you have of me!" Just then, Mrs. Jephcott came in with her tray and a train of youthful assistants. She poured tea from a substantial teapot into clearly her best china cups, sliced a dark, heavy cake into chunks and presented it to the visitors on matching plates and urged them to use the sugar tongs.

"What lovely china, Mrs. Jephcott. I believe it is Wedgwood, from Stoke-on-Trent. Is that right?"

"Yes, Mr. Jephcott brought it home for me two years since, and I don't think you'll see finer, excepting of course in the big houses like Cheveley. There I daresay you have foreign stuff from France or Germany that is finer."

"Only very old things, Mrs. Jephcott, nothing quite so modern and pretty."

The miller's wife preened and removed herself and her children, saying as she went, "Now, seat yourselves, make yourselves comfortable. My boys will care for your horses for as long as you need."

She closed the door behind her to keep in the heat. Rory remained by the window, sipping at his tea. Rosamund sat herself in one of the two wheel-back chairs by the fire.

"Come, Captain, take a seat. You look most uncomfortable standing there."

Rory came forward and sat in the chair opposite Rosamund. He gazed down at the fire, now tenderly licking at a pair of logs in the grate. He took a mouthful of his cake and then another. If he ate and drank, perhaps he might keep his mouth sufficiently full that he would be prevented from saying anything foolish.

Rosamund broke off a piece of cake and popped it in her mouth. It would be easy enough to take umbrage at Captain Buchanan, who one moment flirted outrageously, then the next brooded and glowered. But that would simply be playing his game, and where the captain was concerned, she was not interested in playing games.

SEVEN

The silence between the pair in the miller's parlor deepened, seemed still more profound as it was broken only by the ticking of the carriage clock on the mantelpiece and the hiss and crackle of the fire below.

"Miss Lovelace, I must speak." Rory paused and Rosamund looked inquiringly at him. "You said that I was the sort to do only what served myself. This has been true. But you are making me see that I can and should change my ways."

Rosamund took another sip of tea before responding. "I am not sure I see how, Captain Buchanan."

"You have changed. You have become a most admirable young lady."

"Of course I have changed. I had a good deal to learn and still do. I am flattered that you consider me admirable, Captain, but I do not see how it affects me."

"I admire you as more than a person of accomplishment. I feel something deeper than admiration. I wish to follow your example, strive to become a better, wiser person." Rory smiled wryly. "The tables are turned. Once, it was you who saw me as a paragon. Now I wish to learn from your example."

"Well, I was a fool for suggesting that you were a

paragon, and I think it mighty uncomfortable to be considered one myself."

"I'm making a mull of this. Miss Lovelace, I am leaving for Scotland on the morrow, and I will not be returning this way before I go to Portugal. But might I write to you? Would you correspond with me?"

"I am wary of writing letters to a gentleman. I have done it once and it was not a success. But if you were to write in a spirit of friendship and should not be bored by mundane accounts of domesticity, it is not out of the realm of possibility that I should reply."

"No ardent declarations of passion then." Rory was a little disappointed.

"It is unkind of you to remind me of my past errors."

"I did not mean to—I was merely—you do it on purpose to wrongfoot me." He laughed as he met Rosamund's sparkling eyes. "I believe it is I who would now be making grand statements and you who would spurn them Friendship then."

He reached out for her hand, and she held hers out, expecting to shake his, but he took it and lifted it to his lips. She had taken off her gloves to drink her tea and eat her cake, so the swift, definite impression of his lips imprinted itself on her skin like a brand. She suppressed the urge to yank her hand out of his grasp but immediately reached for her gloves and drew them on.

"We really should be getting back."

"Yes. I to my packing and you to your duties." Rory pulled on his own gloves and they both went out to find their horses now rested and the focus of rivalry between the two boys, each extolling the virtues of the horse of which he was in special charge.

***

Rosamund did not see Captain Buchanan again before he left for Scotland. But a fortnight later, she received her first letter from him, one page neatly and narrowly written, describing the delights of his family home and the highlights of a cousin's wedding in full highland style. He mentioned that it would be best for her to write directly to Portugal, since he was shipping there in ten days.

Although Rosamund had no intention of hiding the correspondence from her family, it somehow did not come to anyone's attention. Generally, the post was brought to her every day and she sorted out those items her Uncle Leonard must deal with and the rest of the innumerable bills and issues of correspondence arising from the management of a house of any size. Leonard Veasey, being inclined to idleness and trusting his niece implicitly, was delighted to be relieved of the charge of going through bills for candles and string and sealing wax and all the other items so necessary to the smooth running of his home. Hero had no interest in the post unless it brought her one of the periodicals to which Rosamund subscribed or a letter from Aunt Lydia about life in Edinburgh.

Naturally, if the correspondence had come to anyone's attention, it might have caused raised eyebrows at the very least. A single gentleman did not customarily write letters to a single lady without there being some interest or attachment that ought really to have been publicly acknowledged somehow.

In her more honest moments, Rosamund knew that there was a significant interest on her part. She had gone from passionate adoration to loathing to a not entirely worthy desire to pay back the captain for his treatment of her and to make him regret that he had not loved her when she loved him. Initially, her letters were full of assemblies attended, dances, flirtations and picnics as the summer wore on and the admittedly limited social circle of Cheveley stretched to its fullest. But gradually, the real Rosamund asserted herself: her wry asides about the flaws of her suitors could not be suppressed, nor could her excitement about the latest books and ideas, her rage against the wrongs she perceived being done whether national or international, her longing to break out of the confines of life as led by the Veaseys, blameless, quiet and regular.

> *Uncle Leonard and Hero are quite happy cultivating their little patch, and I suppose I should be also, but the difficulty is that I do not feel that this is my little patch and so my interest in it is limited. It seems ridiculous to say such things of the place where one has been raised and found nothing but kindness and care, but at times, I feel that life at Cheveley is like living in a chamber where the air is gradually and steadily being pumped out. I daresay to you in the midst of campaigning, where matters of life and death are decided in an instant, my ramblings must be regarded as indulgent maundering, product of a tedious fortnight of steady rain and no outings. What a frivolous and light-minded creature this makes me sound.*

Of course, it took so long a while, weeks and sometimes months for their letters to cross, that often they were writing at cross-purposes. But a rhythm to their correspondence was eventually established, and Rory's letters of marches and skirmishes, inconclusive encounters with the enemy and the bitter hatred of the Spanish for their French occupiers did broaden Rosamund's horizons and made her better able to cope with the occasional tedium of life at Cheveley. He wrote succinctly and elegantly, and intermittently, between the jokes and the accounts of the idiocies of military life, began to express his own hopes for the future, for a return to his family acres in Scotland, the wish to help his father overcome the legacy of debt and mismanagement that had been left by his grandfather, and the fear of being killed before this could occur.

Over the course of a year, or eighteen months, a good deal can be revealed in letters that might otherwise have been concealed. So it was that Rory and Rosamund came to know each other, revealing to each other aspects of character and inclination that were generally hidden from onlookers and acquaintances. There was never any mention of any joint future. Both parties abided by the bargain they had struck in the millhouse, to act as friends, to share ideas and information, to ignore the normal restrictions placed about members of the opposite sex and to treat each other as equals. For Rosamund, it was a lifeline away from the pleasant but somewhat suffocating charms of her home; for Rory, it was a reminder of the world for which he soldiered. Neither was sentimentally inclined; each replied in robust terms to the other's plaints. The tone of their letters was comradely and practical, and at times Rory almost forgot he was writing to a woman, for Rosamund would discuss harvest yields and politics and increasingly, the cross-breeding of sheep, which the Veasey brothers seemed to consider an acceptable field of interest since it produced wool, which women must spin.

It did not occur to him to worry when Colonel Fitzgerald announced just before Christmas that he must return to Brackenbury Park for several months. He had quite forgotten that he had revealed to the colonel Rosamund's girlhood indiscretion. Naturally, the colonel was entirely

unaware that Rory had maintained any links with any of
the Veaseys.

The colonel had been to England and was on his way
back to Portugal by the time Rory received out of what had
seemed a clear blue sky the epistolary thunderbolt that left
him bereft and miserable.

Rosamund's letter was brief and to the point.

> *Sir,*
>
>   *I find that you have not kept secret what should
> never have been discussed and what would not have
> been told by any gentleman. I would be grateful if you
> could return to me any letters of mine you have kept.
> Yours to me I have consigned to the fire.*

Her signature beneath was so firm that the ink had sput-
tered with her vehemence. He returned that evening to
his lodgings. After a simple supper of garlic soup and red
wine, he took the box where he had kept her letters down
from its shelf, unlocked it and took out the bundle of letters. He counted them. Over twenty now, not quite thirty.
Initially just a page, then two, close written, neat, her
pretty handwriting reminding him of her pretty looks.

Now he must return them. To do anything else would be
to betray her trust still further. He wondered if he could
find some clerk to copy them out, a Spaniard who would
not be able to understand a word of them but would be able
to preserve for him their essence. But it would not be the
same as the faint whiff of lavender that clung to the sheets
she wrote on, he would no longer be able to see her bent
over a desk, scribbling in peace or in haste as Hero and
Uncle Leonard pottered on in their usual way.

That night, he reread her letters and tried to commit to

memory some of her livelier anecdotes and turns of phrase. He lamented that he was no draftsman and had never thought to get a likeness of her, though what good that would do him now that she was severing all ties, he could not imagine. He grieved that he had caused her pain, and even now he squirmed as he imagined her rage and discomfort. Of course, he should have confessed long ago to having revealed the secrets of that distant summer to the colonel, but he had put it off and then forgotten about it or felt that she was already too inconvenienced by the duties of her position. In short, he had evaded telling her and it had caught up with him now, just when he least wished to pay the price. Just when he was ready to go to Cheveley on his next leave and ask for her hand in marriage.

He packaged up the letters in brown paper and sealed the parcel, addressed it and tied it up with twine. Their route back to England would be lengthy and circuitous, compounding his sin in her eyes, he had no doubt. He wondered how Fitzgerald had revealed his indiscretion. Inadvertently, he was sure. Rory had done his best to conceal from everyone his correspondence with Rosamund and his growing attachment to her. He was already sufficiently teased by his fellow officers; he had no wish to lay himself open to continued interrogations as to the identity and the whereabouts of his beloved. For Rosamund was, he recognized even as she rejected him, his beloved.

Of course, by the time she received the packet of letters, Rosamund had calmed down considerably. The colonel had long gone, and she simply felt melancholy and baffled as to why Captain Buchanan had thought it necessary to reveal her folly.

The parcel was battered and salt-stained by the time it reached Cheveley, but intact and the seal unbroken. She took it up to her room and locked the door before sitting down with her embroidery scissors and snipping through the string. The paper crackled beneath her fingers as she unfolded the wrapper and saw another wrapper, tied with blue ribbon. She undid the bow and shook out the wrapper. Her letters tumbled into her lap. She looked at the sheet he had used to enclose her letters, but there was not a mark on it. What had she expected? What had she hoped for?

An abject and groveling apology was what she had hoped for, although she had not really expected it. Or even a word. Some sign that he was upset by her dictum that the correspondence should cease. Some acknowledgment of all they had shared in the two years since that breakneck ride to the mill, even though they had never set eyes on each other. Rosamund sat amidst the puddle of papers and could no longer contain a sob, followed by another and another until she was in full flow. She groped for a handkerchief and wiped her eyes eventually, then stacked up the letters and retied them with their blue ribbon. She went to her wardrobe and pulled out a neat mahogany box. She withdrew the key from round her neck and unlocked it. Within was a bundle of letters addressed to her in Captain Buchanan's clear, definite script. She picked up the packet but thrust it back in the box as though it burned, then dropped in the packet of her own letters, locked the box and shoved it back into the darkest recesses of the wardrobe. No good would come of rereading his letters now.

Checking her appearance in the mirror of her dressing table, Rosamund was relieved to see that all traces of her emotional storm had passed. It was nearly four years since she had first seen the captain, and now it was time to put all thoughts of him away from her. It would be unrealistic to expect to blot all memories of him from her mind, but such memories as she did have must be fleeting and swiftly discouraged. She had begun to think there might be something more, that the constant stream of letters cheerful and serious betokened some deeper connection, but the colonel's inadvertent admission that Buchanan had warned him off wooing Rosamund had put paid to that.

There had been talk of Rosamund's accompanying Hero to Edinburgh this year, to participate in a second Season there, but it soon became apparent that Uncle Leonard was not entirely well and she would be needed at Cheveley to manage when his arthritis flared up, so Hero was escorted north by Uncle Anthony. There were dances and picnics nonetheless, and Rosamund spent a cheerful enough summer, sharing happily Hero's letters from Scotland, which seemed increasingly full of a young officer by the name of Valentine Wemyss. There had been no formal offer by the time Hero returned to Cheveley, but the correspondence between the pair was open and acknowledged by his family and of course by the Veaseys and Macdonalds as earnest of the young couple's affections.

Lieutenant Wemyss did mention his fellow officers from time to time, including the exploits of one Captain Buchanan, who earned much respect from his fellows for his courage and common sense under fire and his tricks and jollity when taking his ease. But after three years of steady correspondence, young Wemyss's letters had been increasingly vague and erratic. This had caused Hero no little anxiety. Rosamund could not help wondering if the young lieutenant had come across some other eligible girl while seeing off Napoleon once and for all. There had been tales of glittering balls and all sorts of entertainment while Wellington's army was in the Low Countries, and these had only continued after the decisive battle of Waterloo.

Now, at last, the soldiers were returning, Colonel Fitzgerald would open Brackenbury Park fully and perhaps Hero might have the opportunity to pin down her lieutenant and extract an offer after all. The prospect of Hero's leaving Cheveley to set up her own home filled Rosamund with a curious mix of despondency and elation. When sharing tedious tasks, Hero's methodical mind and cheerful nature were a godsend, but if Hero were safely married off, what horizons might not open up to Rosamund? If the truth were told, her guidance was not strictly necessary to the running of Cheveley, for the butler and housekeeper might easily share the burden of correspondence between them, especially if Uncle Leonard could be prevailed on to employ some sensible young man as secretary to whom he might devolve the bulk of tasks currently undertaken by Rosamund.

Dangling before Rosamund was the prospect of accompanying her neighbors on a trip overseas. Mrs. Carmichael, the widow who had moved into Greenbriar in 1810, was now contemplating a trip abroad. She lived with a cousin and her young son, now fourteen, and while she had been happy to settle back in Yorkshire, the scene of her childhood, she was keen that young Daniel should see something of the world. She had been reluctant to send him away to school, for he was her only child, but this meant that he was a somewhat sheltered individual, his chief education coming from daily lessons with the local rector and, unofficially, from his exposure to Rosamund.

While Hero's grand plans for Uncle Leonard and Mrs. Carmichael had come to nothing—she was too devoted to the memory of her late husband, Mr. Veasey too idle to press his suit in anything more than a halfhearted manner—Rosamund had been very taken with the Carmichaels. When Daniel had come into the neighborhood, he had been a lively and scampish nine-year-old. Both Uncle Anthony and Rosamund made him something of a pet, for his intelligence was considerable, his manners charming and his spirit humorous and merry.

Inadvertently, on one of her earliest visits to Greenbriar, Rosamund had found herself discussing her favorite books and discovered with Mrs. Carmichael and Daniel a shared admiration for Montaigne. Having read his letters in translation, they made it a project one winter to read together his works in the original French, sharing the burden of unpicking the writer's meaning and discussing the rare ambiguities in his prose. Rosamund increasingly regarded Greenbriar as a refuge where she could explore the ideas and theories that truly interested her. Mrs. Carmichael encouraged Miss Lovelace, for she too had wrestled with dear relatives who did not entirely understand that the life of the mind was worth cultivating and exploring.

Five or six years on, Daniel had become a thoughtful and polite boy, deeply attached to his family and the Veasey household, and filled with an enthusiasm for antiquities fostered by both his tutor and Rosamund.

Now that the Corsican menace seemed finally tamed, Daniel had been pressing his mother to consider a trip abroad. Miss Johnstone, the cousin who acted as companion and housekeeper to Mrs. Carmichael, had no interest in foreign travel, but it was at Daniel's suggestion that Mrs. Carmichael thought to recruit Rosamund to her side. There was still planning to be done, but it was hoped that the party might set off in September, if the Veasey uncles could be brought to agree to it. Hero was the only sticking point, for she looked tearful at the slightest mention of losing her cousin to what she termed a tiresome collection of old monuments and foreign places. If she could be sufficiently occupied by plans for a wedding, she would surely raise no further objections to losing Rosamund for a space. Uncle Anthony's news of the imminent arrival of the Fitzgerald party brought succor to Rosamund's increasingly blighted hopes. Although what would happen if it proved that Lieutenant Wemyss was faithless and fickle, Rosamund did not wish to contemplate.

EIGHT

Although Hero was sometimes a little hesitant, even she could not resist the opportunity offered by a glorious April morning to ride along the moor on the way home from visiting Squire and Mrs. Allerton and more important, her great friend Caroline Allerton. Accompanied by Rosamund and the groom, she gamely spurred her docile mare to a canter and was looking flushed and vivacious when all three pulled up their mounts. Some way off, a horn was blowing and a great thunder of hooves seemed to be gathering in velocity and volume.

"It can't be a hunt. Uncle Anthony would have told us, and anyway, it's too late in the season." Rosamund urged Arcturus a little further on and craned up as far as she dared to try to see over the crest of the hill. The noise was getting louder and closer. She hauled her horse to a safer vantage point well out of the central section of the bridle path, leading Hero and the groom with her. Just as well, for mingling with the horn and the great pounding of the hooves of at least six animals were now the cries of men, she thought, and all of a sudden, the mass of great horses burst upon them—four, five, six, no, eight, or was it twelve, in formation, six out front, six behind, at full stretch, their riders upright in the saddle, bellowing and whirling sabers about their heads.

Rosamund had a time holding Arcturus back as the gray horses passed by them in a welter of dust and jingling saddlery, so she could not examine the riders too closely, receiving just an impression of red coats and light bouncing from the swords the soldiers were brandishing. But Hero squeaked out, "Valentine!" and waved furiously, jigging up and down in her saddle with excitement. It was just as well her Dolly was calm to the point of comatose or else the mare would have been bounced into a frenzy by Hero's delighted astonishment. The girls watched as the cavalry gradually disappeared, then eased their horses back onto the path and began trotting homeward. But behind them, more quietly, betokening only one or two horses, came the noise of hooves and someone calling out, "Stop! Stop, please!"

The Cheveley girls turned their horses round and watched as a young man approached, his shako removed, revealing sweat-dampened curls and hopeful, dancing dark eyes. "Hero! Miss Veasey! It was you I saw." He urged his horse over to her, and took her hand, bringing it to his lips. "How happy I am to see you, Miss Veasey. Colonel Fitzgerald promised we should meet again very soon, but I had not imagined that it would be as soon as we reached Brackenbury."

"Mr. Wemyss." Hero blushed and at a little cough, turned to Rosamund and presented her. "This is my cousin, Miss Lovelace."

Valentine bowed in the saddle at Rosamund. "How delighted I am to make your acquaintance. I have heard so much about you."

"Really?" inquired Rosamund coolly. "Who from?"

"Why, Miss Veasey, of course! Her letters have been full of Cousin Rosamund. And Uncle Anthony, and Mr. Veasey too, of course. I feel as though I know you all already, so clearly has Miss Veasey drawn you all. May I call on you at Cheveley very soon?"

Rosamund's discomfort at her own misunderstanding was easily subsumed by young Wemyss's enthusiasm. Her face lightened and she laughed. "We shall be delighted to see you there as soon as you wish to visit."

But her pleasure faded as she identified the rider following behind, sent back to guide Wemyss safely to Brackenbury. She stiffened as Captain Buchanan approached. She met his eyes and strove to appear unmoved. He broke the glance first, doffing his hat and dipping in his saddle at the ladies.

"Miss Lovelace. Miss Veasey. How good to make your acquaintance once again."

"Would that it were good for us, Captain."

Hero gasped at Rosamund's abrupt comment and Wemyss looked at Buchanan, raising a quizzical eyebrow.

"I shall strive to make it so, Miss Lovelace."

"Strive as hard as you may, I doubt that you will succeed. We have little patience here with pretty words when they are spoken by those with indiscreet tongues."

The captain winced and smiled. "My sins are unforgotten and unforgiven. Now I begin to understand the comparison between some women and granite. Unyielding and impervious."

"And I understand the comparison between some men and sugar. It may be sweet at first, but it sickens when taken to excess. We must get home, Hero. Good day to you, gentlemen. We shall look forward to your visit, Mr. Wemyss."

Rosamund spurred her horse away, followed by Hero and the groom calling after her to wait, to let them catch up, how could she be so . . .

* * *

Rory and Valentine watched them as they rode off toward Cheveley, waiting until the girls were out of sight before turning their own mounts back to Brackenbury.

"What sin have you committed, Buchanan? What a welcome!"

"In justice, I have given her ample cause to mislike me. I just did not imagine that war would be declared quite so vehemently and so promptly."

"War? And what will the spoils of the victor be, I wonder?"

"I believe like most wars, this one will end without any real victors and a good deal of woe on both sides."

"You'll come through, Buchanan, I have no doubt. But what do you think of my little Hero. Is she not delightful?"

"I last saw her when she was still a child. She's grown into a very sweet girl. But I am with Miss Lovelace on this: sweetness can cloy."

"No, not Miss Veasey's sort. She is charming and so pretty, so delicate. She was in most excellent looks. I had forgotten how very lovely she was. Skin like porcelain and that golden hair, like guineas."

"Too much the china doll for me. I find Miss Lovelace the true beauty of the family. If only she didn't have a tongue on her like a lash." Rory flicked at his reins and his horse (no longer the faithful Trojan, who had not survived the rigors of the Peninsula) responded by trotting forward.

"What must they have thought of us, howling like banshees and making that ridiculous charge!" Valentine laughed. "But you were right. The chances are we shall now disperse and I for one will be resigning my commission. How strange to think there may never be another charge for us. What are your plans now?"

"I have already resigned my commission. I will see what I can do to help Fitzgerald get Brackenbury in order and then I shall return to Scotland and discover what duties my father has in store for me." This thought somewhat lowered Rory. One of his brothers had been killed in the fighting, the other had experienced a religious fervor and had decided while in Spain to enter a seminary so that he might join the Roman priesthood, causing much ire to their father, who was a strict, even ascetic Presbyterian. This meant that Rory bore the brunt of managing the family lands, and additionally, he missed his brothers. The years of campaigning might have bought him some wealth and considerable honor, but it would be the companionship and camaraderie that he would truly miss. Life in the Highlands was likely to be a tame and somewhat glum affair.

As he rode along, he could not forget that other time he had ridden this way, at breakneck speed, for the most part following Miss Lovelace on Arcturus, down to the Jephcott mill. Even he, with his poor sense of direction, could lead Wemyss safely to Brackenbury, so clearly etched in his memory was that other ride. If only matters between himself and Miss Lovelace had proceeded smoothly, he might even now be preparing to take her home with him. She would have livened up his homecoming considerably.

How clear she had made it that she found his presence irksome. The imp of mischief that so often governed Captain Buchanan determined that while he was here at Brackenbury, he would do his utmost to discomfit the girl. He would not be the only one who would be teased and provoked.

The two soldiers caught up with their fellow men. Of the twelve, six were enlisted men, a couple who had come from Brackenbury, four others heading northward to their homes and offered a decent wage and shelter by the colonel on his land in exchange for some work about the estate over the summer months. In addition to the colonel, Wemyss and Buchanan, they were also accompanied by Macdonald, young lieutenant Lowther and Buchan.

Since they had met over the affair of Rosamund's honor, Buchan had seemed to be a calmer and more pleasant individual, and there was no doubt about it, he was an outstanding soldier, proving competent and cool under fire. He had taken Lowther under his wing, and it seemed that he was a good teacher also, guiding the lieutenant wisely and demonstrating as well as explaining how best to manage one's men and mounts.

The officers' batmen had gone ahead to Brackenbury, their aim to make the place as comfortable as possible before their gentlemen arrived. Although Colonel Fitzgerald had instituted some change at Brackenbury over the years since he had inherited the estate, this was more in the management of the lands and tenancies than in the house itself, which had been run with a skeleton staff. Now that he was returned once and for all from the wars, he intended to make some changes about the place.

Being a man of position and wealth, Colonel Fitzgerald was immediately fêted and courted by all the families in the neighborhood, particularly since he came back to the county with a collection of eligible young men for the spinsters of the area. Fathers and brothers from all over the county were sent to call on the gentlemen of Brackenbury Park and eagerly interrogated as to what—or rather who—was to be found there.

Of course, the colonel was quick to renew his acquaintance with the Veaseys himself, visiting Cheveley on his second day home, accompanied by Lieutenant Wemyss and Captain Macdonald. At the time that the soldiers called, Leonard Veasey was away from the house on business, but the gentlemen were admitted to the music room, where sat Hero, Rosamund and their other visitors, Mrs. Carmichael and Daniel.

Rosamund acted as hostess, standing to greet the visitors, introducing them to the Carmichaels and making all comfortable. She noticed that Lieutenant Wemyss gravitated with gratifying promptness to Hero's side, and how her cousin's face lit up when he did so. They were soon deep in conversation, although Rosamund could not imagine that their conversation was wildly scintillating.

"So, how goes everything in Yorkshire, Miss Lovelace?" inquired the colonel.

"Quietly, but well enough. The weather is very dismal, though. We seem to have had no spring at all, and I fear for the harvest if these rains continue. I cannot remember the last time we had to light fires throughout the house in May."

"I shall have to take care that my guests are kept warm. But we are all hardy enough and can withstand a little damp." The colonel turned to Mrs. Carmichael. "How are you finding life at Greenbriar? I do not believe you had quite moved in the last time I was in these parts, but you were expected."

"It has been good to be back amongst my own people. My family live close enough for regular visits, but not so close that we are perpetually in each other's pockets, which is how it should be. But I am delighted to see you safely home, Colonel, for I have been wishing to discuss with you for some time the coppice that is on the boundary between your land and mine. It is a matter of business, perhaps not suitable for a call, and a matter much too trivial for me to have written to you whilst you were engaged in defeating France, but now that you are returned, I hope you will be able to give some consideration to my plans and approve them."

"I am sure we can come to some arrangement. I shall be sure to call round in a day or so, once I have settled in a little at the Park."

Valentine Wemyss interjected at this point. "Colonel, Miss Veasey is telling me about a dance to be held at Squire Allerton's this Saturday evening. She assures me that we can secure invitations. I wondered whether it would be possible for us to attend, for we'll need carriages of some sort, I suppose."

"We can supply one spare carriage for you, Colonel." Rosamund smiled at Hero, for they had already discussed this earlier; Hero had come down to breakfast clearly having fretted about the question.

"Thank you, Miss Lovelace, we may well avail ourselves of your offer."

The colonel and his officers made a stunning entrance to the Allertons' dance. Most of the company of twenty or so families were assembled when the group of soldiers was announced. They stood in the doorway, their shoulders seemingly broader under the cloth of their scarlet dress jackets, their legs longer in their dark dress trousers with the red stripe, resplendent heroes eliciting a gasp of admiration from the girls in the room and mutters of resentment and envy from the young men. Squire Allerton greeted his guests with pleasure, immediately leading the men deep into the throng, introducing them to suitable dancing partners and ensuring that they were plied with food and drink.

Almost immediately, Valentine Wemyss sought out Hero

and asked her whether he might still escort her into supper and reserve a dance with her. Rory Buchanan took the opportunity to approach Rosamund. She saw him coming and snapped her fan shut.

"Miss Lovelace, might I have a dance?"

Rosamund could not refuse him. If she did, she would not be able to accept any other offers to dance. She glanced at her dance card and sighed.

"I am dancing next with Reverend Saxby, and then with Mr. Bassingham, but after that, I am free."

"I shall wait with pleasure."

"You should not wait, sir. There is an excess of ladies this evening, so please, seek out a partner and put some female however briefly out of the misery of being a wallflower. Anything is better than being accounted unworthy of a dance when there are men to spare." Rosamund's glance made it clear that dancing with the captain could be only marginally better than the fate of being left at the side of the room in the company of the matrons while everyone else was disporting themselves. Rory bowed and withdrew, determined to do as he was told and equally intent on suppressing his inclination to rise at every barb thrown his way by Miss Lovelace.

Buchan was not so obliging. He stuck out, resolutely withstanding the pleading gazes of several ladies, young and a little more mature, and worse crime, detaining Lieutenant Lowther by his side, making barbed comments about the company and laughing behind gloved hands at the dowdy women and frowsty men.

It seemed like an age but could have been no more than half an hour before Rory managed to secure his dance with Miss Lovelace. He hurried over as Bassingham brought her off the dance floor. Miss Lovelace's partner was a corpulent figure, a young man, but a substantial and sweaty one, and he was quick to hand her over to the captain before going in search of lemonade or some other chilled drink.

"Do you need any refreshment before we rejoin the floor, Miss Lovelace?" asked Rory, determined to give her no opening for any of her needle-sharp observations on his character and morals.

"It is good of you to ask, Captain Buchanan, but I do very well. I am sitting out the next dance, so I may rest then."

They were called then to join their friends in a figure that would be completed with their participation. Rosamund's curtsy was perfunctory. Captain Buchanan bowed deeply and she glowered at him as he offered her his hand for the first turn.

"How long is it since we last danced, Miss Lovelace?" asked Rory as they started stepping through their paces.

"I cannot recall, Captain Buchanan," she responded through gritted teeth.

"I believe it is eight years or so. What happy days those were in Edinburgh." Both his face and voice seemed almost boyish with enthusiasm.

"For you certainly, cutting a swath through the ladies of the town."

"Really, Miss Lovelace? You intrigue me. I thought it was only on your account that I became the talk of every drawing room. You suggest that other young ladies were as publicly smitten as you."

"I do not believe you were so very attractive to young ladies. I was thinking more of the ladies *on* the town." As soon as Rosamund had spoken she regretted her archness, which had drawn her into outright indelicacy. She caught a glimpse of Buchanan's crooked eyebrow, eloquent testament to her folly, as he whirled away from her and changed partners. How infuriating it was always to rise to his bait! She must ensure that she had the final word in this sally. By now they had switched partners and must continue down the ranks of dancers until they met up again near the end of the dance, so there was no further opportunity for discussion. Rosamund composed herself to chat easily with her partners as they worked through the sequence of moves, determined to get her own back on the captain at some point before the evening was out. It had been all very well promising herself as she dressed that she would avoid the dreadful man at all costs, but in a company of ninety or so, it was virtually impossible to ignore an individual, especially an individual who was a guest of a good neighbor and family friend. She glanced toward Captain Buchanan. He was dancing opposite Caroline Allerton, smiling down at her with a warm friendliness that brought a sudden lump to Rosamund's throat. Fortunately, Valentine Wemyss distracted her.

"Miss Lovelace, I have not had an opportunity to speak with you before now."

She grinned. "No, your time has been so thoroughly occupied by my cousin."

"How delightfully your cousin dances." He looked dreamily across at Hero, swaying gracefully to and fro in another set.

"She does indeed."

"Do you think . . . ? Could there possibly be any hope for me? Will her father look favorably on my suit?"

"Hero has not been alone in singing your praises. Our Aunt Lydia has been assiduous in forwarding your cause, and her opinions carry a good deal of weight with her brothers." Rosamund wished only that Valentine Wemyss would come up to scratch as soon as possible, for then they might be married, and safe from the influence of the dread Buchanan.

"You fill me with hope. You fill me with resolve, Miss Lovelace."

The dance drew to a close, and Rosamund was brought once again face to face with Captain Buchanan as the dancers and spectators applauded. As the band struck up the next number, Captain Buchanan escorted Rosamund from the floor.

"You said you were sitting out this next dance. May I escort you to the dining room for some refreshment?"

"There really is no need. I am sure that there are other young ladies who would welcome the opportunity to dance with an officer."

"There may be no need, but I feel that it would be far more pleasurable to tease you with my presence than to oblige some other young lady with a dance."

Rosamund's lips tightened a little, but conscious of the eyes of so many of the assembled crowd eagerly observing the actions of all the officers, she knew she could not succumb to any impulse to pull away from the captain or in any way suggest that his presence discomfited her.

"I see my young friend is about to engage himself to your cousin."

"This second?" Rosamund swirled round to try to catch a glimpse of Hero and Lieutenant Wemyss heading off into a private corner.

"No, not this very second, but imminently, I feel sure."

"You do not sound as though you approve the match."

"I approve of no matches at all. I think the married state is most unnatural to a man, and if only you ladies would cease your machinations, the world would be a far more comfortable place."

"You have no intention of marrying yourself?"

"I suppose I must now, for I am the only Buchanan of

our line likely to produce progeny, and my father will wish to see grandchildren ready to take on the burden of our lands. But it is against my inclination, certainly."

"I pity the woman you ask to be your wife." Rosamund's tone was acerbic.

"Rather you should pity the young woman who accepts my offer." Rory raised a nonchalant eyebrow. "Not that it concerns you in the slightest." He reached to the table and procured a glass of lemonade for Rosamund. She sipped before responding.

"Of course not. I daresay you have some complaisant creature in the Highlands, primed by your family to accept as and when the offer comes."

"You shall never know." He sipped at his punch and nodded at the platters of food on the table. "Do you care to eat, Miss Lovelace?"

Rosamund found that she did not. The captain seemed intent on reminding her that where once it was quite likely he would have fully divulged all his plans and hopes for the future to her, she had made it quite clear that such a subject was of no interest to her. But of course, it did interest her and the idea of him finding himself a bride and settling happily with her on his Scottish homestead somehow dismayed her beyond anything else. Perhaps it was fortunate that just then, Mr. Buchan came to claim his dance with her. Rosamund handed her glass to Rory, dropped him a little curtsy and swept away with Buchan without a backward glance. Impassive, Rory watched as she positioned herself opposite the man ready for the last dance before supper. He found Lowther at his elbow.

"Buchan is a fortunate fellow dancing with Miss Lovelace. She is the only girl here worth dancing with, I believe."

"Is that what he told you?"

"I suppose it is. He said she was warm on the eye and in the pocket, and he fancied his chances with her. Better than with her cousin, who is both a milksop and so firmly attached to Lieutenant Wemyss."

"What are your plans now the wars are over?"

"These wars, but I am sure that there will be others. Perhaps we shall serve in India next. I shall stay with the regiment."

"Have a care, then. Buchan has taught you well, but there are other ways of doing things and other ways of seeing things." Rory hoped that this would be sufficient to warn the cub not to become entangled in any of Buchan's schemes, but looking at the hero worship in Lowther's eyes as he followed his mentor's progress in the dance, it was doubtful. Rory's eyes too were led toward the dance floor, where Rosamund, resplendent in her white gown with cerise sash, moved easily in time to the music. He should have known better than to try and bait her: all he had succeeded in doing was to reach the melancholy conclusion that he had entirely dashed his chances with the one woman who might have made him happy.

NINE

For all his charm, Rosamund could not bring herself to like Captain Buchan. She did vaguely remember him from her time in Edinburgh, but she seemed to recall that he was a great favorite of her enemies, the MacTavish tabbies, and now that he was visiting Colonel Fitzgerald, she could not quite shake the impression that he was seeking out a comfortable billet on a permanent basis where he might survey the rest of the world from a superior and somewhat uncharitable vantage point. Although he was not tall, he seemed to look down his nose, which was elegant enough, to be sure, on everyone and everything.

"What a charming little band this is. Are they local favorites or imported from a larger town?"

"They are local musicians. But we try to ensure that they have access to the latest tunes, and they are assiduous in their practicing. Do you find them very rough?"

"A touch rustic, but charmingly so. That has been my general impression of Yorkshire thus far, so it is of a piece."

Fearing that her tongue would lead her astray, Rosamund strove to change the subject.

"What are your plans for the future? Do you intend to stay with the regiment or return to civilian life?"

"I am undecided. I return to Edinburgh and once I am

there, I shall make up my mind." Buchan's rather brusque manner inhibited any further questions on that topic, so Rosamund left it to her partner to raise a new subject. But he did not. So she battled on, asking him his opinion on all sorts of matters, mostly frivolous, feeling that she was exposing herself as vacant and silly, allowing Captain Buchan to assert his superiority at every turn.

By the end of the dance, Rosamund parted from Buchan convinced that his spirit was smaller than his stature, yet satisfied that she had soothed his *amour propre*, for he had taken the opportunity she had offered to talk of nothing but himself, his likes and dislikes, his tastes and his opinions.

Leonard Veasey tended to tire quite quickly at dances, so the Cheveley party left the ball relatively early, certainly before two, leaving behind Uncle Anthony at the whist tables and the officers enmeshed in the dancing.

Hero was exhausted but happy. Lieutenant Wemyss had stayed close by her side virtually all evening and when he had had to relinquish Hero to other partners, had danced only with Rosamund and Caroline Allerton. He had said that he would come calling the afternoon following the ball, and he hoped that Uncle Leonard would be at home. At last, after four years of waiting, it looked as if time and place permitted Hero to achieve her dearest wish.

Of course Rosamund was pleased for her cousin, but she was still more relieved for herself. Never having hazarded her heart since the debacle with Buchanan in Edinburgh, she had limited patience with the desire to analyze a lover's every word and phrase for significance. Even when she had been in love, it had been a matter that required concealment rather than discussion. The constant chewing over the letters and possible thoughts of a young man whom she had never met had been a burden to

Rosamund. Now she had met young Wemyss. Although he seemed exactly the sort of gentleman who would suit Hero, Rosamund found him polite but wearyingly commonplace. Not an original idea did he have in his head, nor any spark of wit. But he seemed kind and deeply enamored of Hero.

So deeply, in fact, that he was the subject of considerable merriment on the way back to Brackenbury Park in the coach that the Veaseys had sent over for the officers. Buchan and Lowther left early, taking the colonel's carriage, but the other four officers were among the last to leave the ball, having repaired to Squire Allerton's study for brandy and cigars once the ladies had retired.

"How many times did you dance with Miss Veasey?" asked the colonel.

"Three times, sir," replied Valentine, glad that the dark carriage hid his blush. "And I took her in to supper."

"Excellent, I've won my wager with Buchan in that case. He thought you would have lost interest in the wench by now."

"I don't think of her as a wench, sir. I mean to ask her to be my wife. If she'll have me." Valentine was stout in his beloved's defense.

"If she'll have you! Of course she'll have you; she's been dangling after you these four years. Unless old Veasey raises any objections, but I shouldn't think he would. You're from a good family and you've a few guineas behind you now, I hope, if you've followed my advice." The colonel settled himself more firmly in his corner and closed his eyes.

"You have no doubts, I hope, Wemyss," added Rory. "It would cause us all grave embarrassment if you were to withdraw your suit. No more loans of carriages, I daresay."

"You are mocking me, but I can stand to be mocked. The only thing I cannot stand is this uncertainty. Wooing a

girl is so fraught with difficulty. Whether she truly cares
for one, or just for one's uniform, whether she is simply a
flirt or genuinely attached, whether her relatives will take
to you or you to them. You gentlemen seem to be sworn
bachelors, so you are safe from these great issues."

Captain Macdonald attempted to comfort his fellow officer. "Not I. Here I am, putting off the evil hour when I
must sue for my beloved's hand in the face of all sorts of
opposition from her family. Still, I'd have thought you
knew Miss Veasey as well as I know my Catriona; you've
been corresponding with her long enough."

"Letters are not the same. One cannot truly learn anything about a girl from a letter. She writes to impress, she
may seek assistance in her phrasing from her friends and
she may consult books on the ideal content for a letter."
Valentine continued his ruminations. "Miss Veasey's letters seem indicative enough of her feelings and her
thoughts, but they have clearly been crafted. They do not
reveal the true personality of the writer."

"What rot!" exclaimed Rory. "Letters reflect the personality more truly than a few dances at one of these infernal
balls. I should have said that it is through writing that one
achieves the greatest understanding of character possible.
There are no other distractions to confuse or muddle the
writer or the reader. A letter allows the truth to be revealed
far more eloquently than standing in a crush and pondering
over whether to eat crab patties or ham pie."

"You speak with such passion, but I have never known
you entangled with any woman, at least not since you bade
farewell to Emily Gillespie." Captain Macdonald paused.
"Unless you have been conducting a clandestine correspondence." Then he laughed. "But no, you would never
exert yourself so far over any woman. You've the most

jaundiced views of the opposite sex, yet here you defend them when your acolyte repeats the lesson you have taken such pains to teach."

"By and large, I believe that women are conniving creatures on a perpetual hunt for some simple soul to coax into marriage. But just as I believe that there are exceptions to the common mass of humanity who are not the customary simpletons and fools, so I believe that there are rare women who are honorable and constant and wise."

"How you can have such complicated thoughts so late into the night, or, I should say, so early into the morning, is beyond me," said Captain Macdonald. "You speak with a voice of experience, yet I never heard tell of you wooing any woman worth offering for."

"Since the woman I would consider worth offering for is very likely a woman of too much sense to accept my offer, I think it unlikely you would have seen or heard of me wooing anyone. I see no reason to expose myself to failure."

"Have you ever met a woman so rare?"

"I have, but she wouldn't look at me. I see no reason to wear the willow, however. I have probably had a fortunate escape." Rory folded his arms, hoping that the conversation would die away. But Captain Macdonald probed further.

"Now you're the sole heir, your father will start pressing you. There's no escape from the altar for you."

"I shall do all I can to eschew it for as long as possible."

"We must all marry." Valentine was quite insistent and quite inebriated. "It is incumbent on us to shackle ourselves and produce progeny as prolifically as poets produce odes."

"You marry then. Propose to Hero, see if she'll have you and report back to us unfortunate fellows who haven't your address," said Rory.

A bounce jolted the colonel awake. "You've chosen well there. Hero comes with a heroic dowry, I've heard. The Veaseys are warm in the pocket and she gets a share of her Uncle Anthony's wealth too."

While this sally was indelicate, it reached the heart of Valentine Wemyss's increasing affection for Hero. She might not be the brightest or most brilliant of girls, but she was pretty and compliant and rich. There had been that other mild flirtation last summer in Brussels, but when Wemyss had discovered that Miss Sutcliffe was dependent on her aging godparent, her attraction for him had waned substantially.

It was not that he was mercenary, but he was by no means rich, not compared to most of his fellow officers. His commission had stretched the family funds considerably and he had been too young to profit particularly in the recent wars from booty, so the least he could do to relieve the burden of his upkeep was to marry well and perhaps be able to provide some sort of Season to his three sisters and improve the quality of the roof over his widowed mother's head.

"He hasn't yet made her safe, though. You talk as if she's in the bag, but he must needs ask her, and he's babbling about the uncertainty of it all. Here's a man who will charge at a regiment of artillery but won't ask a girl to become his wife." Rory was losing patience with the entire topic and finding the journey back to Brackenbury interminable.

"I'll woo her for him," declared Colonel Fitzgerald. "I'll ask her how she feels about a military man. I shall plumb her depths and winkle out her secrets and report back to you immediately. I'll call on them tomorrow and take her for a stroll."

"This is folly. You'll simply confuse the girl and she'll have just cause to spurn you if you play such games with her," said Rory.

"There speaks the man who wishes to woo no one. If Buchanan had his way we'd all end up single and the world would come to a halt."

"Better that than producing more nodcocks prepared to carry out ludicrous schemes."

"Are you suggesting your commanding officer is a nodcock, Buchanan?"

"I've resigned my commission; I no longer have a commanding officer."

Fortunately the coach pulled up at the doors of Brackenbury Park before the discussion could develop any further.

The next day, the colonel was true to his word. Accompanied by Macdonald and Wemyss, he called in at Cheveley, where he found the whole family at home. On the ride over, their strategy had been established. Wemyss would occupy Miss Lovelace, while Macdonald would distract Mr. Veasey and his brother if he were also present, allowing the colonel access to Miss Veasey.

Fortunately, it was a reasonable day, the best for some time in that although it was a little dull, at least it did not rain and it was certainly warm enough for a walk. Captain Macdonald successfully distracted Leonard Veasey while the girls were prevailed on to show Fitzgerald and Wemyss the walled garden that had been established by their great-grandmother. After the officers had left, Hero hurried Rosamund upstairs to the privacy of their bedroom where they might discuss in detail their separate conversations.

"That was the oddest call I've ever known. Lieutenant Wemyss wished to monopolize me, but all he did was talk about you." Rosamund sat herself in the window seat and continued loosening the threads and unpicking the hem of a dress she was adjusting. Hero settled in beside her, knees tucked under, idly rolling and unrolling a piece of blue ribbon.

"Colonel Fitzgerald kept asking me what I thought of soldiers and whether I could ever be attached to one. He was so roundabout and mysterious that I thought he was trying to fix his interest with me. But then he began to speak of Lieutenant Wemyss and all his family obligations and how hard it was to approach a young woman when one was poor and not entirely sure of what path to take now the wars are over."

Rosamund shook her head, exasperated with the machinations of these foolish men. "I'd have thought it was obvious that you wished to ease the lieutenant's way however you might these three years. They think to test you and try you, Hero. I'd have no patience with it."

"Oh, Lieutenant Wemyss is simply a little nervous. It is understandable. It is a great thing to make up one's mind to marry, and it must take a good deal of courage to make an offer for someone. I am so relieved I am not a man. They must do all the work, and we simply have to wait and hope."

"Waiting and hoping for someone who will never come up to scratch is a good deal harder than deciding not to come up to scratch. Men can always go away and do something different if they truly wish to eschew an entanglement. We have no choice. We are approached, and by the time we have realized that the object of our infatuation is unsuitable the entire neighborhood knows of our attachment and awaits the outcome with bated breath. If we accept an offer, we are castigated as foolish and feckless, while if we refuse it, we are fickle and flighty."

"You are so jaded, cousin. You could have your pick of

the young men of Yorkshire, yet you frighten them all off. No one dares approach you for fear of a tongue-lashing. You see the worst in every fellow who comes calling."

Hero's judgment gave Rosamund pause for thought. She supposed she did bite off the heads of any male who was sufficiently ignorant of her reputation to approach her. She had few friends, and those she did have were by and large married or on the point of marriage. She was on the verge of becoming an old maid, although this did not particularly concern her. But she was conscious that with every passing year, her circle seemed to narrow in size and scope. She could predict almost before the opening sentence was uttered the direction in which a conversation would go, because she knew her intimates so well. She had for some time found the day-to-day events in her life dull, repetitive and tedious, but she had thought that she was managing to conceal her boredom and her irritation successfully. Hero's observation suggested otherwise.

Of course, when she had had an outlet for her observations, she had been far less irritable. But the days of writing to Captain Buchanan were long past, and while she regretted the rift between them, she saw no way of healing it. He had behaved despicably in telling Colonel Fitzgerald of her youthful indiscretion and he had never shown any sign of repentance nor any desire to make amends.

Hero bustled off, sufficiently encouraged by Rosamund's account of her conversation with Lieutenant Wemyss to speak with her father about the young man's prospects and whether some suitable occupation might not be found to fill his hours and his coffers now that the wars were no more.

***

As soon as she heard Hero's footsteps fade, Rosamund went to the door and locked it. Then she rummaged in the drawer of her dressing table and dug out a small key. The wardrobe seemed larger than usual, but eventually as she delved she came upon the box she had been seeking and hauled it out. She went to the bed and sat with it on her lap. It looked a very ordinary box now that it was in the light once more, but Rosamund handled it as though it held powder and she the match. She tucked a ringlet behind her ear and cradled her cheek in thought before turning back to the box and slipping the tiny key into the tiny lock and twisting. It was stiff with lack of use and she thought she might have to get a letter opener to help her pry open the fastening, but then it seemed to come unstuck and the lid sprang free.

There they were, still wrapped in their ribbon. Her letters to him, his to her. She slammed the lid down fast and relocked the box. She shoved it aside and took several turns about the room, her arms crossed, her lips narrowed, her impatience with her own folly almost uncontainable. What on earth was the point of reviving these long-dead sensations?

She went over to the window overlooking the approach to Cheveley and leaned her cheek against the frame. Stupid, stupid, stupid to have kept the letters, to be still mooning over a man who had made clear years before that he cared nothing for her, and to be storing away these memories of a time long past and best forgotten.

Just as she was about to turn away, she saw the unmistakable movement of a horse and rider cantering comfortably up the driveway. It was one of the military men, she could tell simply from the sight of the great gray horse and the splash of scarlet coat amidst the acid green of the new leaves. But which of the men, she could not tell, although it did look from this distance too large to be Buchan, which was at least one blessing.

She returned to the bed and picked up the box. Really, she should burn the contents and keep the box out to house some knickknacks or darning wool. Some prosaic use could surely be found for the container of a good deal of prose. But Rosamund made a wry moue and restored the box to its hiding place, knowing full well that it was impossible for her to burn the letters, as it was for Hero not to gush at the thought of the brave young lieutenant.

Soon, Sally was knocking at the door with a firm little rap and panting out in great excitement that there was a caller for Miss Rosamund in the morning room if she so chose to come down and greet him; he was a fine gentleman certainly.

Rosamund checked her appearance in the glass before she went down. Everything neat and crisp, as she liked it, a few stray ringlets of hair escaping as artlessly as Hero had been able to arrange it this morning, no ink on her fingers or cheeks. She picked up her shawl and tried to plan what she might say to Captain Buchanan if indeed it was he who had come, if he did plan to attempt a long-overdue apology.

But downstairs, it was Captain Macdonald who waited for her, tall, certainly, although not so tall as Captain Buchanan and his thinning mousy hair utterly unlike Buchanan's unruly blond thatch.

"Miss Lovelace, your servant."

She dropped him a curtsy, hoping she did not look too stern or vexed. It had been the work of an idiot to imagine that Captain Buchanan would come calling after her chilliness. She sat and indicated a chair for Macdonald.

"I've come to ask if there is anything you or your cousins would like me to carry to Mrs. Macdonald. I'm leaving for Edinburgh the day after tomorrow, and I thought I'd leave you a little time to prepare a letter or a parcel."

"Thank you, Captain Macdonald. We'll certainly have something for you, but I promise it shan't be very bulky." She watched him for a second or two, then added, "I had imagined you would stay a little longer at Brackenbury Park."

"No, it was just a convenient place to rest. I must go home and sort out my affairs. You will know that I have long wished to marry a certain lady, and at last, I am in a position to please her by addressing her and please her family with my increased fortune. I do not wish to put this off any longer."

"I wish you all the best, Captain Macdonald, and if you choose to make your wedding trip extend as far as Yorkshire, we should be delighted to make both you and your bride welcome."

"You are very kind. I daresay by the time I return, the colonel's visitors will still be at Brackenbury. I do not think anyone else is intent on leaving so promptly."

"Surely their families must be waiting for them? At least you have the excuse of a family connection hereabouts. And Brackenbury, despite the colonel's improvements, is still far from being a comfortable billet."

"For some of us, I think the prospect of leaving our soldiering is more fearsome than the moments before the bugle is sounded and we start our charge."

Rosamund ceased hedging and fencing. "What about Lieutenant Wemyss? Is he so frightened by the prospect of a peacetime existence?"

"I cannot speak for Wemyss, you know that. But I do not believe that Miss Veasey has anything to fear. Very soon, he will wish to secure his future." Macdonald met Rosamund's eyes without guile or constraint.

"Do you know his family? His sisters or his mother? Hero has heard of them of course, in his letters, but nothing of substance. Few men seem to know how to write of what concerns them most nearly. We know he has family, but we know very little about how they truly are." She tapped her foot with impatience.

"Gentlewomen. I have met them. They live a little retired, there is not a good deal of money, but they are merry souls, much the same as other young women, interested in the latest dances and fashions, fond of novels, sketching, sewing, all the things that girls do. They will welcome anyone into the family circle who has the best interests of their brother at heart."

"Would they be willing to come here?" Rosamund stood and walked about the room. "I think Uncle Leonard would feel the loss of his daughter deeply. He speaks about releasing her happily enough, but I do not believe he has appreciated the real consequences of Hero leaving us." She paused again and watched Captain Macdonald carefully. "If Mr. Wemyss's family could come to Cheveley, perhaps it would make matters smoother. Unless he has land of his own he must manage? There are houses hereabouts they could take quite easily."

"I do not believe he has ever considered such a possibility. I could, if you think it right, put this suggestion to Wemyss. It is a great thing to ask people to remove themselves entirely from their usual sphere, but if there is nothing else to tie them to Fifeshire, they might be willing. At least to come and visit." Captain Macdonald eased a finger round his collar. Miss Lovelace's rather direct views were bound to require him to chivy on his hesitant friend.

"I daresay Lieutenant Wemyss has thought nothing of any of this. He imagines that Hero will be able to follow him, and her fortune with her. But her fortune is all at Cheveley, and perhaps he needs to come to understand this."

Shocked by Rosamund's blunt view of his junior, Macdonald was quick to defend the young man. "It is not simply her fortune that attracts him. I believe he loves her."

"Then let him show it by making his offer for her. She has waited long enough."

"You wish me to convey this message?"

Rosamund went over to the piano and neatened the piles of music on top of it. Of course the man should convey this message to Wemyss, but not directly. If only she and Buchanan had been on terms, he would have understood her perfectly. "Not exactly. Perhaps you had best say nothing. Perhaps I should speak to Lieutenant Wemyss if he comes calling tomorrow and monopolizes me instead of Hero."

Macdonald shook his head. It was all he could do not to turn tail, mount his horse and head directly to Scotland. Good luck to Wemyss, joining any family with Rosamund Lovelace at its center.

"I shall make sure that we have prepared something suitable for Aunt Lydia if you care to call tomorrow, Captain Macdonald."

It was a relief to make his bow and stride out to the stables. He did not envy Wemyss, who was to share a home with this determined female.

TEN

Captain Macdonald rode back to Brackenbury as though furies or Frenchies were on his tail. He found his fellows in the garden, busy with their short swords. Fitzgerald had come across a set of foils and masks in a trunk and the gentlemen were now reviving their skills with an enthusiasm that generally made up for their lack of ability. Buchanan was far and away the most competent fencer, although, as usual, he looked as though he were taking no trouble at all. He disarmed first Lowther and then Wemyss, then stepped back to allow Buchan and Fitzgerald a turn with their juniors. He sheathed the foil he had been using, then went over to Macdonald.

"Have you been over at Cheveley?"

"Aye. Wemyss has them all in a tizzy."

"God, I'd wish he'd offer for the chit and have done. He's promised to come up to Lomond with me afterward, otherwise I'd join you on the way north. But I must needs wait until he's sure of Miss Veasey."

"Miss Lovelace wishes to speak firmly with him."

A rare, ripe smile flitted across Rory's face. "Does she, by God?"

"I pity the poor fellow she snares. She may be a beauty,

but she's a managing sort of female, headstrong and calculating."

"Still, I'm surprised she's still unspoken for."

"Are you?" Macdonald looked sharply at Rory. "I'm not. She may have money enough, but she's not a comforting sort of creature. You should know; wasn't she chasing you all over Edinburgh that year she visited my brother?"

"Will you look at Buchan—he's trouncing that poor lad. There's no need to go that far." Buchan had somehow managed to force Lowther down to his knees and now held his foil at the boy's neck. "That's a nasty trick he has, but it's easy enough to get out of if you have the knack. Mmm, she did have a crush on me once, but it didn't make her uncomfortable. A little importunate."

"Do you think we should warn Wemyss she's on his warpath?"

Rory had been about to go forward and intervene between Lowther and Buchan. He shook his head. "Let her have her head; she might put a fire under him and then I can be on my way home."

In the end, there was no need. Fortified by his colonel's assurances that Hero had no eyes for anyone other than him, Wemyss returned to Cheveley the very next day and spoke to Hero, then went in search of her father. Leonard Veasey instantly sent over to Brackenbury, inviting the colonel and all his men for a celebratory dinner. To add a greater female presence, the Allertons and Mrs. Carmichael were also summoned to join the festivities.

Hero was walking on air, her dearest wish these four years finally fulfilled. She wanted only to find a mate for her cousin for utter delight. Rosamund was carefully adjusting her ringlets while Hero dithered between turquoise and amethyst sash, necklace and hair ornaments.

"Wouldn't it be glorious if we could be married together, a double wedding? We could start our new lives at the same time, and the officers would look so fine in their red coats. Do you think we shall process out of the church through their ranks, with their sabers forming the arch?"

"I daresay the swords can be arranged if you truly wish it. But you may leave me out of your matrimonial plans, my sweet. If Uncle Leonard allows, I shall join Mrs. Carmichael on an expedition to Italy once you are safely off our hands. I can scarcely wait. You must fix on a date very soon."

"Valentine wishes us to marry without delay. Valentine. How long I have wished to speak his name, and now I may." Hero waltzed about the room intoning her beloved's name in swooping tones. "Valentine, Valentine, Valentine. What a beautiful name. He has such a kind soul too. He asked if his mother and sisters might visit, and he suggests that if it suits, he might take a house for them hereabouts."

Rosamund stifled a knowing grin and said as innocently as she could, "Does he now? What a capital notion! I hope you will like them and they like you. Sisters can be very jealous of their brothers, I have heard."

"Oh, but Valentine's sisters will be charming! Captain Buchanan said they were, and though I find him a little fearsome, I would trust his word implicitly."

"Would you? I wouldn't! He's not the type I'd consider reliable." Conscious that she had given away too much, Rosamund closed her mouth and concentrated on her toilette. But it was too late. Hero came over and sat beside her on the bench before their shared dressing table. The younger girl started fidgeting with her cousin's honeyed tresses and stroking at them with a brush.

"You really seem to dislike him inordinately. What can he have done to you that was so wicked and disagreeable?"

"Nothing." Rosamund's lips compressed with the effort of holding her tongue. She snatched the brush from Hero's grasp and wrenched the bristles through her locks. "But he thinks he is a great deal cleverer than he actually is. Is my neckline too low? I lowered it a little in line with that picture you showed me, but I'm not sure it isn't more immodest than alluring."

"No, you look charmingly. That red suits you; I told you it would."

Rosamund gave her cousin an affectionate kiss and patted her on the hand. "You have an unerring eye for stylish colors and patterns. I shall trust you in this. Come now, coz, let's descend with great aplomb. They should all be present. I told Carrington to show guests directly to the music room."

The two girls linked arms and did make a lovely picture as they entered the music room, Rosamund resplendent in her ruby satin, Hero delicate and exquisite in her ice blue taffeta. The gowns were not so very new, but the gentlemen need not know that, and there were no unfriendly eyes to give the game away.

In the music room, the whole company apart from the Allertons was assembled. Uncle Anthony, a fair accompanist, had persuaded Daniel Carmichael into performing a violin sonata. The boy was an assured and dedicated musician, although it had taken a little persuasion to encourage him to stand up before such a company and perform. The officers were just applauding his efforts when the girls entered the room. Fitzgerald was the first to catch sight of them and left off his applause at once, coming over to bow to the two girls. Only Rory Buchanan made no move toward them, going up to Daniel instead to congratulate him on his efforts.

Rosamund circulated round the room, greeting the guests, gravitating toward Mrs. Carmichael, with whom she hoped to have a comfortable conversation. Buchan tried to detain her, but she sidestepped him and headed toward her goal.

"Rosamund, my dear, you spurn the redcoats for a chance to chatter with an old friend you may see any day of the week." Mrs. Carmichael was standing by the piano, idly looking through the sheets of music there.

"Officers are all very well, but they come and go. One's true friends are always there and consequently should be valued above temporary delights." Rosamund guided her friend to a love seat under the window.

"Mrs. Carmichael, I have wonderful news," she said in low tones. "Wemyss does not wish to delay the wedding. We may begin planning our trip very soon. He is going to leave with Captain Buchanan next week, and he has written to his mother and sisters to prepare themselves for a journey south. As soon as they are all here, within four weeks, he says, we may celebrate the nuptials!"

"So you will be free to accompany us on our travels?"

"I have not yet broached it with my uncles. In principle, as you know, they have agreed to my leaving for Europe with you, but in practice, I wonder whether they will be quite so sanguine once Hero has gone."

"There is no hurry. We may travel at any time. I'd prefer to make the Channel crossing in clement weather, but that is simply a question of waiting at Dover for a pleasant day. Otherwise, whatever the season, travel is full of discomforts, as I have said to you before."

"What is full of discomfort?" inquired Rory Buchanan, coming up to the ladies in an effort to escape the general hubbub of wedding-related prattle.

"Oh, Captain, you may reassure my companion here, it is possible to travel at any season and each season has its disadvantages. The summer is dusty, over-hot and one is plagued by insects, while the winter is muddy, freezing and the roads can be impassable."

"Certainly, but this year, the omens do not look promising for a decent summer. We seem already to have had inordinate rain. Are you planning to travel extensively?"

"Indeed we are. With my husband, I have been to France, some of the Habsburg territories and Venice, but I long to see Greece as well as show my Daniel all the places his father introduced me to. Rosamund has kindly consented to accompany us."

"Kindly? I begged and begged you would allow me to go with you."

"How long do you intend to be away?" asked Buchanan.

"At least one year, possibly two. I do not believe we can do justice to all the places we should see if we try to cram too much into too short a space. There is no real rush, I think, is there, my dear?"

"None at all," replied Rosamund. She met Captain Buchanan's eyes, which looked suddenly quite chilly. She glanced away. What business this was of his, she could not imagine, and why he should disapprove of her intention to travel with the Carmichaels was even more mysterious.

"Your relations will miss you." He bowed and made to withdraw. "I shall leave you to your plans."

As he sauntered away, Rosamund could not help watching him. Mrs. Carmichael did not fail to notice.

"Are you fond of him?"

Rosamund's head twisted round sharply. "Fond of Buchanan? Why should I be? I scarcely know the man."

"How odd. He seemed most put out by the prospect of your traveling. He had the air of a disappointed man."

"I cannot be the cause of his disappointment. We met in Edinburgh many years ago, but I have scarcely had any dealings with him since then." The knowledge of the box secreted upstairs in her cabinet seemed to burn like a brand, but Rosamund barreled onward in her determination to dismiss Captain Buchanan as of little account.

Mrs. Carmichael shook her head, a little baffled. "Of course, it may have been my imagination. You know how vivid that can be." She then turned the subject once more to their prospective travels, and soon enough the Allertons were announced and the company shifted to take their seats in the dining room.

Rosamund had been in charge of the seating plan, but she saw that Uncle Anthony had been tinkering with her placement, and she found herself to her annoyance seated between Captain Buchanan and Valentine Wemyss. Sharing a meal with a love-struck ninny and a cantankerous campaigner was hardly her idea of a lively evening, but she stifled her sighs and set out to make the best of it, waxing lyrical to Wemyss on the subject of her cousin's manifold virtues and charms, and firmly declining to discuss anything with Captain Buchanan other than the weather and the food. She had much rather have been seated where Mrs. Carmichael sat, between Squire Allerton and Colonel Fitzgerald, and successfully charming both. Or down at Uncle Anthony's end of the table, where he had as always monopolized the young and lively members of the company, notably Daniel Carmichael and Caroline Allerton.

As Rosamund plied her knife and fork, she could see

that Ned Lowther was making heavy weather of the meal and the company. He seemed to be quite taken with Caroline Allerton but kept glancing toward his mentor, Captain Buchanan, for approval, much as a dog hopes for scraps from the master's table, its head cocked and its eyes large with longing.

"Who are you watching now?"

Rosamund started slightly as Buchanan interrupted her reverie. He continued. "It is like entering the world you described to me. I hadn't realized just how accurate an observer you are."

"I'd prefer not to discuss it."

"No, you'd prefer me to stick safely to comments on the succulence of this rib of beef, or the inclemency of the day and how long I think the rain will continue, and whether we shall ever have anything like a summer. But I'm afraid I cannot oblige you with idle nonsense."

Rosamund stiffened. "I do not imagine that you are able to indulge anyone in any way other than yourself."

"I am able to do so, but I generally do not choose to. Much too much effort and for so little return."

It was Rosamund's turn to give a tight, chilly smile in response to her neighbor's comment. She could have said more, but she knew she was on the verge of losing her dignity and possibly her temper. This was the celebration of a betrothal, not an argy-bargy, and she would not forget herself so far as to stoop to Captain Buchanan's light and sarcastic sally.

"Tell me more of your intention to travel."

"It has long been an ambition of mine, wanting only a congenial and experienced chaperone. In Mrs. Carmichael, I hope I have found a person who will satisfy my uncles' desire for propriety and my desire for knowledge and adventure."

"You have no wish to follow in your cousin's footsteps and find yourself an acceptable suitor?"

"None. Now that you gentlemen have done us the very great favor of ridding us of the tiresome tyrant Bonaparte, it would be churlish of us civilians not to profit by your work in traveling far and wide, enjoying the fruits of your peacemaking."

Then Wemyss turned once again toward Rosamund, demanding to know what local customs and traditions he must keep to on his wedding day and inquiring as to whether Miss Lovelace knew of any suitable lodging or house he might take for his mother and sisters.

"They must come and stay here, of course. We have many rooms and not so many relatives scattered about the countryside demanding to attend the marriage."

"That is very kind of you, Miss Lovelace, but they cannot stay with you indefinitely."

"Of course they would not wish to. It is most uncomfortable to be forever in someone else's home, obliged to go on according to their customs and traditions. But I thought if in the first instance, Mrs. Wemyss and the Misses Wemyss stayed with us, then they might have the opportunity to take a leisurely look about them and find exactly the right house for their needs. Gentlemen are generally less likely to understand what those might be."

"You're right, of course. I might choose a house for them, but I know that it would be the sort of place that I would wish to live in and probably all wrong for ladies."

Buchanan interjected here. "It would certainly be all wrong, Wemyss. The needs and tastes of a single man are vastly different than those of four women. Better to leave them to find their own home, if they choose to remain here in Yorkshire."

"You've agreed with me, Captain Buchanan! I thought it was your policy never to agree with anyone but always to have your own opinion, which must differ and, of course, which must be right." Rosamund's smile was glittering as she spoke, but inside, she was kicking herself for giving way to the impulse to needle the captain.

"I don't believe I did agree with you entirely, Miss Lovelace. You suggested that men do not understand what women require. I was simply suggesting that there is a difference in requirements, not a lack of comprehension over what those requirements might be." Whether he did it deliberately or not, he seemed to imply that in his view, it was women who did not understand men.

"I've met very few men who ever put themselves to the bother of understanding what it is women require."

"But the female sex is very simple. You need occupation and pretty things to divert you from the mundanity of that occupation. You need stalwart affection, but it must be dressed in high-flown words of passion, and when you are actually offered passion, you fly from it as much too dangerous. You need a good deal of discussion to make minor decisions and virtually no discussion where major ones are concerned, and you must be protected from your flightiness without being made aware of the protection."

"You have a very jaundiced view of our sex, Captain Buchanan."

"I didn't understand one word in ten you spoke, Buchanan, but it did seem a little harsh." Wemyss returned to his plate with renewed relish.

"I prefer to think of myself as realistic, but if I seemed unduly hard, so be it."

"Thank heavens your fellow men are less rigorous in their judgment, or else there would be no more marriages."

"Since you have no interest in marriage, Miss Lovelace, I don't suppose it matters to you one way or the other."

"I don't believe I said I had no interest in marriage, Captain Buchanan, simply that I have no current interest in finding a suitor. There, each of us has put the other in his place."

"So you hope to marry eventually?"

"If I find the right man. Not one who believes that we women are so contrary and superficial."

"Could there be any creature so rare as the right man?"

"Of course. But I shall leave it to you to work out what his character and ideals must be. It will tax you a little, I daresay, since such a man would be very different from yourself."

By this time, the meal was drawing to a close. Prompted by a glance from Rosamund, the two footmen had ensured that everyone had a full glass. Leonard Veasey stood and tapped his knife against the crystal and the room fell silent.

"It is with great pleasure that I see so fine a company assembled here tonight. You all know why you are here. It is with delight that we celebrate my Hero's betrothal to a fine young man. Let us raise our glasses to toast the happy couple."

Everyone stood and gave the energetic cry, "The happy couple!" before sipping or downing their drinks. Young Wemyss remained standing as everyone settled down again.

"Thank you, Mr. Veasey, for a fine toast, and a better daughter. May I ask you all to drink to our fine host?"

Again the company stood and drank. Rosamund looked at Mrs. Carmichael, then caught Hero's eye. In the lull as the officers were finishing their glasses, she pushed her chair right back and said, "It is time we ladies withdrew so that you may enjoy your port. We shall be in the music room when you are ready, and we hope that you will be ready for some hearty singing."

It was while Rosamund was in deep conversation with Mrs. Allerton that Miss Caroline Allerton, Mrs. Carmichael and Hero tentatively explored the reaction between Miss Lovelace and Captain Buchanan. Caroline Allerton raised the subject, having observed how closely Rosamund was watched by the captain.

"He scarcely takes his eyes off her, yet when they speak, they brangle."

Hero Veasey dismissed the notion that there was anything between them, and of course, since she was virtually Rosamund's sister, surely she must know if there was something. But Mrs. Carmichael took a sip from her coffee cup and carefully placed it on the side table before considering the question a little more profoundly.

"She was most adamant that she scarcely knew him, yet there is some sort of familiarity between them. They seem half to expect what the other will say, each one capping the other as best they can. I noticed it again as we were eating."

"I believe we should smoke them out," murmured Caroline Allerton, casting a careful eye toward Miss Lovelace and her mother. But the two were still deep in discussion.

"How might we do that?" asked Hero, her imagination as usual not quite allowing her to comprehend this turn of events.

"Simple, Hero. We must tell Miss Lovelace that the captain is languishing after her and has proclaimed himself in love with her, but that she is too hard-hearted to consider him worthy of her."

Mrs. Carmichael considered acting as the voice of reason but then she remembered that sticky moment when Rosamund had so vehemently denied any substantial acquaintance with Buchanan. Something had not rung quite true there, and it would be interesting to see if her young friend were a little less immune to the opposite sex than she claimed.

"Perhaps," she suggested, as innocently as she could, "perhaps, Hero, you might inquire of Lieutenant Wemyss whether Captain Buchanan has ever shown the least partiality for Miss Lovelace."

Miss Allerton, somewhat more abundantly gifted in gray matter than her friend, grasped Mrs. Carmichael's implication immediately. "We should get the other officers to tell Captain Buchanan that Miss Lovelace is passionately in love with him." She grinned, for all the world like a scampish boy. "What a wicked trick, but wouldn't it be amusing if we could persuade them both that each is mad for the other? It must be the officers who suggest it; he's not the sort to discuss such things with ladies whom he scarcely knows."

"I might raise it with Colonel Fitzgerald. His relations with his men seem positively avuncular. If anyone can persuade Buchanan of such a story, it will be him, and I am sure I can interest him in such a trick." Mrs. Carmichael was quite ready to approach the colonel, for she had seen in him a mischievous bent that very likely would relish such a hoax. She could not see that it would lead to any catastrophic result. It might simply encourage both parties to speak to and of each other with greater civility, which could only ease things given how very likely it was that

Captain Buchanan would be returning to the neighborhood to socialize and shoot with his old companion at arms.

It did not take the gentlemen long to finish their port and wend their way toward the music room. The animosity in which Buchan held both Buchanan and Wemyss made it uncomfortable for the gentlemen to spend any length of time in each other's company. Fitzgerald was hoping that Buchan would speed himself home as soon as possible, but the wee fellow seemed inclined to linger, and as for Lowther, why he hadn't returned to the ample and fond bosom of his family, Fitzgerald could not fathom.

Rosamund was pressed into service at the piano. The newly engaged couple were immediately required to give voice to a sentimental ballad of waiting and waiting, waiting and waiting, until hope was rewarded and love might flower. Mrs. Carmichael had managed to snare Colonel Fitzgerald into sitting beside her. Once they had applauded Hero and Valentine, there was a pause as Buchan and Miss Allerton sought out a livelier song to share with the company. Mrs. Carmichael seized the opening lying before her.

"Miss Lovelace is a fine accompanist. I believe Mr. Buchanan was quite taken with her skill at the pianoforte."

"That's all he sees in her, I seem to think. Those two are forever bantering with increasingly sharp effect. I cannot remember seeing two such finely matched wits sparring with such gentle but deadly venom."

"Perhaps that is merely a symptom of some deeper affection."

"I've heard of such things, but I am not sure I believe in them."

"I understand that Miss Lovelace has a deep but unspoken attachment for Captain Buchanan."

"I'd be surprised, Mrs. Carmichael. They knew each other once and I believe she might have had a girlish crush on his fine red coat and his shiny boots, but she's much too sensible a girl to get herself tangled up with a military man with more acres than assets and the temperament of a Pyrenean wolf."

"Is he so very fearsome?"

"He's ferocious and loyal, like the best of the species. But love? Well, I'm not sure. I'm not sure at all."

"What if you were to tell him that Miss Lovelace is devoted to him and his cause?"

"He'd probably call it poppycock. But then again, he swears so vehemently that there is nothing between them, it makes one suspicious."

"It does indeed, Colonel. It does indeed. And here is our dear Rosamund, eager to inveigle you to the piano. I must cease monopolizing you."

The colonel rose from his Sheraton seat with a flick of his coattails and a slight bow toward Miss Lovelace, who was approaching fast. He was not sure whether he should do anything with the intelligence so kindly supplied by Mrs. Carmichael, but he would keep a close eye on his subordinate, that was for certain.

ELEVEN

The opportunity to discuss Miss Lovelace with Captain
Buchanan presented itself to Colonel Fitzgerald far sooner
than he had anticipated. A couple of days after the celebratory dinner, the colonel, accompanied by Buchanan and
the faithful Wemyss, set off to ride to Northallerton to attend a cattle market and see if a few more hands could be
found to help on the estate and in the house. It was Wemyss who brought up Miss Lovelace.

"Hero tells me that Miss Rosamund Lovelace is pining
after some gentleman."

"Really?" inquired the colonel. "Is this a recent affection?"

"I believe so, sir. It is only since we came into the
county that she has lost her appetite and apparently begun
to play love songs in a manner quite unlike herself. Or so
says Hero. I do not imagine that Hero would lie to me."

Buchanan seemed to be studiedly remaining silent. The
colonel edged his mount forward so that the horses' paces
matched. "What do you make of this, Buchanan? Which
of us has the *beaux yeux* to have attached Miss Lovelace?"

Curtly, the captain responded, his thighs unmistakably
tensing about his saddle and quickening the pace of his
horse. "I cannot imagine. Miss Lovelace has not seemed

to me particularly enamored of anyone, but then, I hardly know her."

The colonel shrugged and drew the conversation along different lines, but his curiosity was piqued, and when he next encountered Captain Macdonald, later that afternoon, they decided to share a pipe in the garden.

"There's this old tale about Miss Lovelace and her attachment to Buchanan. Could that have been revived?" The colonel inspected a wall for damp and decided that it was dry enough to sit. Macdonald sat beside him and they struck up their pipes and began puffing contentedly away.

"Miss Lovelace, you say?" Macdonald inclined his head toward an arbor some few yards from them, its frame coated in dense vine leaves, fresh green from the incessant rain. Fitzgerald returned his gaze with a knowing smile. He too had glimpsed a pair of polished boots that had drawn themselves out of sight at the sound of Miss Lovelace's name. The vine leaves gave an extra rustle, then settled.

"I believe it could," continued Macdonald. "She does not strike me as the sort of woman who loves lightly. Even though she was very young when she first encountered Buchanan, she made a great push at the time to enter into his interests and follow his thoughts. But he is so dismissive of any gentler emotion, I am surprised she is not immediately discouraged."

Fitzgerald shook his head and sighed exaggeratedly. "His view of the fair sex is so disenchanted as to verge on misogyny."

"I'd say he was more inclined to misanthropy. His view of his fellow men is altogether jaundiced." Macdonald gave up on his pipe and knocked the ashes out by tapping the bowl on the sole of his boot.

"Indeed. I pity the poor woman who does love him, and can only hope Miss Lovelace is entirely recovered from her interest in him." The colonel frowned a little. While he was somewhat exaggerating for effect, there was some truth in his words, which made him feel more uncomfortable than he had expected. "He must jest and quip and turn a person's words round; he is ever eager to lead his unsuspecting interlocuters into some trap or trick that he may mock."

"He would certainly be quick to ridicule any tender passion. I have heard him so often decrying the gentler emotions. Why, only this morning, he was teasing poor Wemyss for his affection for Miss Veasey."

"Perhaps the time will come when he himself succumbs to the charms of a lady who will not countenance his suit."

"I think he is more likely to drive some lady to an incalculable frenzy. He is made of hard-hearted adamant." Macdonald watched the colonel, who nodded in response and they wandered from their theme onto less lively topics.

As soon as they had left, Buchanan emerged from his hiding place. It was lamentably true that eavesdroppers never heard good of themselves, but he had not thought to hear quite so damning a picture of himself. Hard-hearted! Mocking! Misanthropic! And was Miss Lovelace's interest in him truly revived? That had been the most interesting titbit. For his interest in her certainly had not diminished. She remained the most fascinating woman he had met.

But he could not change in his approach to her. She would smell a rat, or something more noxious still. She did not give the appearance of giving two hoots about him. She had rated him finely, and what had her final sally been—that it would take him time to work out the characteristics of her ideal man because he possessed no characteristics in common with such a figure.

Perhaps he had been a little blunt. Or rather, very blunt. Perhaps he had been a little dismissive of her plans. It was true that he approached women with a wary cynicism. They were always so expensive and so irrational. But she had never been either. She had a fortune, but she was modest in her appearance and her behavior. He had noted that her gown was not entirely new. It was a very fine gown, a very fetching gown, that suited her coloring and brought a glow to her skin, and was neither missish nor vulgar. But it had not been the very latest thing. He had known enough women who demanded only the latest thing to recognize that Miss Lovelace was not the sort to waste her allowance on a tide of apparel that would be worn only the once.

What would her ideal man be, after all that? Not some milksop like Wemyss. Nor a ferret-faced individual like Buchan. She would seek a fine-looking man. She would seek a man with ideals and a charitable disposition. An intelligent man. He remembered her letters, bright and full of ideas, not just notions bought by the yard from some bookseller, but theories that she had considered and explored, to which she had given full weight. More than appearance, she would be interested in the life of the mind and the state of the heart. She would require a man whose heart had some capacity for warmth toward his fellows.

If she truly still had some regard for him, he must deal more kindly with her. There had been reason enough for her anger, after all. He searched his soul and was forced to admit that he had shown no outward sign of repentance, although inwardly, he had regretted his rash tongue more frequently than he cared to remember. Thus resolved, he emerged from the arbor and sauntered back into the house.

***

It was a merry band of Hero's intimates that gathered to help prepare her trousseau. In the wilds of Yorkshire, it was incumbent on the local ladies to assist in perusing the magazines, producing helpful sketches and sharing notes on the latest fashions espied on any recent forays to sites as forward with the world as Harrogate or Scarborough.

Of course, Mrs. Allerton and her two daughters, Caroline and Mary (the latter not yet out at dinners and dances), were present, along with Mrs. Carmichael and Mrs. Cameron Robertson, another lady with Scottish connections who had recently returned from Edinburgh. It was while Rosamund was hidden behind a screen, trying on a dress that had the cut and draping that Hero liked and wished to see on her bridesmaid, that she could not help but hear an exchange between Mrs. Carmichael and Caroline Allerton.

"I am sure Miss Rosamund will look very well in this garment. She looks well in everything she wears." Despair tinged Miss Allerton's assertion, for her girth was a little generous, and she did have to avoid certain colors and cuts if she were not to appear over-substantial.

"That is her own flair married with Hero's impeccable eye."

"They are so fortunate, the pair of them, equipped with looks and wealth, good humor and good health. I wish them all the happiness in the world." Again, Miss Allerton could not entirely suppress a wistful sigh.

"I am sure Hero will find it, she is a simple, straightforward soul, but I am not so sure about Miss Lovelace." Mrs. Carmichael paused, and Rosamund craned to hear her somewhat lowered tones. "She is so very particular in her requirements that I begin to think she will never find a man to suit."

"Not even Captain Buchanan? He is such a fine figure of a man, and he gazes after her with such fondness. Why, she is virtually his only interest and he seems always to be able to turn a conversation so that she must be brought into it and praised."

"I too have noticed a distinct partiality there, but I fear it can come to nothing." Mrs. Carmichael sounded very definite. "I have heard her say that she could never develop a tendre for a military man, for even if they have sold their commissions, they must be restless and forever on the move."

"How strange a prejudice! I would have thought a military man more reliable than most. Especially one such as Captain Buchanan. He is temperate and charming and makes so many jokes that only he and Miss Lovelace seem to wholly understand."

"But have you not heard her when in his company? She can be cutting, positively biting. And he is so chivalrous a soul, he simply allows her to voice her most scathing thoughts and accepts them as though he merited them."

Rosamund longed to lean round the screen and deny that he was so amiable as they suggested or she so rag-mannered, but she contained herself and simply cleared her throat, then emerged in her splendor. The gown she wore was midnight blue, not entirely suitable for a wedding, but the cut was such that she appeared positively Olympian.

"Ah, Pallas Athene, except you have such bright blue eyes instead of gray!" commented Mrs. Carmichael, a knowing curve to her lips and a twinkle in her eyes. "Hero, my dear, it isn't the color, but you are quite right, it is exactly the cut.

Now, what material have you in mind for Miss Lovelace's ensemble?"

"I thought a mint-green bombazine, trimmed with swansdown. In this delicious color, and with the ermine, it is too much a winter gown, but I believe that the swansdown will give it a lighter touch, and the paler color makes it suitable for summer. What do you think, Rosamund?"

"My dearest, it is your wedding, and you may have me decked out in whatever you please, whether it is a milkmaid's shift or the presentation robes of the Princess Carabou."

It was not long before Rosamund developed a most wearisome headache and had to withdraw from the ladies and their chatter. She caught sight of a maid in the corridor and asked for a chamomile tisane and a cold compress, to be brought up to her room. It was a relief to reach her bedroom and lean back against the door, her eyes closed, the tension draining from her neck and shoulders. She unlaced her slippers and climbed onto the bed. As she lay there waiting for the remedy to her ailment, she pondered the conversation she had overheard.

Had she really been so very acerbic in his presence and about his presence? She supposed she had. But what was Mrs. Carmichael suggesting? That Captain Buchanan held her in high esteem? If that were the case, why was he so ready to bite back at her every sally? It was perplexing. She did not wish to drop her defenses against the man. It was most unaccountable, but he did seem to bring extra vividness to any company he entered, and one's eyes could not help but be drawn toward him.

However, he was, like most military men, full of his own consequence, and of course he had done her an injury in the eyes of the colonel. Still, it would be interesting to know his plans for the future now that he had resigned his commission. There was land, she seemed to remember, and talk of a somewhat irascible and reclusive father.

There was a knock at the door, and one of the girls brought in a tray. Rosamund thanked her and drank down the chamomile tea, then lay with the cold compress over her forehead and eyes, resolving to watch Captain Buchanan more carefully and handle him a little more kindly the next time she saw him.

It was with some anticipation that Captain Buchanan's and Miss Lovelace's friends looked forward to the next social gathering, which would bring this pair in close proximity. They did not have long to wait, for the announcement of Hero's engagement brought a deluge of invitations to both the gentlemen at Brackenbury Park and everyone at Cheveley as the county vied to throw ever more magnificent parties in honor of the happy couple.

There were only two dissenting voices to all this jollity and enthusiasm, but the pair of naysayers were careful to limit the expression of their distaste for all the fuss to each other. Captain Buchan found the whole business tiresome, considered the bride provincial and simple and the groom unfairly fortunate both in his favor with the colonel and in his choice of wife. None but Lieutenant Lowther was aware of Buchan's general discontent and growing irritation.

Resolutely avoiding the eye of any of the unattached females gracing the edges of the room where they were watching the dancing at yet another bumpkin's ball, Buchan expounded to his junior officer, "There, look on her simpering up at him, and he gazing into her great hangdog eyes. I suppose there are those who like that sort of prettiness, but I find it blowsy and liable to run to fat at the first sign of a baby. But she's not the only one. I suppose Wemyss's great friend Captain Buchanan will be securing the other great fortune at Cheveley. You'd have thought Miss Lovelace would have learnt her lesson the last time she was tangled up with our courageous Buchanan."

"What do you mean?" inquired Lowther, who had still been a schoolboy eight years previously.

Buchan rolled his eyes and proceeded to recount the tale of poor Miss Lovelace's lovelorn letter and how it had so filled Buchanan with scorn and panic that he had up and left Edinburgh within hours of receiving it. Naturally, no mention was made of Buchan's role in spreading its contents, nor of the duel he had fought with Buchanan, let alone the ignominious wound he had received from his colleague.

"I am astonished that Captain Buchanan should have behaved with so little chivalry. He has been such a model of propriety, an exemplar for all of us in the regiment." Lowther smothered an unmistakable snigger. It was always a pleasure to see the mighty in the regiment brought a little closer to the ground where more normal mortals trod.

"The most unexpected individuals may lapse. Why, take Miss Hero Veasey. I daresay she has more than one dark secret which if exposed would end her current happiness." Buchan crossed his arms and leaned against the wall, one ankle elegantly crossed over the other, cooler than the sorbet served at supper.

"Miss Veasey! I would sooner believe the Great Cham of China could lapse. Of all the girls hereabouts, she is one of the most virtuous, the most innocent."

"What would you say if I could prove her to be a bawd?" Buchan was careful to speak casually. Eagerness might frighten off this fish.

"Infamous! You could not."

"Could I not? What is it worth to you?" Again, Buchan quelled his own excitement, striving for an air of calm detachment, aware that he was reeling in his catch but did not yet have him on dry ground.

"A bet? We should not wager on a girl's virtue." But Lowther, even as he acknowledged what he should not do, was eager to act upon the suggestion. "Forty guineas."

"Forty guineas to prove the girl's a double dealer."

"We should record the wager," said Lowther, but he shifted as he spoke, avoiding Buchan's eyes. It was just the sort of gamble Buchan favored: so disreputable that its participant would be unwilling to admit to it and eager to pay it off.

Of course, he had no way of showing Lowther that the girl was easy in her morals, but that had never prevented him from making similar bets before. It would be easy enough to bribe a Cheveley maid to snaffle a pelisse and a bonnet that unmistakably belonged to Miss Veasey. Get some girl to wear the clothing and take a tumble in the stables of the local inn, show the sight to Lowther and he'd be warmer in the pocket by forty guineas before three days were out.

Buchan excused himself from the evening's entertainment and went in search of a tavern girl to assist him in executing his plan. There were low inns in the locality where such girls might thrive, welcoming the chance of a pound or two and a roll in the hay with a man of their choosing rather than a client. The trick would be in persuading the fellow to address his doxy by Miss Veasey's name. The promise of half a crown would almost certainly do it.

Preoccupied by the orchestration of his deception, Buchan did not consider that Lowther would have been so astounded by his tale that he would have tattled it immediately to the colonel. For Fitzgerald, espying one of his men avoiding the opportunity to dance had made it his business to seek out young Lowther and question the boy, who had one of the longest faces this side of payday he'd ever seen.

"I have been deeply shocked, sir. I know not what to do." While it was true that Buchan's assertion had shocked, Lowther was also operating under the influence of a small imp of mischief that he had learned of the captain, a sprite that could not help causing him to wonder what Wemyss would do once he discovered his heiress was secondhand goods.

"What has caused you such offense?"

"I scarcely know how to say, sir, save that it concerns Miss Veasey."

Fitzgerald gave Lowther a sharp look. "How does it concern Miss Veasey?"

"Perhaps I should say nothing. But I have heard this very night a most disquieting rumor. I have heard that she is . . ." Lowther paused, looked about him and whispered to the colonel, "Well, that she is free with her favors!"

"Miss Veasey! Preposterous! Who spoke this rumor? Some thwarted youth, perhaps, or a disenchanted damsel envious of her fortune in securing a match with Wemyss. But I have known Miss Veasey for years. She is sheltered and pure, I would swear on it."

"I demanded proof, of course."

"Proof? How can proof be secured of something so impossible?"

"I am told that it can be proved."

The colonel calmed down a little. He shifted as though his dress jacket had become too tight for him. "I do not like this. I do not like it at all. Proof, you say! Well, I shall come and see your proof, and if it proves to be founded on truth, we must get Wemyss out of this match."

These Cheveley girls, thought the colonel, seemed to bring nothing but trouble to his men. He could not believe this rumor that Lowther had heard, but equally he was wary of dismissing it out of hand, particularly since he knew that Miss Lovelace had been capable of great forwardness in her youth. Of course, she gave no sign of lightness, still less any tendency toward light-skirtedness, but it paid to be vigilant, and if Lowther claimed to have proof, it must be explored before any action could be taken.

He looked out onto the dance floor and the first couple to catch his eye was Miss Lovelace and Buchanan. They were looking less warily on each other, he thought. One could not say they yet approached warmth, but certainly she was less rigid and he was less frowning than hitherto. This rumor must be nonsense; the Cheveley ladies were respectable, sheltered and entirely pleasant. In which case, the rumor must be scotched, and the easiest way, it seemed to the colonel, to achieve that end was to examine Lowther's so-called proof and disprove it at the earliest opportunity.

On the dance floor, Captain Buchanan was smiling at Miss Lovelace.

"I have lost count of the number of times I have danced this last week. How many more parties must we attend before Wemyss can excuse himself so that we may head northward and collect his family?"

"Not many, for I believe we have been fêted by all the main families in our county. Have you found it hideously wearisome?"

"By no means, Miss Lovelace." He glanced round the room. "My chief entertainment has been identifying the people you used to mention in your letters to me."

Rosamund felt the heat mount in her cheeks, which fortunately could be ascribed to the exertions of the dance. "I'm astonished you remember them so clearly. It is years since we corresponded."

"I have regretted the lapse of our correspondence virtually every day since you ended it, with every justification, I might add."

Rosamund could not quell a glint of suspicion in her eyes. "Are you going so far as to apologize?"

The captain's grin was saucy. "I am not sure. Only if it will persuade you to look on me with a forgiving eye."

"If that means you expect further letters from me, you are mistaken. Whenever I have written to you, it has caused me only trouble."

"Now that is unjust. We corresponded without any difficulties for nearly two years. That can hardly be said to be trouble. Apart of course, from the incursion on your time." He did hope that she would find something good to say about having written to him.

"It was no incursion. It was a pleasure, and you know it. I too have missed our exchanges." For once, Rosamund did not sound merry or mocking. She was rewarded for her honesty by a breathtaking smile from the captain, a smile that seemed to warm her from her head to her toes and fill her with a glow of happiness. Just then, they were forced by the motion of the dance to swing away from each other on the arms of different partners, but they held their gaze until the last second they were able. This did not go unnoticed.

"Mrs. Carmichael, I believe you were absolutely right about Miss Lovelace and the captain," said Miss Caroline Allerton, standing in the doorway between the dining room and the ballroom. "Look, they are almost incandescent. I believe they would glow even if every candle in the place were doused."

"Good heavens! I never expected our carefully chosen words to take effect quite so swiftly. He seems entirely won over. And Rosamund! I've never seen her look like that. What have we done, Miss Allerton?"

"A good turn if it serves to bring happiness to Miss Lovelace. She has been so restless these last months, it has been like sitting in the same room as a caged lynx."

"I hope I will still have a companion to help me round the Continent with Daniel."

Miss Allerton sighed wistfully. "If only I could persuade Mama and Papa that a young lady requires a grand tour. I would come with you in a minute if you weren't able to take Rosamund."

"Who knows, Miss Allerton! If our little trick does not end in a nuptial there, I shall grill my bonnet and eat it with mustard."

The dance ended, the dancers and their audience gave their muted round of applause, their hands muffled by their gloves, and Rosamund curtsied to her partner.

"I will call on you tomorrow, if I may, Miss Lovelace." Rory swallowed. "I believe I have something very particular to ask of you."

Before Rosamund could do more than nod in agreement, she saw Hero holding her pelisse in the doorway, signaling that their carriage was ready and Uncle Leonard was eager to be home. She nodded mutely at the captain and wound her way through the crowd of dancers preparing for the next melody, astounded into silence by the suddenness of this development. She was unusually quiet on the journey back, responding only with "mmms" and "ahs" to Hero's cheerful review of the evening's highlights as Uncle Leonard dozed fitfully. Hero scarcely noticed her cousin's passive responses, moving onto speculation about the wedding, about the Wemyss family, about all the good things that were to come her way now that her Valentine was safely on the road to matrimony. Even if Rosamund had been less absorbed by her own dreams of what Captain Buchanan might say the following day, it would never have crossed her mind that Hero's happiness was so soon to crumble to ashes.

TWELVE

When Rosamund woke, it was late morning, after ten. The curtains had been drawn and she could see that the ewer on her washstand was a new one. She rose and rinsed her face in the tepid water in the jug and wandered over to the table where the maid had also left her a pot of tea and some toast. She lifted the lid of the teapot and sniffed at the brewed concoction within. It was quite cold. She had asked to be roused at half past eight, but clearly someone had taken it upon themselves to ignore her instructions, and much better she felt for it too. She had not immediately been able to sleep. In fact, she had tossed and turned, listening to the clocks throughout the house chiming the quarter hours with an unsettling unevenness, which had her determined to go round the house and reset them all the next morning, until she had finally dozed off properly between a quarter to four and the hour itself.

Of course, Captain Buchanan had been the chief cause of her insomnia. Would he truly come and offer for her? Would she accept if he did? What of her plans to travel, and her general wariness of men, and her specific wariness of Captain Buchanan? The questions whirled about her brain, his smile wafted in and out of her memory, his sudden and inexplicable civility baffled her and she was in a state of some confusion.

She shrugged on a robe, went to the bell pull to summon a girl, then over to her favorite window seat and gazed out over Cheveley's acres. She was sitting there, gazing into the distance and fiddling with the ribbons when the maid came in and helped her dress. When she went downstairs with the tray, the girl told the amazed kitchen staff that Miss Rosamund must be in love, for she was in the doziest state imaginable. One might have asked for the rest of the week off and she'd likely have agreed without a murmur.

It caused Rosamund some amusement to find herself dithering over her choice of clothing, her hair, her shoes, whether to go downstairs or stay upstairs, whether to read a book or do some stitching, whether to seek out Hero or remain alone. It was by this time half past eleven, and her air of indecision was gradually being eroded by a growing awareness that Captain Buchanan would be coming soon.

She could put off her descent into the day no longer and at last left her room and went to the little study where she and Hero spent so many hours toiling over the management of the house, the organization of meals and the ordering of their lives. Hero was not there, but Rosamund set to work, examining the post that had been left on her desk, taking out her account books and recording all the minutiae of the day before that had resolved matters or raised fresh ones.

The room was quiet, but Rosamund had left the door open, partly to show that the room was occupied and partly so that she could hear if anyone was admitted to the house. Soon enough, she heard the front doorbell and the steps of a footman to answer the call, the low tones of a masculine voice and the response of the footman showing the caller into the garden room. It was all Rosamund could do not to leap up and scurry down the corridor immediately. But the footman's steps came down the corridor past her study. He walked past the door, checked and poked his head in.

"Miss Lovelace! I was just looking for you. It's Captain Buchanan to call on you. I've shown him into the garden room."

"Are Miss Hero or Uncle Leonard with him?"

"They're out, miss, seeking out possible houses for Mrs. Wemyss, I think."

Rosamund carefully wiped her pen and laid it down, shook sand over the document she had been amending and stood, hoping she showed no sign of how her heart was beating. A school of tiny fish appeared to have taken up residence in her diaphragm, and she breathed in deeply before saying as calmly as she could, "I shall be along directly. Bring us some tea and some of Mrs. Harris's parkin, if you please."

"Yes, miss."

The footman went his way and Rosamund went hers, walking steadily, the excitement within her seeming to mount with every step. The door to the garden room was closed. She paused, breathed in again and then turned the handle and entered.

Captain Buchanan was standing, looking out across the park, his hands behind his back, imposing in his red coat, clean white trousers and polished black boots. He was bareheaded, and he whirled round on hearing the door open.

"Miss Lovelace. The lad told me he was not sure you were in."

"As you see, I am in, and happy to see you, Captain Buchanan."

A little of the tension in his shoulders and back seemed to seep away. They looked at each other for a second; then Rosamund broke the gaze and cleared her throat.

"Please, do sit down."

The captain looked around and walked over to the love seat on one side of the fireplace. Rosamund came and sat on the sofa opposite him.

"I have asked for some tea. And parkin. I hope you like parkin."

"It is one of the many cakes you have here in Yorkshire that I enjoy."

They gazed at each other in silence. Rory looked away. His knee began to jiggle furiously. The door opened and in came the footman with the tea tray. He positioned it on a side table near Rosamund, but she was still obliged to stand so that she could pour out the tea for the captain.

"Do you take sugar? Or milk?"

"Neither. Just the tea." She came over with the cup and saucer and in the other hand, a small plate with a slice of parkin. He took them and waited until she had served herself and was once again seated opposite him.

"Do you remember when we raced up on the ridge way and we went to tea at the mill? It seems so long ago."

"It is quite a long time ago—some years, at any rate." Rosamund's smile was wistful and her air a little abstracted.

"Miss Lovelace—" Rory broke off. Then he rushed on as if he could hold back no longer. "Miss Lovelace, we were friends then, and I wish we could be friends again. I wish you could be so much my friend as to call me by my given name."

"What sort of friend do you wish to be, Captain

Buchanan?" Rosamund noticed the disappointment in his eyes. "Rory."

She was rewarded with another of his rare, full smiles. "I wish you to be the sort of friend that I see each day. The sort of friend to whom I am able to tell everything. I thought we were so companionable, and then I spoilt it, out of jealousy and fear. When Colonel Fitzgerald came to me, inquiring about you, I could only think that he meant to ask for you himself. I didn't have the courage to claim you for my own, so I told that ridiculous story. And as a consequence, I lost you. At the ball last night, for the first time, I thought there might still be a chance for me."

Rosamund looked down at her teacup. Friendship was not what she sought from Captain Buchanan.

"Miss Lovelace?" She looked up and met his eyes. She looked wary but not hostile. "Is there a chance for me?"

"Captain Buchanan, I don't wish to seem foolish or silly, but I must know exactly what you mean by a chance. I want no confusion between us, only honesty. There has been confusion enough."

He placed his cup and saucer on the table beside him with some care. It was now his turn to avoid her gaze. In one easy movement, he stood, then knelt down on one knee before her and took her cup away from her before taking her hands in his and finally raising his bright blue eyes to hers.

"Miss Lovelace, will you do me the honor of becoming my wife?"

For a long moment, a moment filled with the awareness that his semirecumbent position was not particularly dignified, Rory watched her face as confusion and uncertainty warred there. Her hands tightened about his. She looked very dubious.

"Really? Are you sure?"

"I've never asked anyone before. Of course I'm sure."

Her grip loosened. "You look very silly and quite uncomfortable."

"Are you going to give me an answer or must I stay like this forever?"

She laughed and pulled her hands away, only to cover her mouth. Her eyes were dancing but she could not contain her giggles and threw her head back and laughed with delight and amusement. In exasperation, Rory rose and strode over to the window.

"No wonder I've never proposed before. It's the most humiliating business."

Rosamund leaped up. "I didn't mean to make it so. I just couldn't believe it."

Rory came back into the middle of the room. "You must believe it. I never imagined I'd meet a woman like you. You are so bright and so sharp. Sometimes I feel as though I'll cut myself on your blade. You make me feel more alive than rising on the morning before a battle, and for a soldier, that is something."

"Captain Buchanan—" He quirked an eyebrow at her. "Rory. You make me feel the same. I have a feeling we shall be perpetually wrangling and brangling, but no other man I've met has ever held a candle to you."

He took another step toward her, until they were standing very close, as close as they might be standing if they were to waltz. Except that she could scarcely know what a waltz was. He could teach her. But for now, he was content to press a kiss on the corner of her mouth and whisper against her skin, "Say yes, darling girl."

The warmth of his breath against her skin sent a tingle of sensation through her whole body. She felt as if even the finest of hair, every strand on her body, were standing to attention, and she breathed in sharply. His lips were almost touching hers, as if he were waiting to catch the word as she spoke it. She felt surrounded by him, the scent of his cologne, and beneath that, a more masculine, warm smell, of skin, warm wool, lemon and musk. She inhaled deeply as if gathering strength.

"Yes. Yes, I'll marry you."

His arms came round her waist and his mouth closed in on hers, and Rosamund received her first kiss, a slow, delicate play of lips.

Rory closed his eyes and leaned his forehead against hers, keeping her tight in his embrace. "I don't know what I'd have done if you'd refused."

"I don't know what I'd have done if you hadn't asked."

"I was such a fool. I was going to ask you on my next leave, but then Fitzgerald kept talking about how he would see you and what a sensible woman you seemed to be and what a suitable helpmeet you'd make, so I wanted to deter him from thinking of you as remotely acceptable as a wife. Thank God you've forgiven me." This time he kissed her with the desperation he'd pent up for so long, with the passion he'd suppressed and the love he had still scarcely admitted to himself he felt. And miracle of miracles, she was not frightened or disgusted but seemed to share his urgency. He broke off to sweep her into his arms and carry her back to the love seat, where he sat, holding her emphatically in his lap so that she could not escape, and began to kiss her thoroughly again. Eventually, they calmed down a little, although both could give only sharp, shallow little breaths.

"Well, well. I tried hard to imagine what it would be like

to kiss you, but I never imagined it would be like that!" Rosamund grinned. "Is it very indelicate of me to say so?"

"I don't care whether it is or not. I like to hear you say so. I shall strive to make you say such things every day."

"Will we truly see each other every day? It seems so strange, we have known each other for so many years, and yet we've spent very little time together."

"If I had my way, I'd sweep you off this minute and we'd never spend another second apart." Rory sighed as he felt a tension cause Rosamund to pull away slightly from him. "Damnation. I've woken you up to all the calls on your time and the demands of the real world."

"We can't announce it yet. We mustn't say anything. It would look as though I were trying to steal Hero's thunder. We must keep it quiet until she is safely wedded."

"But that's over a month away! We can't hide how we feel for that long. At least, I don't think I could." Rory turned Rosamund so he could look directly into her eyes. "Could you truly conceal what you feel for me? When we were dancing together last night, I felt as though all the world could read exactly how we felt about each other from our faces. It's what gave me the courage to come to you today."

"Whether we are so transparent or not, we cannot announce it yet. We cannot even tell the Veaseys. They'd insist on making a fuss and having a double wedding or some such nonsense. But that's not what I want. It's right for Hero because she's going to be mistress of Cheveley, but it isn't right for me."

"I see. I do understand. If you say anything now, they will make a great song and dance about it."

"Yes. But I'm not like Hero. She adores all these parties, and she loves to introduce Wemyss everywhere, which is how it should be because he will be in charge of Cheveley when the time comes. But I should hate to be the center of so much jollification." Rosamund pulled a face. "I like a dance well enough, but this incessant visiting is wearing in the extreme. I just want a quiet, family celebration."

Rory sighed. "I know you're right. And I should do my father the courtesy of telling him before we announce it also. It would make your life very difficult if I were to fetch up with you on my arm, having given him no warning whatsoever." He winced as he imagined the forthright reception he'd receive from his father. It would be no way to introduce a bride to her new home.

Rosamund reached her arms around his neck and pressed a kiss to his lips. "You are sensible, and it is one of the things I love about you. You know what is romantic and wild and tempting, but you are able to resist the temptation in favor of doing what is right. Neither of us may wish for it, but we cannot give way to our impulses and do as we truly desire. But at least you could come to dinner with us tonight."

Rory grinned. "I think you may find yourself a little shocked when we do give way to our impulses." His grip on her waist tightened and he could not resist showing her exactly what he was talking about. He kissed her again, then his lips moved gently, tenderly along her neck down to the hollow at the base of her throat and she gave a little murmur of desire that nearly undid him. He pulled back and collected himself.

Rosamund nestled with her head against his shoulder. Her breathing was shallow and she was astounded by how every nerve ending seemed to have become sensitized.

"I feel as if I was sixteen again. It reminds me of how I used to watch out for you and when I first caught a glimpse of you, my heart would come into my mouth and my pulse would race. It's ridiculous." She gave a little chuckle, then pulled away from him, stood up and shook her skirts out. He leaned back and watched her, his arms crossed, his legs crossed to stop himself from rising up and fetching her back to sit where she belonged, close to him. She went to the mirror and removed a pin or two in an effort to tidy up her disheveled hair.

"Rosamund, what made you look favorably on me again?"

She turned back to him and cocked her head to one side. "I shouldn't have shown my inclination if it hadn't been for something I overheard. I don't think I was meant to hear it, but someone suggested that you might hold me in some affection, if only I weren't so prickly. So I thought I would be less prickly next time we met and see what happened."

Rory laughed. "I believe someone has been having a game with us both. I was eavesdropping also when I heard about your affection for me. How curious it should be that we should each hear such similar tales."

"Who were you listening to?"

"Fitzgerald and Macdonald. They speculated on whether you were still attached to me, but they were rather blunt about my shortcomings."

"It was the same in my case, but it was Mrs. Carmichael and Miss Allerton talking. If it is true and we are the victims of some conspiracy, I am glad of it, for I do not believe we would ever have found our way to each other without such a glaring piece of guidance."

Just then, they heard a flurry of activity in the hallway. Rosamund looked around the room, as if to check that there was no evidence of the joyful meeting she had just had with the captain. He stood also, ready to greet the Veaseys.

"You have not yet said whether we will have the pleasure of your company at dinner. Will you come?"

"Of course. I shall be here promptly. But here comes your cousin."

Hero bounced into the room, her brown eyes sparkling with excitement, her cheeks flushed pink, gloves still in hand and bonnet swinging by the ribbon with her reticule. She paused on catching sight of Captain Buchanan, then smiled and thought no more of it.

"Rosamund, I believe we've found the ideal house for the Wemysses. You know the one, we've often remarked on how pretty it is, just the other side of the crossroads past the churchyard and the school? Well, it's available for rent, and we may have it on a short lease, and if it suits, they'll extend as long as we wish." Hero rambled on about its advantages and perfections, then suddenly turned to Buchanan.

"You must forgive me for going on so, but I am so looking forward to meeting Valentine's family and having them around us. Would I be trespassing if I were to ask you to carry a note to him at Brackenbury, asking him to come and see the house as soon as possible?"

Rory bowed and agreed at once. Hero went to a writing desk in the corner of the room and continued to chatter away as she scrawled her missive. Rosamund asked after Uncle Leonard, which set Hero off on another digression about his digestion and his arthritis and how he had had to go straight up to his room because the chill in the air did not seem to be dissipating and wasn't this weather impossible and utterly unspringlike.

It did not take Hero long to write her note, and once she had handed it to the captain, he felt as though he really had very little reason to remain at Cheveley. He was careful to make the same formal bow to both ladies as he left, and he wondered if Hero had noticed anything in either his or Rosamund's demeanor to give away their secret. But she had seemed much too carried away by her plans for her prospective in-laws to have noticed anything closer to home. It felt odd that he should remain silent about something that he wished to crow to the rooftops, but he knew he had to until Rosamund was ready to announce the match, and besides, he must write to his father. Even if he and Wemyss started off for Scotland in two days' time, a letter would probably arrive there more swiftly, and somehow it would be easier to arrive with the news of his attachment already under discussion than to have to break it himself.

But all of his musings were immediately forgotten on arriving at Brackenbury Park. For there, he was summoned at once to Fitzgerald's study, and feeling like a schoolboy discovered playing truant, Rory went down the paneled passageway to the small room where the colonel had established his headquarters. He knocked tentatively, looked inside and found Fitzgerald in anxious conclave with Macdonald.

"Thank heavens you're back, man!" The colonel indicated that he should sit and broached his concern straight away.

"Lowther has come to me with some wild tale of Miss Veasey, and I do not know what to do about it. I need your advice, man, before I next see Wemyss. I daresay he's with the chit even now."

"I believe not. She has sent me a note for him, hoping he will go over to Cheveley this instant to look round a house for his mother and sisters."

Fitzgerald shook his head and glanced at Macdonald. "It's a bad business, wouldn't you say?"

"I don't believe a word of it. I can't see why Lowther should have cooked up such a story, but I don't think it is anything more than a story." Macdonald was most emphatic. "My sister-in-law would never have tolerated a lightskirt in the family, and it must have come out during her stay in Edinburgh, or here. I haven't heard a word against her in either location. Lowther's cooking up some mischief. He's so much under Buchan's thumb, and it's just the sort of nonsense that that gentleman would cook up in an instant, simply for a little pother."

Rory felt increasingly baffled but at Buchan's name sat up. They had never been on good terms, but since their duel eight years before, they had studiedly avoided each other as much as possible and preserved as dignified a front as possible. On the whole, they had succeeded, and while Rory still felt somewhat uncomfortable with the man in social circumstances, he could not deny that Buchan was a brave and competent soldier, reliable under fire and careful of his men.

"Explain, please, gentlemen. What exactly is this tale?"

"Lowther came to me and said that he had heard that Miss Veasey was less than virtuous. I spoke of it to Lowther this morning, and he places no credence in the lieutenant's account. But I feel that one ought to see the proof he claims to have."

"And do what? Tell Veasey before or after we have accused his affianced wife of easy behavior?" Macdonald continued. "They have signed the settlements, he is committed, whether she can be proved to be loose or not. The contract is near as binding as the vows in church, man. Whether she is free or not, he must marry her, and what is the use of disillusioning him before the wedding?"

"I thought I was cynical!" exclaimed Rory. "Good God,

Macdonald, we cannot leave Miss Veasey to be slandered
so. She is virtuous and what Lowther thinks he's about I
have no idea." Rory leaped out of his chair and paced the
room. "It is our duty to get to the bottom of this rumor and
scotch it."

"Lowther tells me he will have proof this very night. I
am going to accompany him to examine his proof, and
then we shall decide whether to tell Wemyss."

"I've never heard such folly. You should summon
Lowther now and get the whole tale out of him before
he causes any further damage. We've been here more
than once, the Veaseys have been enormously hospitable
and we repay them by giving credence to this vile little
fabrication! It is monstrous, sir, and I beg you will establish the truth at once. I always knew Lowther to be a
foolish puppy, but to besmirch an innocent girl's name
in this way in unconscionable."

But Fitzgerald and Macdonald disagreed, suddenly forced
into agreement by Rory's uncompromising defense of Miss
Veasey. It was agreed that Rory would go as promised to
Cheveley but that the other officers would accompany
Lowther that evening to whatever shady rendezvous he had
agreed to attend. And there, once and for all, they would establish Miss Veasey's reputation. It was with grave misgiving
that Rory went in search of Valentine to pass on Hero's note,
a note that seemed to have been written in a time of inno-
cence that quite suddenly had been swept away and was
perhaps gone forever.

THIRTEEN

The regular customers at the Griffin Inn were not an observant bunch, dedicated as they were to ale, dice, song and the fine women on offer. Well, perhaps not so very fine, in fact, rather coarse and certainly well-used, but still, in the dim light and after a pint or two, acceptable. But the women were observant, for they watched out for each other, and anyway they were on the *qui vive* this night. So when a group of four smart officers from Brackenbury Park appeared just after nine o'clock, they perked up. These were the gents who were to be sent to the stables for a show. They'd get a show all right. It was good to think of some stuck-up miss getting her comeuppance, especially since it seemed, from what that other gentleman had said, that she had been poaching on their territory.

The four men found a quiet corner and sat themselves gingerly on the wooden settles, watching the proceedings with faintly disgusted eyes. Lame Meg was performing her regular routine to roars of approval and cries of "Gerremoff." It was next to impossible to hear anyone talk, so they looked down at their tankards, reluctant to sully their lips on the indisputably filthy rims. Captain Macdonald was drumming his fingers on the table, Fitzgerald was examining the material covering his knee as if it were a masterpiece, Valentine was simply baffled as to why his commanding officer had chosen to frequent this insalubrious tavern while Lowther looked about anxiously for some sign of Buchan.

At last Lame Meg's interminable siren song came to an end, the applause died down and it seemed there would be a pause in the evening's entertainment, allowing the clientele of the Griffin to order their next round and hear one another speak for a brief spell at least, which was when Buchan came in. Macdonald watched him approach their table with distaste and suspicion. He slipped into the seat beside Lowther and bent close to the table to confide in his fellows.

"She is in the stables even now. I must prepare you for a most upsetting sight. Wemyss, I hope you will not hold it against me that I brought this to your attention. It was more than I could stomach, seeing a fellow officer so taken in."

"What do you mean?" Valentine looked around at his friends. "What is Buchan implying? Who is in the stables?"

Fitzgerald rose up, reluctant to follow Buchan but determined that the truth must be uncovered. "Wemyss, my dear fellow, I fear that you will be mightily upset by what we are about to witness, but I could not let you proceed down your current path without discovering the true nature of your intended."

"Come on then, let us see what Buchan has to show us and be done with this vile business." Macdonald stood and followed Fitzgerald. Buchan shook his head and led the way out of a side door of the tavern. The light faded and the men were instantly buffeted by a needle-sharp burst of rain and wind. They bent their heads and tightened their grip on their cloaks as they strode single file down the passageway into a courtyard behind the main building of the inn. Buchan indicated that they should quietly take the stairs up to a hayloft. Lowther went up first, followed by Fitzgerald, then Wemyss, then Macdonald. They each ducked to enter by a low hatch, then crouched in the dark.

There was a muted light below from two lanterns swinging from the beam supporting the hayloft. First they were conscious of the unmistakable sounds of a couple in congress. Then as their eyes became accustomed to the dimness, they saw the shadow, a wavering, rocking shadow. By this time, Buchan was in the hayloft. He brushed aside some of the residue of grass and seed and uncovered a place where there had once been a knot in the wood but that now provided a peephole to gaze down on the couple below. He nodded at the colonel, whose lips tightened in revulsion but who bent down and watched for long seconds. He jerked upward, his face full of pain and misery, and beckoned to Wemyss to look. Valentine leaned forward and positioned himself so that he could see clearly. He was still, but then the man below called out, over and over, in soft, quick pants, "Hero, Hero, Hero." Wemyss recoiled from the spy hole, wild-eyed. Buchan clamped his hand over the boy's mouth and Lowther took his arms to prevent him from flailing about and catapulting himself over the side of the hayloft.

As quietly as they could, they wrestled him out of the hatch and into the fresh air. The rain had finally ceased, but the air was still damp and clammy. It seemed to calm Valentine down, but he was still taut as a tiger with rage and confusion.

"You saw it, you saw it too! How could she do this? Has she always been so? Good God! That I nearly married with this creature!"

"I cannot credit it!" Macdonald was quick to spring to the girl's defense. "How can you be sure it was Hero? Peering through some tiny crack in the wood like a Peeping Tom, how can you be sure of anything you saw?" His question was equally directed at Fitzgerald as at Wemyss. The colonel was swift to defend himself.

"Macdonald, I wish I could say otherwise, but I have seen Miss Veasey wear that same pelisse and bonnet before now. It is most distinctive, a dark red color with a gold embroidered hem and matching bonnet, again stitched in gold thread. I could not have mistaken it. And then you heard the man yourself!"

"Did you see her face? Or her figure? Was there any definitive distinguishing mark? Or just shadows and faded colors in a darkened spot? That's no proof. Anyone might have picked up her pelisse, what's to say she hasn't given it away herself to some indigent?" Macdonald was determined to defend his sister-in-law's niece, not only because of their family tie but also because he could not imagine Miss Veasey being so duplicitous, so conniving a creature as to give herself freely to some man in a stable while engaged to another. It went against everything he knew of the girl.

"I saw her wear that same coat only yesterday, Macdonald." Wemyss sounded a broken man, his voice weary, his heart sore. "She has not handed it over to some poor slut to ward off this dreary weather. I did not see her face, it's true, but I am persuaded that it was Hero there."

"We should ride to Cheveley this instant and see if she is there. If she is not, then you may start accusing her of infidelity, but until then, until you have absolutely cast-iron proof, you should not doubt her." Macdonald was emphatic.

Buchan intervened. "It's after ten now. We can hardly go to Cheveley and rouse the entire household."

"On a matter so grievous, I think we can. Veasey should

look to his daughter, and he should certainly look to his daughter's reputation if she is safely there."

"No, I think we must deal with this matter in the morning. We are due there tomorrow for this assembly. Let us repair to Brackenbury. We can do no good here."

"No good? Why not wait for her to emerge and beard her here, so that we may establish once and for all the chit's identity?" Macdonald was becoming increasingly exasperated with his comrades-in-arms. They seemed so defeatist and so certain of their facts, but as he saw it, his lawyerly inclinations coming to the fore, there was no conclusive proof against the girl, and ample opportunity to acquire exactly the proof one might need to settle this business once and for all. But he was overruled, and the sodden, miserable party trailed away toward Brackenbury, much to Buchan's relief.

None of the party slept well. Fitzgerald was clear in his duty, which was to remain with young Wemyss and control his rasher impulses. Buchan knew he needed to continue stoking the fires of doubt and fury that consumed the young lover, and consequently remained with the colonel and the lieutenant. This meant that Lowther also decided to stay up. Macdonald abandoned them to their fruitless, circular speculations and went in search of the only sane man left at Brackenbury. But it transpired that Buchanan had gone to dine at Cheveley and had been prevailed upon to remain there rather than risking the road alone in the dead of night.

Of course, since the cavalrymen had broached more than one bottle of brandy to fuel their discussions and oil their woes, they were not capable of rising early the following morning. Macdonald was down early and in a quandary as to whether he should ride directly to Cheveley to warn the Veaseys of the impending storm, or whether he should wait until Fitzgerald led the charge there in an attempt to mitigate the wilder accusations that no doubt would fly about when all were gathered at Cheveley.

In the event, he set out promptly enough, but his horse went lame on the way over and by the time he had settled the poor mare in the Cheveley stables with a poultice and constant attendance from one of the stable boys, guests of all sorts were pouring down on the place with the persistence of the rain that had thus far wrecked the summer. The place was in an uproar of conflicting demands and calls for shelter for the carriage horses and hacks that had carried the assembled company for this betrothal luncheon. As he emerged from the stall where Lucy had been settled, he saw the backs of Fitzgerald and his cohorts marching toward the house in grim determination.

He hurried after them, struggling his way through a mass of guests. He hadn't realized that half of Yorkshire had been invited to this blasted party, half of Yorkshire in all its finery, ladies with wildly decorated hats and expansive gentlemen taking the opportunity to catch up on the latest gossip about manifold plows and the coal mine that Kirby had stumbled across in his west field, scarcely aware in their excitement of a stranger working his way through their midst, following the four red coats that were striding forward inexorably toward a confrontation that was going to cause utter disaster.

None of the guests from Brackenbury Park had understood just how great an occasion this party was to be. It had started out as a small gathering designed to introduce Wemyss to some of his more influential neighbors-to-be but seemed to have become a great assembly of all the finest families in the county. The footmen were weaving their way through the crowds bearing trays of champagne, orgeat and

lemonade. A small orchestra had been assembled from local
musicians, some amateur and some professional. They were
now scraping their way through a divertimento by Mozart.

Hero stood in the great stateroom at Cheveley, a room that
had played host to lords, lieutenants and royalty making pro-
gresses about the countryside (at least, to a royal duke and
prince of the blood), her father on one side, her uncle the other.
Macdonald caught a glimpse of Rory Buchanan turning his
face, at first startled and then anxious as he absorbed the stern
mien of his commanding officer and his friend Wemyss. He
bent down to murmur something in a feminine ear, which
Macdonald recognized as belonging to Miss Lovelace. She
looked up, her calm features suddenly marred by a frown.

By now, Wemyss and Fitzgerald were standing before
the Veaseys, surrounded by guests, all looking on benignly
as Hero gave a great beam of pleasure at the sight of her
fiancé. Then Macdonald saw her smile falter and the light
fade from her features. The musicians squeaked their way
to their finale and a hush fell over the room.

"Miss Veasey, I demand that you release me from our
engagement. I find I cannot give you my name, since I
have discovered you have none of your own."

Hero reeled as if she had been struck, and Rosamund
gasped audibly before rushing to her cousin. Hero looked
up at Wemyss with the eyes of a stricken puppy, confused
at receiving pain from a trusted source.

"What do you mean, sirrah?" demanded Anthony Veasey.
Rosamund was ready to echo him, except that she found her
arms full of an increasingly heavy Hero, whose knees had
buckled. The two girls sank to the ground in a welter of petticoat and satin, and Hero passed from consciousness.

"Ask her where she was last night. Ask her who she was
with. Ask her and discover her true nature." Wemyss's voice

cracked in its extremity and he turned on his heel and left the room. Fitzgerald looked first one way, then another, realizing that Lowther and Buchan had melted away also and had left the chamber hurriedly, followed by Anthony Veasey demanding to know exactly what was going on, who had slandered his niece and what sort of misdemeanor could make acceptable such entirely outrageous behavior.

Rory wrestled his way through the gaping mass of bodies to Rosamund and Hero. He bent down and said quietly, "I can carry her. Let me take her." He scooped up the stricken girl and rose gracefully. "Where should I go with her?"

Rosamund had risen too by this time. Unsteadily, she raised a hand to her brow, rubbed her temple and shook her head slightly as if to clear the dense fog that had settled there. "Follow me. I'll lead you to her room."

The guests parted like the Red Sea making way for the Israelites, and Rosamund had an impression of avid, stunned and intrigued faces, as well as the intent, infuriated features of Captain Macdonald. She caught his eye and inclined her head slightly, so that he made his way to the forefront of the throng and entered Buchanan's slipstream.

They none of them glanced back, where Leonard Veasey was clutching his arm and visibly paling, unable to go forward and make any move to assist his daughter, and soon enough was attended by his doctor.

Despite the burden of the unconscious girl in his arms, Rory took the steps to the first floor of Cheveley two at a time, with Rosamund and Macdonald at his heels. Within seconds, they were at Rosamund's door, and placed Hero delicately on the bed there. Both Buchanan and Miss Lovelace rounded on Macdonald instantly.

"What on earth is going on?" they demanded in unorchestrated tandem. They glanced at each other and their lips twitched, but the seriousness of the situation suppressed any sense of the absurd that they shared.

"It's preposterous. Last night, Buchan led us to some low tavern, where he showed us a sight which I cannot mention before ladies, except to say that it seemed that Miss Veasey was a key participant."

Rosamund was incandescent. "What on earth? What nonsense! What can have possessed them to believe this farrago?"

"Only Fitzgerald and Wemyss had any true view of this supposed encounter. I've tried and tried to persuade them that they were mistaken, but they are certain that they saw Miss Veasey most grievously compromised."

From the bed, Hero gave a low moan. Rosamund had the wit to gather up the basin from the washstand before going to her cousin, who promptly evacuated the contents of her stomach, retching and weeping.

"You cannot remain here. For heaven's sake, leave us. I will come down directly, but you see how she is! See if you can find a doctor downstairs."

Both Buchanan and Macdonald were relieved to be dismissed. They tracked down the family doctor, who had been attending Leonard Veasey, then repaired to the terrace.

"Explain to me once again, how does Buchan have any involvement in this tawdry business?" Rory was pacing the tiled surface of the terrace, his hands clenched behind his back, every muscle rigid with tension.

Macdonald told him the full tale of the previous night's excursion to the Griffin Inn and watched for Buchanan's reaction, which came promptly enough.

"What an unholy mess! And you know the worst of it? Miss Veasey was out last night. Her father cannot prove she was present and accounted for because she had gone out to dine with neighbors. She came in after eleven. I was playing billiards with Anthony Veasey and we heard her return home."

"You didn't happen to see her and find out whether she was wearing this infamous red pelisse, I suppose?"

"No. We didn't go out of the billiard room, nor did she come to seek us out. But you know, the footmen will have seen."

"They may well have done, but Wemyss and Fitzgerald will simply say that since these men are in Veasey employ, their word cannot be trusted."

"That may be so, but at least you and I can begin to build a case against them. That it has come to this! How sick she was, as well!"

The two men poked their noses indoors, watching as the guests ebbed away, for no more scandal seemed to be emerging as the afternoon wore out its course, and there was certainly nothing to be celebrated in the fact that both Leonard and Hero Veasey were upstairs in their bedchambers under medical supervision.

Rory and Captain Macdonald went among the guests, at first suggesting that the whole business would be speedily cleared up, then easily suggesting that it was some great insult to the county as a whole that one of their own should be spurned so publicly by some upstart Scot. This notion was swiftly taken up, so that the guests as a whole were indignant as they left about the insult offered to Hero Veasey and very much upset with the colonel and his subordinate at their want of manners in creating so unsightly a scandal when the whole business might easily have been dealt with discreetly, if indeed it was a business that needed dealing with at all.

Miss Lovelace came down as the last of the guests were climbing into their carriages. She sought out Buchanan

and Macdonald, who were by this time uneasily waiting in
the library for some direction.

"What idiocy is this? I knew Wemyss for a fool, but I
hadn't taken him for a blackguard! How could he treat her
so? I've never seen Hero so ill. It breaks my heart."

"And what of Mr. Veasey? We saw him being taken up
by his servants, looking most unwell," said Rory.

"Uncle Leonard is never entirely fit when there is any
fuss, especially a fuss which might force him to take any action. He will be healthy enough in a day or two. In the
meantime, we have Uncle Anthony to rely on for our honor."

Once again, Macdonald found himself explaining a somewhat censored version of the events of the previous night.

"Wearing her red pelisse? Thank God we can prove her in-
nocence. She was not wearing her red pelisse last night
because it had disappeared, along with one of the wash-
house girls. Our maid went down to fetch it from the laundry
room yesterday afternoon when she was helping Hero get
ready to go out and it couldn't be found anywhere. She wore
my blue cloak, I can testify to that, as can Pam, our girl."

Rory cleared his throat. "Macdonald has, um, suggested
that perhaps such evidence will not be sufficient because you
will be partial. Is there anyone not connected with the household who might have seen Miss Veasey in this blue cloak?"

"Of course. She went to the Robertsons' house. She and
Mrs. Robertson are thick as thieves when it comes to clothes
and she was once again intent on a consultation over her
trousseau. Heaven help us!" Rosamund started pacing, her
hands clasped tight, her head bowed in thought. "She left
here at half past six. She would have taken half an hour to
reach Holden House and must have been there for supper. I
don't imagine she reached home much before eleven, which

means she must have left there sometime around half past ten. When were you at the Griffin Inn?"

The three of them pieced together the evening's events and established exactly which people they needed to rebut this slur against Hero's character. Soon, Captain Macdonald left for the stables to call up his and Buchanan's horses, ready to gallop out in search of Mrs. Robertson and the missing laundry maid.

Alone with Rosamund for the first time that day, Rory went to her immediately and held her close. "My love, we'll clear your cousin's name, and then I'll thrash Buchan from one end of the county to the other."

She broke free of his embrace and paced the room. "God, that I were a man, I'd do it myself and whip your friend Wemyss with him. How could he behave so shabbily on so little proof?"

But this, Rory could not answer. If he had been in Wemyss's position, he would never have believed Buchan. But Wemyss did not have the benefit of ten or twelve years of exposure to Buchan's wiles and tricks. Besides which, Buchan's familiar, Lowther, was able to spend time dripping additional poison in Wemyss's ear.

"She has been so happy. It has been four years that she has loved him and she has been so faithful, so true. For him to malign her so is beyond wickedness."

With this, Rory entirely concurred, but he did wonder what the implications were for his own attachment to Rosamund. If anything grievous happened to Hero, Rosamund would be entirely occupied in setting matters to rights. How long it would be before he could claim her, he could not tell. His exasperation with Wemyss and Buchan increased.

"Is the doctor still with her?"

"I left him up there with firm instructions to see me before he left."

"Rosamund, look at me." She raised her eyes to his and he continued. "You know I would never doubt you thus."

Her lips curved a little. "I know that." She reached for his hands. "I do know that, my dearest friend. First of all you are too sensible to believe such a tale without corroborating it thoroughly, and second of all, you know me well enough to trust me. But Wemyss has broken something in Hero and I do not know if it can ever be repaired." For the first time that afternoon, tears threatened Rosamund's composure.

There was a knock at the door and the doctor bustled in, forgetting his usual bowing to all and sundry, his voice harsh and urgent, utterly unlike his usually emollient tones. "Miss Lovelace, your cousin is grievously ill. Some sort of brain fever. I must ask you to sit with her constantly this night. Her pulse is disordered and her temperature wild. I have left a maid up there, but you will need assistance to keep her from harming herself. I've never seen a girl so beside herself."

"Go up to her at once. I shall seek out Macdonald and together we will do all we can to right this wrong. Dear girl, take care, and be brave." Disregarding the doctor, he dropped a kiss on her temple and left. Rosamund hurried upstairs to Hero, the doctor at her heels hurling instructions for the sick girl's care. But when they reached her room, the maid was sobbing in a chair, and Hero was stretched out on the floor, her pulse fading fast, her state entirely comatose.

FOURTEEN

The news of Hero's collapse soon spread far and wide, and as with the best gossip, became increasingly garbled as it oozed through the county. It caused a good deal of ill feeling against Brackenbury Park, where in any case, both Fitzgerald and Wemyss were peculiarly shaken by the disappearance of Buchan and the appearance of Mrs. Robertson on their doorstep the morning after the disastrous confrontation with Miss Veasey.

The footman was very clear in delivering the colonel's instructions. No visitors were to be admitted, the master was definitely not at home. But Mrs. Robertson brushed this aside with increasing indignation, and lurid as a cockerel's wattle, brazened her way into the colonel's study.

"You have been a party to the greatest folly imaginable, and how you are to repair the damage I cannot imagine."

Fitzgerald winced, for it was only what Buchanan and Macdonald had been telling him repeatedly for the past hour or more.

"Miss Veasey was at my house from seven in the evening until thirty minutes past the hour of ten. I can tell you exactly what we ate and who else was present and the fact that she did not come wearing her usual pelisse, although why this should be of the slightest importance I cannot imagine. Your captains have come to me and asked me a great many impertinent questions, everyone is in complete uproar and how that We-myss boy thinks he can remain in Yorkshire and show his face is beyond effrontery. I warn you, Colonel, you misjudged your target when you attacked the Veaseys. They may look as tooth-less as hens, but they've friends and they've influence."

Fitzgerald was later to report to Macdonald that the old besom kept up her harangue for a good twenty minutes be-fore demanding to see Wemyss himself. When the boy appeared, she had rested sufficiently to give him a good jawing for a further half hour. Fitzgerald escaped and went out immediately to apologize to the Veaseys.

Fortunately for the colonel, he did not cross paths with Rory, who had ridden over to Cheveley first thing, only to be told that Miss Lovelace was still with Miss Hero, hav-ing had no rest the previous night. Miss Veasey's condition appeared to have worsened further. It was in an ill temper that Rory returned to the stables, thwacking his crop against his boots as he waited for his horse to be brought out, and riding off in a set, determined frame of mind. The ride back to Brackenbury did not succeed in dispelling his displeasure. He went directly up to his room and hauled off his boots, hurling them into a corner and then fetching them and standing them neatly in a corner of the room for his man to polish, his ire mounting as he considered the stupidity of both his friends and the deep trouble they had brought not only on that sad figure, the Veasey girl, but much more important, to his own dear Rosamund.

He was interrupted by a knock at the door.

"Come!" he barked. The door opened warily and in sidled Wemyss.

"How is Hero?"

"What do you care? You've driven her to her sickbed."

"I care a great deal. It seems we were hasty. If I should lose her!"

"Good God, man, of course you've lost her. I'd be astonished if any of the Veaseys allowed you anywhere near her and I can tell you her cousin wants to hunt you down, coat you in honey and stake you out for the ants. I would be inclined to assist her were I in the vicinity. Particularly if Miss Veasey does not recover. She's very ill indeed."

"What have I done?" Wemyss sat in the chair by the fire, cradling his head in his hands, abject and full of remorse. Or self-pity, Rory found it hard to distinguish.

"You've been a complete ass. Ably assisted by our noble colonel, who I'd have thought had more sense than to believe anything presented to him by that menace Buchan."

"What can I do to mend matters?"

"Find Buchan and punish him. Lord, man, must everything be explained to you? Have you no brain of your own? No, for if you had, you'd have seen at once this was some low trick, you'd have trusted the woman you purport to love and you'd have swatted Buchan like the tiresome fly he is."

Buchanan was towering over Wemyss by this time, shouting down into the lieutenant's guilt-stricken features. A flicker of feeling stirred the lieutenant.

"Are you saying I am stupid?"

"I didn't realize I must spell it out. I thought even you had wit enough to work that out for yourself."

"There's no need for you to insult me." Wemyss stood.

"Since you are so capon-brained as to need me to explain that I *am* insulting you, I think there is ample need for me to tell you what a fool you are since you are certainly too woolly to do it for yourself. If I had treated a woman as you have treated Miss Veasey, stupidity is the least sin of which I would be accusing myself."

"What should I do, Buchanan?"

His rage finally got the better of him. "Leave Yorkshire immediately and seek out some other heiress to insult but at least wait until you've safely married her. Then you may treat her as ill as you please."

"Now you are saying I am a fortune-hunter."

"Aren't you?"

"If I were, I'd marry Miss Veasey regardless of her reputation."

"There was nothing to disregard until *you* started mangling her reputation." Rory went to the door of his room and held it open. "Go before I forget myself and give you the thrashing you deserve. I've had enough of you."

"You've had enough of me! You rant and rave at me and expect me to accept your slurs," spluttered Valentine, finally reacting as Rory had intended. "You shall answer to me, sir. Name your seconds."

"Macdonald will act for me, and Anthony Veasey, I daresay. What about you? Are you going to go running to Fitzgerald? Who will you name? Buchan and Lowther, those reliable souls who skulked away the instant you'd thrown your grenade?"

Wemyss's lips tightened and he turned on his heel, finally allowing Rory some privacy in which to berate himself for giving way to the impulse to needle and nag at Wemyss. Provoking the boy into fighting a duel was a displacement of the ire he should more correctly have aimed at Buchan. But Buchan was nowhere to be found.

It was not long before he was troubled by the other idiot, as he now apostrophized his senior officer. Fitzgerald sent up a man, asking Rory to step down to his study. He hauled on his boots again and went downstairs.

The colonel was nursing a tankard of ale. There was no life in his voice.

"We played directly into his hands, didn't we?"

"We?" asked Rory.

"The girl may die. I saw Anthony Veasey at Cheveley. He says she's been unconscious since last night." He sipped his beer. "I only glanced. I couldn't bear to take a longer look. It all appeared so plausible. Buchan made it so. But he's made things so before, hasn't he, and I should have been alive enough to his ways to see that."

"You may as well know, I've managed to provoke Wemyss into an encounter."

"Just to add to my troubles. Still, I have brought this on myself, I suppose. And we cannot track down Buchan, not for all the bucks in Yorkshire chasing him down with considerable enthusiasm. He and Lowther appear to have made good their escape."

"Have you checked the Griffin Inn? Might they not have concealed themselves there until the furor died down a little? They must know that we're all baying after them. They'd be identified and brought before you if they stirred, so they're lying low."

The colonel was galvanized by this notion. "Go there, man, go there at once, will you, and see if you're right. Even if you're not correct, you might discover something more about this debacle."

So Rory set off once again, his thoughts full of Rosamund, imagining her at Hero's side, mopping the girl's brow, shaking up her pillows, that faint fresh scent of lily of the valley hanging about her. He would no more have doubted Rosamund than he would have doubted the rising of the sun or the position of the stars. She was steadfast, and it would take more than the sight of her

pelisse and a man calling her name to make him suspect
her of any infamy. Even if he had not loved her, he would
have known her to be incapable of such wickedness, just
as he knew Hero to be innocent. It baffled him how Wemyss or Fitzgerald could have been so taken in, but
perhaps they were genuinely foolish. Or simply suspicious of the opposite sex. After all, what did Fitzgerald
know of women? As for Wemyss, he had been writing
regularly to Miss Veasey and still had initiated that flirtation with Miss Sutcliffe in Brussels. She had been
livelier than Miss Veasey, that was certain, but poor and
a little vulgar. She was just the sort of girl who might be
found in a stable with her skirts about her ears, but how
Wemyss could be such a noddlecock as to confuse the
two personalities, Rory could not imagine. He wondered
what Hero and Rosamund would have to say to the dis-
covery of Wemyss's little infatuation. There was far more
substance to that relationship than this nonsensical slur
against Miss Veasey.

With such musings occupying his thoughts, Rory found
he was at the Griffin Inn more quickly than he anticipated.
He did not expect to be there long, so he simply tethered
his horse to the post by the drinking trough rather than taking it round to the stable yard.

The inn was quiet and its shabbiness undisguised in the
afternoon light. He half-expected to find the place locked
and barred, but the door opened, its unoiled hinges squeak-
ing. He stepped directly into a taproom, rancid with the stink
of stale beer and smoke and sweat. The room was empty and
dark. A passageway seemed to lead through to another room.
He made his way down it, calling out for assistance.

The corridor opened out into a marginally cleaner area
where three women in various stages of undress were sitting,

one sewing, the other two playing at cribbage. The sewing woman looked up and nudged the woman seated beside her.

"Hey ho, Becky, here's a customer for you."

Becky looked up and grinned. It was intended to be a beguiling smile, but her lack of a complete set of teeth somewhat impaired its charm. Her hair was a wild, knotted tangle and she kept poking the mass with a forefinger and scratching vigorously.

" 'S another officer. Positively swarming with officers we are." She rose and swung away from the bench where she'd been sitting. Her corset was tightly laced, and she wore no blouse or dress, simply her chemise beneath the corset and several layers of petticoats, all rather gray and stained. "It's two shilling for the half hour, half a crown for a full hour."

"I am willing to pay you for information, but not for your time. That isn't necessary."

"Better spoken than the other ones." Becky's card partner had turned round now to inspect the captain. "I should take the money, Becky. It looks as though he'll pay you on the spot 'stead of on tick."

"When I need your advice, Patsy, I'll ask for it. Till then, shut your face."

"Oooohhh, touchy, aren't we?" Patsy gave a grin marginally less toothless than Becky's. "You'll find yourself in trouble with all the schemes you've got yourself into and then who'll you turn to?"

"I have a guinea for you all if you can help me." Buchanan silenced the trollops before their dispute could get out of hand by holding up a single gold coin. They all three looked at him in wonder and blessed silence.

"I'm looking for two officers, one captain, one lieutenant. The senior is small and dark, the other is younger, in his

early twenties and sporting sideboards. Have you seen either
of them? They were here two nights ago with other officers."

The women exchanged a significant look but said nothing. Rory waited, idly fingering the guinea and avoiding any
eye contact with the ladies. He started flicking the coin as if
playing at heads and tails, catching it with a clean smack
against the leather of his glove. He started humming a ditty
about a fox being chased from morn to night.

"You aren't the only one looking for the officers." Becky
gave a little smile.

"I'm sure I'm not, but I should think I'm the only with
a guinea in hand and the promise of another if you can provide me with the answers I'm looking for."

"The lady's upstairs already, having a chat with our dear
Aunt Moll. She was full of guineas too, and I'm sure we
can find a way of unburdening you both." Becky's chin
had an impudent tilt to it, and her eyes were calculating.

"What lady?" he asked, although her exact identity was
dawning him with increasing horror.

"Why, one of the ladies from Cheveley. Shocking, isn't
it? A lady talking with trulls. But she found us, and she's
prepared to pay a lot more than two guineas between three
of us to find your two officers."

"Where is she exactly?"

"Up the stairs, at the end of the passageway, the door on
your left. Hurry now, or Auntie Moll will have recruited
her to our game."

Rory did not pause to take in their final sally, which
was accompanied by gales of cackles and knee slapping.
He hurtled through the inn and up its stairs, pausing only
before the low door to which he had been directed, force
of habit preventing him from barging in. He listened and
heard the harsh tones of an older woman, followed by

a lower, more educated voice. It was, he was certain, Rosamund.

He opened the door and entered. As he had suspected, Rosamund was standing in front of a table where sat an older doxy, a woman well wrapped in shawls with a bonnet that might have been respectable if the face beneath it had not been painted with a bright blue powder on her eyelids, great pools of rouge on each cheek and a scarlet smear smudged over her lips. The woman's grin was predatory.

"You'd give a good deal to find these gentlemen, I take it. Or their light-o'-love?"

"I can pay you well whatever information you give me. Obviously, the more you can tell me, the greater the sum I can offer in recompense for your trouble and your time." Rosamund examined the tassels on her shawl. Her voice was calm and she did not glance round as Rory came into the room, a shabby little place, dust-filled and cramped with the overspill of broken chairs and boxes of dented, chipped china.

Aunt Moll did look up, however, and at the sight of Rory's uniform seemed a little agitated.

"This lady is certainly able to offer you a handsome sum, and so am I. Of course, if you find yourself unable to remember any of the events of the night before last, or the whereabouts of any of the participants, not only will there be no money, there will almost certainly be an uncomfortable visit from the watch."

Rosamund smiled. "Yes. Perhaps Mrs. Wetherby has forgotten that there are several Cheveley men on the watch."

Moll Wetherby's lips tightened and her eyes were resentful. "Show me your money. Show me your gold guineas."

Rosamund reached into her reticule and withdrew a small but weighty-looking purse. She loosened the drawstrings and carefully counted out five gold coins. She placed them on the table in front of Mistress Wetherby in a tidy column. She spoke once more, her voice quiet but tempered with contempt and fury.

"The first one is for explaining to us the request you received on Tuesday afternoon. The second is for encouraging the woman who participated in this masquerade to come forward and tell her part. The third is for doing the same for the man. The fourth is for telling us the whereabouts of the two officers who initiated this plan, and the fifth is for keeping our investigations into this matter a secret."

All three people in the room knew that the bawd was looking at a sum of money equivalent to a month's takings. Her eyes slid about the room like a cornered beetle. Rosamund concentrated hard on keeping her composure. She wanted nothing more than to take the grubby creature by the shoulders and give her an almighty shake, but Rory's presence steadied her. He was radiating a similar tension, but she had a feeling that in addition to waiting for Mrs. Wetherby to take up her offer, he was summoning the strength not to dress her down thoroughly for being so foolish as to have visited the Griffin Inn in the first place.

At last, Mrs. Wetherby reached for the money. Swift and sure as an eagle, Rory caught her wrist before she could touch the pile of coins. "Speak now."

So she did, her arm held steady by the man's grasp. She told the whole sorry tale, how Buchan had come equipped with the coat and bonnet, how she had recruited a girl, how the girl had found her mate. But she could not tell where Buchan and Lowther had gone. They had spent the previous night in her hayloft, that same hayloft where Valentine and Fitzgerald had been so misled, but this morning the old fellow who looked after the stables had taken porridge up to the two men and found the hayloft deserted. They had absconded without paying her the sum they had agreed, and Aggie and her man had come round trying to dun her for the sovereign that Buchan had promised them.

Rory released her wrist and watched her as she swept the coins off the table and into the palm of her hand, nursing them closer to her breast than a mother with a new baby. Rosamund spoke.

"I know you deal in the basest of trades, Mistress Wetherby. I know what that trade is. I understand it entirely. And the next time you attempt to besmirch the name of an innocent, I shall encourage your persecutors in every way I can and wave you away to the transport ships with a far clearer conscience than I have now. Make do with the living you make now and do not seek to expand your business interests again."

Turning on her heel, Rosamund marched down the passage and stairway, not pausing to see if Rory was following her. The prickle of the down on the back of her neck was more than enough to tell her that he was, compounded by the firm rap of his boots on the wooden boards behind her. She headed directly for the stable yard behind the inn, where her horse was tethered. He had not followed her out here. She leaned her head against the warm pelt of Arcturus and paused for breath. Now she must seek out Agatha Dobson and her lover. And set the watch on the trail of Buchan and Lowther. And return to Hero's side, to watch her sinking closer and closer to oblivion. Rosamund's head came up and she suppressed her inclination to cry. Hero would not die.

She mounted her horse neatly, accustomed to organizing

the voluminous folds of her habit for herself, and trotted through to the front of the inn where Captain Buchanan was waiting for her, also ready and mounted.

"I'll accompany you back to Cheveley. I take it you dispensed with an escort on this particular outing."

"The grooms were all busy setting the place to rights after yesterday's crowd."

"Of course."

Rosamund encouraged Arcturus into a gentle canter. She knew she would not be able to shake Rory in his determination to scold her for her visit to the inn, so she made no attempt to race him. Besides which, Arcturus was older and slower than he had been when he had so soundly shown Trojan the way to the mill.

But as the silence built between them and Captain Buchanan's anger vibrated between them, she began to think that it would be better to have the confrontation over before they reached Cheveley. They had entered the park and were still in the wooded area of the estate, quite some distance from the main house, a grassy glade sheltered by oak and beech trees. Rosamund reined in Arcturus and dismounted. Rory came to a halt and looked down at her.

"If you are going to tell me off, it is better that you do it out of earshot. I understand that you may wish to retract your offer to a woman with so little modesty and patience as to visit a brothel, but I'd rather it happened now than at the house with every prying ear alerted to your anger."

Rory looked at her, still grim-faced. Then he nodded and slipped off his horse. He slipped the reins over the horse's head and allowed the animal to graze. He crossed his arms and contemplated his feet for a long moment before finally raising his eyes to meet Rosamund's gaze, a little apprehensive, a little abashed, but steady.

"How is Miss Veasey?"

Rosamund covered her face with her hands and sank to the ground, desperately trying to stifle first one sob and then another. But Rory's simple question had broken her control. He came down on his knees and held her close as the misery wracked her frame. At last the storm subsided and she rubbed her now-itching eyes and gave a great sniff. Rory reached into a pocket and found his handkerchief, a large lawn square. Rosamund blew lengthily and noisily into it before giving a blustery sigh. Then she removed her riding hat and dropped it to the ground before smoothing back her hair and rubbing her temples.

"I take it your cousin is not well at all." He still held her close.

Rosamund shook her head. "She has not emerged from this comatose state. She fell into it last night and nothing can rouse her or penetrate her consciousness. It is as if she has closed her body down. How can she do this? The doctor believes it is shock or some latent condition which was brought about by shock. We have not yet dared tell Uncle Leonard." She twisted round slightly, so that she could look into Rory's eyes. "All I could do was watch and watch, but she lies there, still as death, just giving tiny, shallow breaths. I could not endure it any longer. I had to do something."

"I cannot believe you allowed yourself to do something so utterly sock-headed! To go to so low a place and speak with such creatures! I admire your gall but I deplore your naivete." He picked at the grass, plucking up a strand and peeling away its casing.

"I do not know that it would have gone half so well if you had not appeared at so useful a juncture. I never was so surprised in my life."

"You did not show it. You stood there as cool as marble, as if you'd planned my entry. Remind me never to play at cribbage with you."

"Are you very cross with me?" She met his gaze evenly.

"I ought to be. To put yourself in such a position, it was folly in the extreme." He reached out a hand and took hold of one of hers. "But then you are *in extremis*. Hero is as good as a sister to you and to see her so wounded and so helpless must be bitter. I just wish you had come to me in the first place, before ever deciding to go to that low **dive**."

"But you must admit that together we worked most effectively on that vile old woman. What a terrible creature she is! And how many innocents does she corrupt or lure into her wicked plans, do you think? If I hadn't needed to bribe her, I'd have gone to Uncle Anthony on the instant and demanded he arrest her."

"You cannot distract me. You should not have gone there, and if you were determined to go there, you should not have gone alone. My darling girl, she has henchmen, unscrupulous fellows who'd harm anyone she ordered them to attack without a scruple. You have no idea how dangerous she might be." He reached out and traced the line of her cheek. She knocked his hand away and curled up, her knees under her chin, her arms wrapped tight round her legs, gazing deep into the wood.

"No, because you men keep such things to yourselves. It is a vile business."

Rory had to agree. Then he turned the subject. "You know it was Buchan who made all the trouble years ago in Edinburgh?"

"Was it?" She thought for a moment, then turned and looked at him, her cheek against her knees. "If you know that, how is it that he is such an intimate of Fitzgerald's still?"

"I challenged him to a duel. I pinked him. A graze, nothing more, but we both thought honor was satisfied. I believed him when he promised to do no more mischief. He opened your letter for me, you see. Then he spread the contents about the town. I wish I'd finished him off."

"No more than I. How troublesome we are, we Cheveley folk."

"You are indeed." Rory paused. "I'm meeting Wemyss."

Rosamund uncurled herself and reached for him. "You can't do that! Oh, how dreadful this whole business is. Such dissention between friends, such misery, and all due to one man!"

Rory pulled Rosamund close to him. "I must do it, Rosamund. Wemyss is a fool for mistrusting Hero so and he has brought such woe to you and yours, I could not let it pass. I know he has been my friend and companion at arms, but that is nothing beside your happiness."

They looked deep into each other's eyes and inexorably found themselves drawing closer still.

FIFTEEN

Rosamund's lips found his mouth first. She kissed him hard, then pulled back and said, "You mustn't. This isn't your quarrel."

"I must." With some unwillingness, he extricated himself from her embrace. He held her hands as he spoke. "I did not accompany them to the Griffin Inn that night. I came to dine with you at Cheveley, and I have been kicking myself for it ever since. I refused to take part in their petty voyeurism because I wanted to be with you and see you, but I should have gone, because with me there, Macdonald might have swayed the day and the whole debacle might never have occurred."

Rosamund shook off his hands and stood up. "You are talking complete nonsense. They had made up their minds almost before they reached the inn, and I doubt if you could have talked them round. You aren't indispensable to anyone except me, and what if Wemyss wounds you?"

Rory looked up at her, standing over him, her arms akimbo, her unruly honey hair escaping from its pins, her eyes narrowed. She looked magnificent. "Am I really indispensable to you?"

"How can you try to divert me from the nub of the matter at a time like this? You should not flatter yourself. I have simply become accustomed to you, like a familiar rug or a comfortable pair of shoes."

His hand snaked out and he grabbed at her hand and hauled her down beside him once more. "Miss Lovelace, you are cruel and unkind to compare me to tedious household items. You have not answered my question."

"You have not answered mine. What if Wemyss wounds you? Or worse still, what if you manage to kill him?" Any lightness of tone had vanished from her voice entirely.

"Let us hope it doesn't come to that. In his current state, if he can summon two seconds, it will be a miracle. I have always been better with a pistol, and I daresay I can aim well enough for a flesh wound."

"You take it very calmly."

His hand strayed to her neck and he cupped her face and pulled her close to him, this time kissing her. It was easy to deepen the kiss, to distract himself as well as her from the muddle in which they now found themselves. A trace of a thought flashed across his mind as he kept her close to him, that this might be his last opportunity to kiss her, that if something did go wrong and Wemyss managed to hit him, or he to kill Wemyss, he could never see her again. He broke off the kiss quite suddenly, horrified as this thought seemed to solidify in his mind. What good did it do to duel and preserve some faded code of honor? After all, what really mattered was to share the rest of his life with this particular woman.

"What is it?" asked Rosamund, a little affronted.

"I don't take it calmly, Rosamund. I don't take it calmly at all. I've come to see how foolish it all is. But backing out now would be impossible."

"You men!" she exploded. "With your honor and your scruples and your codes and rules and utter stupidity!"

"I agree. And I faithfully promise that once this business is settled, I will resign my commission, marry you and we shall live as merry as grigs the livelong day, avoiding society and men and all the ridiculous conventions by which we govern our little world. But until this business is settled, I must abide by the laws that society has dictated for us."

Aware that if he had not spoken thus, he would not have been the man she loved, Rosamund sighed.

"What sort of marriage would Hero have had to this fellow, if he is so untrusting and doubting? Perhaps, if she can be mended, we will find it just as well that he emerged in his true colors before the wedding."

"Do you think there is truly no hope for Wemyss?"

"How can there be? Hero may recover, but I doubt she will ever wish to see him again, and even if she does, my uncles will bar him from the house."

On this gloomy note, Rosamund and Rory rose and made for Cheveley once more, each downhearted and afraid for the future. If Hero died, there could be no question of a marriage for at least a year, and if she survived, Rosamund would be needed to keep her poor cousin in spirits. It would not be kind to start making arrangements for a wedding hotfoot on the ruins of Hero's attachment.

Back at Cheveley, there was little change to report. Hero was still unconscious, Uncle Leonard was unaware of that fact and Anthony Veasey was pacing the flagstones of the orangery with ill-concealed temper at his own impotence. But when he heard that the pair of ruffians who had been instrumental in maligning his niece might be tracked down, it galvanized him into a frenzy of activity and he vanished off like a hummingbird after fresh blossom.

***

Rory bade his love farewell and returned to Brackenbury Park, wondering what fresh mess Fitzgerald and Wemyss might have created in his absence. He was relieved to find the place deserted apart from Captain Macdonald, who was packing in preparation for the ride northward.

"I'll set off as soon as you've fought this damned fool duel with Wemyss," he declared, rolling up a sheaf of papers and wrapping up a small velvet jewel box. "We've fixed it for tomorrow. He wants to fight at dawn, I cannot think why. It's deuced uncomfortable rising at four in the morning. Are you agreed?"

"Yes. Has he chosen his weapons?"

"Small sword. He knows you're the better fencer, but then he also knows you're the better marksman and there's less chance of a fatal wound with a sword than with a pistol."

"I wouldn't put it past him to try and spit himself on my saber in a fit of remorse. Especially if the girl dies."

"Is she likely to die?" Macdonald was astounded by this intelligence.

"All I know is that Miss Lovelace is deeply troubled. Miss Veasey fell into an insensible state on the evening of the party and no one has managed to rouse her yet."

"Miss Lovelace? How do you come to know Miss Lovelace's state?"

"I may tell you, but I hope you will tell no one else. She and I are contracted to each other. Heaven knows if we shall ever find the time or the place to make our feelings known to her family, but I love her, and I hope to make her my wife eventually."

Macdonald was quite dumbfounded by the success of his stratagem with Colonel Fitzgerald. He had hoped to witness a thawing of relations, a little light flirtation between two apparent enemies. It had never occurred to him that Buchanan might feel more deeply toward Miss Lovelace than he had admitted.

"This is very sudden."

"Of course it must seem so, but the truth is, I have loved her for a great many years, but one way and another, I have never been able to declare it."

"The last I knew of it, you were apostrophizing her and all other women as tiresome beyond all bearing."

Rory cleared his throat with no little embarrassment. "Yes, well, I must have been mistaken. I believe her to be a very fine woman, the finest in fact, and I have held that opinion for some years. It was simply not possible for me to act on that opinion."

"Well, well! I can only congratulate you, Buchanan. Your choice has fallen on a woman as wise as she is lovely, a real prize. My sister-in-law holds her in the highest esteem and regards as Rosamund's only lapse her brief infatuation with you eight years since. It is to your credit that you have been able to bring her round."

"I don't see why a fondness for me should be regarded as a lapse. She has shown remarkable steadfastness, if you ask me. I am fortunate indeed to have earned her trust, her affection and her admiration."

"Yes, well, there's no accounting for women."

Rory's discomfort was increasing with every exchange in this uneasy discussion, so he turned the subject to Buchan and Lowther and the hunt that Anthony Veasey was organizing for them. It was very likely that the men would be caught soon enough, but exactly what was planned for them was less clear.

"I've no wish to participate in a lynching, yet they both require stiff punishment. To impugn the name of an innocent girl and destroy a match so favorable to both the Veaseys and the Wemysses is unconscionable."

"That's why Buchan has embarked on this sorry course," said Rory, somewhat impatient with the captain's roundabout approach to matters. "He has no conscience and an infinite appetite for mischief and mockery."

It was curious that most of the men in the regiment would have thought of Rory Buchanan as a far greater source of tomfoolery and ridicule than Buchan, who had always been a simple malcontent. Buchanan was far more popular with men and officers alike, he had a way with words and a sharp tongue on him that he shared liberally, but he also had a core of compassion and a fundamentally warm outlook on the world and his own place in it. Buchan, by way of contrast, was always watching out in case someone passed him over or slighted him, and displayed little or no sense of humor. At last, after so many years, Buchan had shown his true colors, and Rory could only wonder how many other schemes he had concocted of a similar unpleasantness and perhaps with no ill effects. There could not be many people as gullible as Wemyss to take in and trust every word that Buchan chose to feed to him.

But what punishment could be devised for Buchan that would bring him at once to an awareness of his own misdemeanors and of his own place in the world? He would be unlikely to continue in his military career, not having so utterly destroyed his credit with his commanding officer. Whether the end of his life as a soldier was sufficient retribution for having so injured an innocent girl was another question. Somehow, Rory hoped a stickier end could be arranged for Buchan.

However, first the creature must be captured. Macdonald

and Buchanan set off once again into the afternoon drizzle
to assist in the hunt for the captain and his lieutenant.

At Hero's bedside, Rosamund was becoming increasingly
agitated as her cousin continued to slumber on, oblivious to
the tumult around her. Uncle Leonard had finally emerged
from his sickbed and had been fully updated on the state of
his daughter. He had summoned the strength to visit her, but
on seeing Hero lying so pale and so still in her bed, no sign
of life about her, he had all but collapsed and retreated, baffled and full of lamentation, to his own bed.

Uncle Anthony had disappeared on his hunt for the
propagators of the rumors about Hero and altogether,
Rosamund was feeling frustrated, helpless and apprehensive about her own future. She could not concentrate at all
on her book, nor on her petit point nor on her darning and
mending. So when in great agitation, one of the footmen
was brought before her, she was quite relieved to be distracted from her thoughts.

"Miss Veasey, I have found traces of two fellows living
in the old folly."

"Traces, Jameson?"

"Aye. I believe they are still there; there are saddlebags
and food still, but there was no sign of the men themselves
when I was there earlier."

Rosamund could scarcely believe the effrontery of
Buchan and his lieutenant. To come onto Cheveley land
while seeking to escape from the consequences of their actions seemed the height of contempt for the Veaseys and
all their business.

Of course it occurred to Rosamund that she should at
once summon Colonel Fitzgerald and his fellow officers,

but she dismissed the notion out of hand. She would not waste time sending for the Brackenbury people; but lay hands on Buchan and Lowther immediately and bring them into the house, where they could be confined until their fate had been decided.

She summoned the four stoutest footmen to accompany her and Jameson to the folly. Surely five men would be sufficient to subdue the two soldiers. But just in case, she decided to equip two of the men with shotguns and the others with stout cudgels.

Silent, initially adjusting their pace for Miss Lovelace, the five men walked out of the house past the terraces of flowers, the walled garden, the lawns and parkland, heading southwest up a slight incline toward a stand of chestnuts. There, squat and gray, sat the little folly, constructed by Leonard Veasey's grandfather after a trip to the Continent, a miniaturized imitation of the Pantheon in Rome that had lost the grandeur of the original without imparting any charm through the reduction in scale. With no discernible function and sited out of the way of the main house, the folly had been left to molder for years. Periodically, the local surveyor inspected the building for soundness, but it was more foolish and less used than many follies.

The footmen spread out as they approached the building, in case the inmates heard them and tried to break out of the building. It had only the one entrance, a double doorway that one had to stoop to use, for it was only five feet high. The dome rose a further three feet high, allowing perhaps one or two men to stand within the windowless walls. The approaching group saw smoke emerging from the oculus. Then they saw that the man or men inside had broken into the building by wrenching at one of the doors and pulling it off one of its hinges. It had been hauled back into position, against the beastly weather, Rosamund assumed, which was fortunate because it meant that whoever was within was in darkness apart from the fire and unable to see out or observe the advance of her men.

The concealed men were strong, or perhaps desperate. It could have been any number of wanderers, for the countryside was full of returning soldiers, dispossessed farmers, rebellious souls unable to find work when their own labor had been replaced by machines in the great mills farther south. But Rosamund was sure that it was her enemy and his protégé. She indicated to the men to stand on either side of the doorway, ready to trap anyone who emerged.

"Who's there?" she cried out. "Whoever you are, you are trespassing. If you need food and shelter, we can provide it at the main house."

There was no movement or sound from the edifice. She came closer, going up the shallow steps to stand by the pillars, and called out again.

"Please come out and leave this place. It is private property."

There was a shove within, then another, as though someone was tussling first with the door and then with some obstacle. Rosamund waited. The door scraped open a crack and a smutty face emerged. It was Lowther.

"Lieutenant Lowther!" Rosamund feigned astonishment. "What are you doing here? We have not seen you for some days; we thought you had gone home."

He hurled himself at the door to try and widen the crack a little, but the wood was heavy and he seemed very weak. It shifted a little, then stuck on the stone steps again.

"Help me, please, I beg!"

"Goddamn you, boy, no one can help you now!" came a

howl of rage from the darkness behind him. There was the report of a gun, a wild, echoing crack that seemed to make the whole temple reverberate and Lowther's pale blue eyes were huge with shock. He opened his mouth, but blood came out, and he raised his mouth to his hand and saw the blood on his fingers before slumping down, a faint astonishment crossing his features before he fell away from the door. Rosamund was transfixed, unable to move, staring at the place where Lowther's face had been seconds before. The door burst open and Buchan emerged, kicking out of the way the outstretched limbs of the young lieutenant, his gaze and his pistol arm steady. Steady, and directed at Rosamund, only a few feet away.

"This weapon is freshly primed. Do exactly as I tell you and I will not fire it."

"What lunacy is this, Captain Buchan? Do you think I have come unprotected to your hideaway? I have only to lunge away and the chances of your hitting me are miniscule. I suggest you surrender your weapon and your person and we shall treat you gently, as befits a war hero."

He took three swift steps and was on her, his left arm looped about her neck, his right arm keeping the pistol against her temple.

"Lunge now, my dear and you will find yourself *hors de combat,* like my poor friend Lowther there." He hauled her back and dragged her into the folly. The footmen all sprang forward, and he cocked the pistol. They fell back immediately. He stopped in the doorway and gave his instructions.

"Go. Run for help. Lowther is past aid. But I want a horse, and I want money. Place the money in a saddlebag, as much cash as Veasey has on the premises. Bring it here in the next hour or I shall shoot her as I shot that spaniel Lowther. Go now!"

Jameson turned and sprinted back toward the main house. The other four servants, Rosamund and Buchan all watched him hurtling headlong toward Cheveley, his arms and legs pumping faster than a steam engine. And then he reached the house and disappeared within. Buchan dragged Rosamund into the pantheon, the pistol remaining dauntingly secure at her temple.

Inside the folly, Rosamund was finding it hard to sustain her self-control. The chamber was wretched and stinking. Lowther and Buchan had been there only twenty-four hours, but in that time, they had cooked in the space and left the customary detritus of human occupation. And now there was the stench of a dead man, a smell Rosamund had never before encountered, but one that she would now never forget. The fire in the center of the building sent shadows flickering about the columns and pediments that her ancestor had insisted on reproducing so exactly. She was rigid with fear, certain that if she made any undue, unexpected movement, Buchan would not hesitate to dispatch her as he had dispatched his erstwhile friend. She swallowed.

"Why did you shoot him? What did you hope to gain?"

"I shot him to prevent him from whining and whimpering so incessantly. He wanted to surrender. He wanted to give in. All I want is some peace."

He spoke through gritted teeth as though every word must be extracted from the dense rock that had become his world. Rosamund stifled her impulse to yell at him that his every action was guaranteed to create dissent, hounding and disgrace. But if any complaint or comment were to be seen as whining or whimpering, it would be wiser to hold her tongue. She looked around the dark little temple. Rain came through the oculus, spitting into the fire beneath. She could not see much wood, certainly not enough to keep the

fire burning more than an hour or two. There were saddlebags and rumpled blankets dumped in a curve of the
building. Close to Lowther's body, she could see the pistol
that Buchan must have discharged when shooting the poor
boy.

She tried to work out what might happen next. Jameson had clearly reached the house and the alarm would
have been raised. He would come back to the folly with
numerous men and the horse with the money, but how long
it would take she could not tell. It had been nearing four
when she left the house. It must now be past five. It would
remain light for another two or three hours.

Rosamund considered the possibility that Buchan might
lose his patience and shoot her. Or once the horse and the
money were safely in his hands, he might try to keep her
hostage, or shoot her as he left the grounds. She could not
see him, of course, for he was behind her, his arm still
looped about her neck, his elbow resting on her shoulder
as he kept the pistol pressed against her skin.

"If I promise to go exactly where you tell me, may I sit?"

He pushed her down and away onto the tumble of blankets. She curled up her knees under her chin, her arms
locked tight about her legs. She was now able to see the
sprawled body by the doorway, near enough to touch if she
stretched out her arm. In the narrow shaft of light from the
wrecked door, she could see that Lowther's eyes were still
open. She glanced toward Buchan, who was in the shadows opposite her. The fire illumined his shabby uniform,
his unruly hair, his calm, nerveless hands, clutched about
the pistol, which was aimed directly at her. She thought
she might be able to roll away if he decided to fire, but she
prayed she did not have to put this to the test. He was not
watching her, so she looked again at him, noting the

grooves of strain about his mouth and the deep smudges beneath his eyes. He appeared to be a man *in extremis*. Still, she could summon no sympathy for him. He had brought this unholy mess on himself, and how it was to end, Rosamund could not imagine.

"What are you looking at, slut?"

She did not look away. "I would prefer it if you did not insult me."

His laugh was derisory and mocking. "Until you hold a loaded pistol aimed at me, my dear, I shall insult you any way I please."

"Even if you escape now, do you imagine you will not be hunted down?"

"I'd rather be hunted down than hanged for that idiot's death." He started to cough but soon suppressed it.

"What have you to gain from this business? Maligning my cousin, destroying Wemyss's hopes, killing Lowther: with every turn you seem to have placed yourself more irrevocably on a path to ruin."

"You are very cool, Miss Lovelace. I admire that in a woman." There was something in the tone of his voice that chilled Rosamund and she prayed that he would remain on the opposite side of the fire. And then she prayed that Jameson would not be long in coming, that the Veaseys would have the wit to meet Buchan's demands, that help would be at hand very soon. Buchan came toward her.

"Why are you so curious, Miss Lovelace?"

"I've read about people destroying everything in their path, about people so bitter that they could not stand to see anyone else happy or settled. But I never expected to meet such a person."

"Am I that sort of person? A visitor of destruction?" This vision of himself seemed to please Buchan, for he checked in his advance across the floor of the folly and paused to consider Rosamund's words. "There is no such thing as happiness. Our existence is brutish and miserable. I am only helping the more naive amongst us to understand that. I find it . . ." He groped for a word, "aggravating, I think, when people seem to be content with their lot." He coughed again. This time the cough lasted a little longer.

"I cannot disagree with you. It is true that much of human existence is fraught with trouble and trial. It is irritating to be surrounded by optimists and smug individuals who cannot see that our lives are nothing but tribulation. But most of us put up with it."

"Put up with it? Why should we? And you are as bad as the rest. What do you know of the ways of men, Miss Lovelace, the thorough vileness of which we are capable? Nothing. You have not seen a village destroyed, its inhabitants massacred, its women and children violated and bayoneted. You have not seen the things that I have seen. If you had, you would hate your fellow men as much as I do."

He coughed again, and this time the cough went on longer, and he could not maintain his aim. Rosamund waited until silence had fallen once again. She listened out, wondering whether anyone had yet come to her rescue. She was not strong enough to hold off Buchan and open the door. She was certain that although he was somewhat debilitated by his cough, he was still far stronger than she was. But if she could keep him talking, if she could distract him a little from his purpose, it would give someone time to stop him from his crazed course.

SIXTEEN

In the house, Leonard Veasey was proving as ineffectual as usual. First he wished to summon his brother, Anthony, then he wished to act on his own, then he thought it best if Colonel Fitzgerald were summoned, then he wanted the local watch called up. While he dithered, Jameson fidgeted, finally reaching breaking point when Veasey thought once again that perhaps it would be best to send for his brother.

"Might I suggest, sir, that we send at once for the officers at Brackenbury Park. They will know how to deal with a fellow soldier gone on the rampage, for it seems that that is what has happened. I have heard of such things before, sir, soldiers who cannot quite forget their soldiering."

"Yes, yes, you are quite right, Jameson. Thank heavens for a sound man in a crisis."

Gathering courage, Jameson continued to make suggestions. "Perhaps, sir, it would be best if you sent one of the stable boys over to Brackenbury. You might write a note explaining the urgency of the situation. While we are waiting, perhaps I should go with some food back to the folly. I could tell him that we're looking out all the gold we can find and the fleetest horse we can muster. Show willing, sir, if you see what I mean."

"I do see what you mean, Jameson." Veasey looked relieved to relinquish the initiative and nodded. "Off you go then, Jameson, and I will set about writing that note. Be sure to get the boy to collect it."

It was with some relief that Jameson returned to the stable yard, where Thwaite, the chief groom, was sitting polishing some harnesses. These were forgotten in a heap by the time Jameson had finished recounting his sorry tale, and before he could make the request, Thwaite was shouting orders about the place, summoning up all four of his boys, sending them running to the four winds in search of tack and first the fleetest pony so that young Jim might ride over to Brackenbury. Then Thwaite turned his attention to Buchan's request and chose the fanciest of Leonard Veasey's hacks, a showy creature that looked well enough but was a sluggard in pace and nature.

"Let's hope he's as easily fooled as the master into taking Centaur for a marvel."

Jameson agreed before heading for the kitchen, where he set about raiding Cook's larder, despite her growing shrieks of indignation. Finally, he rounded on her.

"Miss Rosamund's held hostage by a madman and you want to preserve your pork pie? What sort of a fool are you, woman? Help me get the choicest picnic for this man and keep your wailing to yourself until we have just cause for wailing. He's killed one man. Who knows what he'll do to the girl unless I'm back there with something to distract him double quick."

At which Cook agreed that he should take not only her pork pie but also her chicken and veal pie and some apple dumplings and the marzipan sweetmeats that were left from the great gathering the day before.

Matilda, one of the more sensible of the kitchen maids,

helped him pack up the provisions in a basket, along with a bottle of claret and some ale.

"What about some spirits? Do you think he'll be more dangerous the drunker he gets or do you think he'll lower his guard easier?"

Jameson decided on a bottle of brandy, for the villain could not become more dangerous, he thought, but the hard drink might make him less capable, which should increase the odds of rescuing Miss Rosamund.

As he was about to leave again, Miss Veasey's maid came down in great agitation.

"She's roused! She wants something to drink, tea or some such! Thank heavens, she's come round. I thought she was a goner for sure, but she's bounced back alright."

"For God's sake, don't tell her what's happened to Miss Lovelace, will you? It'll send her right back where she was. Still, it's the first thing that's gone right in days."

Jameson shouldered the basket and left the kitchen posthaste. But his suggestion that Rosamund's plight be hidden from Miss Veasey gave him the seed of an idea. He was not sure that it would work, but it might create a distinct disadvantage for Buchan.

His strides were long as he left the house, but as he approached the folly, he shortened them and slowed his pace. The four men he had left behind called to him, asking him what was up, why the long face. He came closer and closer to the folly and now lowered the basket so that he had to lug it with both hands up the steps to the portico. Puffing and blowing, he bent double in an attempt to recover his breath. He listened out, then shouted up at the doorway.

"I've brought you some food. The horse and the money will take a little longer, for old Mr. Veasey has forgotten where he's hid his cash."

Buchan had grabbed Rosamund once again and had her in his grasp.

"I've got the girl here, ready to kill if you try to play any tricks with me. Do you understand?"

"I understand, sir."

"Open the door carefully. Slowly and carefully. Then I want you to take away this putrescent corpse. Once you've dragged Lowther away, push the food inside. Is that clear?"

"Yes, sir." Jameson went up to the doorway and hauled at the door. Slowly, with a rasping grinding against the stone, it opened up. He could see Lowther's legs in the patch of light that could now enter the temple.

"Can I open the other door too, sir?"

"No. Pull him out, devil take you. He reeks and I don't want him in here anymore." Buchan began to cough again, and Jameson, recognizing his diminishing patience, was quick to grab at Lowther's legs and maneuver the poor fellow out of the folly, leaving copious blood and some flesh behind him. As soon as he'd hauled the body out, two other men came forward to lift him onto some grass a little way off from the temple.

"Bring the food in here. Careful not to dump it in the blood. How long will it be before I get the horse?"

Jameson followed his instructions. As he straightened, having deposited the basket of food by the fire, he spoke again.

"I couldn't say, sir. Everyone at the house is mighty upset, sir, for Miss Hero has passed on."

Rosamund lost her breath. She protested at Jameson's news, exclaiming that it could not be true before her throat tightened and she ranted and railed against Wemyss and his stupidity, then turned and harangued Buchan for his villainy. Jameson stood frozen. Buchan's arm tightened about her.

"Stop it. You can't cry now. Cry later, if you're alive. Otherwise I can arrange for you to join her if you wish."

She collected herself instantly, turning on her captor, "You had better arrange it immediately, sir, or believe me, I shall hunt you down and see you spitted."

"Great God, I tire of you," he yelled and pushed her away. She stumbled to the floor, then rose up. But before Rosamund could stand, Buchan took a mighty swipe at her and knocked her back down again. Her head cracked back against the wall of the folly and she slumped against the wall and collapsed to the floor. Buchan held the pistol on Jameson.

"Check her pulse, man. No games, or I shoot you."

Jameson bent down over Miss Rosamund. She would have an almighty headache when she roused, but she would rouse, for her pulse was surprisingly strong.

"She seems to live yet, sir."

"So my escape from this place is assured. Go now. You've roused the alarm with Fitzgerald, haven't you? Is Hero Veasey really dead, or is it some trick you play on me?"

Jameson's voice broke. "Why should I lie to you, sir? What have I to gain from telling such a tale?"

"Christ knows, I certainly don't. Very well, I believe you. So there's more blame they'll lay at my door. Get the horse here before sundown, and the money, or she is dead. I don't intend to spend another night in this dreary mausoleum."

That left an hour, perhaps a little more, for the Brackenbury folk to arrive, for a rescue of some sort to be effected. It was past five now, and the sun would set just before seven. For the first time, Jameson felt afraid, a sensation deepened by the gruesome task of dragging Lowther's body away from the folly. He looked down on the face of the unfortunate creature, a face that seemed uncertain and unformed, the visage of a boy who had failed to grasp the ways of the world. The situation had assumed a gravity that he had not previously been able to comprehend. It was with some relief that he saw Thwaite riding up, leading Centaur at a neat trot.

"Captain Buchan!" called out the footman. "The horse is here, if you want to leave now."

The captain peered out through the doorway. He saw the flashy chestnut and said, "Good. Bring it up to the steps of this infernal building."

Jameson followed his instructions, carefully maneuvering the beast toward the folly. Hoping against hope that he had done so in a way that concealed the approach on foot of Buchanan round the east side of the building, Fitzgerald and Wemyss coming from the west.

Buchan's boots scraped against the stone and he emerged with Rosamund no longer unconscious but still dazed by the blow to her head. He had hoisted her over his shoulder, but it was clear that she was starting to struggle. It was no easy matter for him to position her so that she slumped onto the horse's withers. He leapt nimbly enough into the saddle and clapped his heels to Centaur's sides. The horse staggered a little under the unexpected weight of two bodies, then loped off in an uneven canter. Miss Lovelace's arms dangled and bounced as they moved away, and he could not sustain the pace he had initially set. And then, roused by the motion, and the discomfort of the pommel digging into her abdomen, she began thrashing about, only to have Buchan force her head down. But the horse would not put up with it. For the first time in Centaur's idle and pampered life, he was angered and he reared up, so that Rosamund tumbled back onto Buchan before gravity and the balance of her body weight hauled her to the left. Realizing that it had failed to rid himself of his tiresome riders, the horse continued bucking and rearing, unable to go forward, incapable of retreat. At last, he managed to shake off the loose weight of Rosamund, who crumpled into a ball as the horse, now disburdened, shot off.

Never had Centaur moved so fast. Fitzgerald and Macdonald gazed as the horse galloped at full pelt into the dell of trees to the east of the folly, clearly crazed with confusion and fury. But Rory ran toward the small navy heap that was Rosamund.

As he reached her, she stirred, slowly but definitively. She made to sit up, but the knock on her head and the shock of her horseback ride and fall dizzied her and she found herself ignominiously and copiously regurgitating her lunch.

Rory stroked her back as she retched and shuddered, murmuring as he would to an animal or a sick child, "There there, there there."

At last, Rosamund turned to him with great bruised eyes and a throbbing discoloration to her right cheek. "But it isn't 'there there,' is it? Hero has died. That is what Jameson said."

Rory called the footman over. "Is it true, what you told Miss Lovelace? Is Miss Veasey truly dead?"

Jameson gave a warning glance toward Fitzgerald and Wemyss. He shook his head once as if to clear it, then nodded and muttered something that sounded like an affirmative.

"Hero is dead?" asked Wemyss. "Hero is dead. Oh, dear God, that I should have been such a fool." And he sat down on the step with a heavy thump, cradling his head in his hands and beginning to moan and rock.

"Chase him," came Rosamund's voice, still faint, but definite. "Chase him now and catch him before he can get a head start."

Jameson nodded at his mistress's instructions. Thwaite dismounted from the horse he'd used to accompany Centaur from the stables. It was Arcturus. Jameson was onto the gelding's back and cantering away before any of the officers from Brackenbury could raise any objection. But Wemyss was roused and ran for his horse, crying out that he would take Buchan or see them both die, for there was nothing left for him now that Hero was gone. Fitzgerald followed, determined to prevent his junior officers from causing further mayhem.

Cradling her head in her hands, Rosamund spoke, fighting back the waves of weariness that seemed to wash over her. "Wemyss is a fool. Jameson knows there is no escape; he can cut off Buchan. Our park is walled, there's no escape for the man. He'll bring him back here. We must call the magistrate and have him taken into custody. Unless he should be court-martialed for murdering a fellow officer."

Rory stood and scooped her up in his arms. There seemed to be no place to put her down, for she shivered as he approached the folly. In an attempt to distract he asked, "How came he to shoot Lowther?"

"Do you know, I am not quite sure. He seemed to be exasperated by the poor lad. No other crime. Lowther was repenting, I think, and Buchan could not tolerate that." Rosamund could not continue, for shock took her over. She was shaking uncontrollably, very pale now and clearly close to the limit of her endurance.

"I must get you back to the house."

"Let me try to walk."

Rory stifled the urge to tell her not to be ridiculous, for it was nearly a full mile back to the house. "My horse is here. We concealed them when we came up to the folly."

"Perhaps now we have good enough reason to demolish the ugly place."

Macdonald brought forward Rory's horse with his own, and they mounted, Rosamund secure in Rory's embrace. Macdonald gave them a wry glance and trotted on ahead. Rory's arms tightened about her as the horses ambled back toward the house. Buchan's instability might well have cost her her life.

"I should be raging at you for being so foolish as to go to that place without a proper guard."

"Rory, I went with five footmen, two of whom were armed. I am just grateful they did not attempt to fire, for I feel sure that would have caused additional carnage."

"I suppose the fact that twice in the past twenty-four hours I've found you in locations where you had no business being is an indication of what I may expect for the rest of our married life."

"I believe it is a sign, yes. Do you mind very much?"

"Don't be ingenuous, it doesn't suit you." Rory squeezed her tight and eased his horse into a trot.

Once they reached the stables, Thwaite and his boys gave them a rousing cheer of welcome, even though Macdonald had told the stable staff that Miss Rosamund was safe. Rory insisted on carrying Rosamund inside, for she appeared battered and worn. He took her along the corridor to the garden room where he had proposed so short a time before. Macdonald cleared their way of obstacles and opened the door with a flourish, and they swept in, only to come to a dead halt. For there, his pistol this time held at Leonard Veasey's head, was Buchan. The French windows were open, the curtains billowing gently into the fresh air. The old man in the armchair was immobile apart from his eyes, which switched from speaker to speaker, his hands clawed round the arms of the chair.

"Not again, Mr. Buchan? How very unimaginative," drawled Rosamund. "I suppose you realize that even if you get off your one shot, there are more than enough of us to hold you, particularly once we are joined by an irate Wemyss."

"It's all very well for you to mock, safe in your hero's arms. Now you've finally got what you've always wished for." Buchan was warming up, readying himself for further invective when Wemyss raced up the shallow steps from the terrace into the house. He paused, taking in the scene.

"Buchan, once again threatening those who are weaker than you. You worm! How dare you tell such lies about my poor Hero?" He lunged for the captain, halted by Rory's abrupt command.

"Stop this instant. He has a pistol trained on Mr. Veasey. Do you want to contribute to the death of another member of this family, Wemyss?" This checked the lieutenant. "May I put my burden down, Buchan? She is not an excessively buxom woman, but she is a little heavier than a feather."

"Just keep her well away from me."

Rory took Rosamund over to the love seat where he had held her on his lap and deposited her there. Buchan could see her, but to aim and fire at her, he must swivel from his position by Leonard Veasey. Better still, Rosamund had a clear view of the entire proceedings, including a small door leading to a servant's passageway in the corner of the room behind Buchan.

Macdonald examined his nails idly. "You know, Buchan, I believe you must surrender eventually. Or your concentration will give way and we shall overcome you, Wemyss, Buchanan and myself. You wouldn't like to be overcome by us, believe me, for none of us is feeling charitable toward you just at the moment. Man, you're playing shinty on a thawing lake."

"Must we listen to your Caledonian witticisms? Can you none of you leave me in peace?" The whine of hysteria began to tinge Buchan's voice.

"Peace?" growled Rory. "We'd be delighted to leave you in peace but you're the one who keeps putting pistols to people's heads and maligning young girls. You've always been erratic, but now you've run mad. I suggest you plead insanity and they'll maybe allow you to be kept under lock and key by your own family."

"You want an explanation? You wish to understand why I have chosen this path?" Buchan glanced round the room and shook his head as if to clear it. "I don't see why I should explain anything. Let my actions be a source of speculation and mystery."

"If that's all that's left to you, man, you might as well shoot yourself now and save the courts the bother of trying you." Macdonald managed to sustain his disinterested tone. "We don't care why you're such a miserable, malingering mischief-maker, we just wish to see this nonsense come to an end. We want Miss Veasey's name restored to her, even if it is in death, and we want you to suffer for the misery you've caused and the wounds you've inflicted. But if anyone catches you, it will be to hang you for the death of poor Ned Lowther."

They kept him talking. Imperceptibly, without giving any sign of working in tandem, Macdonald and Rory distracted him and began to close in on him. He explained exactly how he had come to recruit an impostor for the sordid scene at the stables of the Griffin Inn, he crowed about opening Rosamund's letter to Rory so many years before, he blustered about the iniquities of his career, the promotions he had missed, the booty he had been cheated of, the tedium of army life, and he recounted the numerous times he had sought to destroy the reputation of perfectly blameless individuals, some known to his fellow officers, others being complete strangers. It seemed that Buchan was eaten alive with spite and envy, malice and loathing of himself and his fellow men.

Rory and Macdonald were careful, but even Buchan, wrapped up in his own grim world of deceit and misery, noticed their approach. He cocked the pistol and held it closer to Leonard Veasey.

"No closer. No closer."

At which moment, the corner door opened and in glided a slim, trembling figure in a white shift. It kept its gaze fixed on Buchan and moved inexorably toward the center of the room, silent, pale and accusing.

Wemyss was the first to exclaim in wonder, "Hero!" The girl in her white shift stopped and raised her arm to point accusingly at Buchan, from whose trembling fingers the pistol slipped, landing on the floor with a great report as the terrified soldier backed away from Veasey. Rory and Macdonald saw their chance and leaped on Buchan. Rosamund had risen to her knees in wonder and Wemyss walked slowly toward Hero. Amazement and apology warred in his features. He reached her and dropped down on one knee. He reached out and touched her gown. She looked down on his bowed head, her features unreadable.

"My Hero, I wronged you in life, but I will serve you for the rest of my days in your death."

"You fool. I am not dead. Jameson tricked you all. He thought it might lead Buchan into an error, and now we find he was right. Come, Rosamund. Come upstairs and I will bathe your poor face and we shall leave these men to sort out their own mess."

Rosamund rose and went to her cousin and hugged her close. "I've never been so glad to see you in all my life, my sweet." And the two girls, entwined, left the men. They left by the door that Hero had used to enter, passing Jameson as they headed for the servants' stairway.

"Are you all right now, Miss Hero?" asked the footman. She turned to him and smiled wanly.

"I'm as well as can be expected. I think it is Miss Rosamund who needs our care now, for look, Buchan has treated her cruelly indeed."

"I'll go for the doctor, shall I?"

"I don't believe I need the doctor. But I wish to congratulate Jameson on his good sense and courage throughout this afternoon's nonsense. You will be amply rewarded."

"I need no reward, miss. I'm just glad to have helped capture the villain."

Rosamund was too tired to discuss Jameson's hopes and dreams, but she said to Hero as they climbed to their bedroom, "We must not forget Jameson. It was he who conceived of your ghostly appearance, I take it?"

"Yes. He had heard that I had come to earlier. He thought the whole thing up." They went into their room and Rosamund lay on the chaise longue under the window, while Hero went and poured some water into a basin and dampened a cloth for her cheek. "He came up to our room in a terrible panic, saying that Buchan had gone into the garden room and had Papa at gunpoint. Matilda was there, and she helped us, she found powder, stored away from the days when people used to wear wigs, and made me pale. Then we went downstairs, and by that time you were all in the room, and Buchan was boasting and boasting about his dreadful exploits. Then he stopped, and Jameson told me to go."

Rosamund reached up to hug her cousin close. "How brave you have been, my darling."

"Not so brave as you. You were trapped with him all afternoon, with him and poor Lieutenant Lowther."

"Poor Lowther!" exclaimed Rosamund. "Next you will be telling me that you forgive Wemyss!"

Hero did not meet Rosamund's eyes. She looked down, then blankly into the distance. "We were so happy. I was so happy. Was it a fool's paradise, Rosamund?"

"I don't know, my sweet, but I do believe that Wemyss is contracted to meet Buchanan tomorrow. They are to fight a duel over your honor."

Hero rolled her eyes. "Heaven help us. What weapons have they chosen, Rosamund?"

Rosamund looked at Hero in wonder. "You are not fainting or going into hysterics?"

"Why should I? I suppose I might have before all this, but do you know, I think I am a good deal more sanguine and rather less susceptible than I used to be."

Rosamund closed her eyes while her cousin, for the first time that either of them could remember, took charge and arranged for hot water, sustenance and calming tea to be brought up to their room.

SEVENTEEN

Downstairs in the garden room, Fitzgerald and Wemyss had been abandoned by Buchanan and Macdonald, who had followed Jameson, bearing between them the wriggling, resistant Captain Buchan to a secure cellar. There they would guard him until the local watch could be summoned to remove him to the jail in Northallerton or Ripon until he could be tried at the assizes.

Leonard Veasey gradually relaxed as the yelling officer was removed from the garden room, then looked round at the two uneasy men remaining in the room.

"What on earth possessed you to think that my Hero was dead?"

"We had heard it from Jameson."

"Curious indeed. She might well have died. She was near total collapse. We are quite fragile, we Veaseys." He looked at Wemyss as though emerging from a dream. "Mr. Wemyss, I am very sorry to have to ask this of you, but I must request that you leave Cheveley and do not come here again. After all that has happened, I do not really believe that you are suitable marriage material for my daughter. I had overlooked your lack of fortune because your name is good and of course because Hero regarded you with such warmth. But I do not believe that she can now look on you so favorably and I consider your actions dishonorable and foolish in the extreme."

Wemyss looked helplessly at Fitzgerald, who did speak in defense of his officer. "Sir, I entirely understand your sentiments, but I must beg you to reconsider this ban on my lieutenant. He has shown generally the greatest devotion to Miss Veasey, and if she is prepared to allow him a second chance, I feel sure that he has learnt his lesson. He was tricked by a wily and most persuasive individual."

"From all that I heard in the course of my ordeal with your Buchan, relatively few people have been tricked by this scoundrel, and if you had only listened to men of sense such as Buchanan and Macdonald, my Hero would never have been exposed to so vile a calumny. Besides, whatever Buchan did or did not arrange, it was Lieutenant Wemyss who chose to spread it abroad in the widest possible forum. Under my own roof. Now good day to you, gentlemen. I wish to see my daughter and my niece."

Giving the cavalrymen no further space to argue their case, Leonard Veasey hobbled out of the room.

Wemyss sat, his head cradled in his hands. Fitzgerald went over to him and placed a hand on his shoulder.

"Shall we get back to Brackenbury?"

"I suppose we must."

Their ride back was somber, both men confining themselves to gnomic utterances about their horses, about the weather and about dinner. Preying on Wemyss's mind now was the whole question of the duel he was to fight the next morning, while Fitzgerald was preoccupied by the social discomfort he must face this evening with Wemyss and Buchanan facing each other across the dinner table and thereafter as his part in this distasteful episode with Buchan was unfolded throughout the county.

Naturally enough, the colonel's worst fears were miti-
gated. Macdonald and Buchanan returned from their task
of handing Buchan over to the watch in high good humor,
for the stout yeomen who composed the peacekeeping
band were less disposed to behave as gentlemen must to
their captive. The news about the deception practiced on
Wemyss and Hero's disgrace were widely known already,
but when the two soldiers had revealed Buchan's iniqui-
tous act of shooting his junior in the back, not to mention
holding hostage both Miss Rosamund Lovelace and Mr.
Veasey, their indignation knew no bounds and Buchan was
subjected to rough treatment and considerable indignity.
His wrists were shackled and he was slung on a mule like
so many pounds of potatoes. He had started to protest
against this treatment, but one of the fellows had whipped
off a grimy necktie and gagged him with it.

The gentlemen were on their second bottle of claret when
the seriousness of Buchan's situation hit home. It was indeed
a nasty business, and no one emerged from it with particular credit, that was for sure. Except possibly Hero Veasey,
who had shown herself to be truly heroic and astonishingly
stalwart under fire. Oh, and Miss Lovelace. It was somewhat
apologetically that Buchanan confessed that he was, unofficially at least, engaged to Miss Lovelace, for Wemyss had
explained that Leonard Veasey had barred him from Cheveley, and the captain felt a little embarrassed at sharing his
happiness when Wemyss must confront his own folly.

The men toasted their companion, but this intelligence
depressed Wemyss, who had been buoyed up throughout
the evening by the ebullience of his seniors. First he
lamented the disastrous collapse of his alliance with Hero,
and then he expressed his genuine fear of the meeting he
had forced on Buchanan.

"That at least, we can mend," said Rory. "We should still meet, it would raise your credit in the neighborhood if we do. But we can use buttoned foils, surely. No one but our seconds ever need know, and honor will be satisfied. For I shall trounce you, no matter how much claret we have this night."

"Trounce me?" Wemyss was indignant.

"He has experience and coordination on his side, Wemyss. If you were fighting with unbated weapons, you should genuinely fear engagement with our Buchanan. Surely you've heard of his reputation?" Macdonald asked.

"I have, but I've never had the opportunity to see him in action. We never seem to have practiced together, and swordplay in the midst of battle is a very different matter."

"My concern is that Miss Veasey and Miss Lovelace will somehow contrive to prevent us from meeting. I spoke to Miss Lovelace about this engagement and she was scathing. If she believes it is progressing, I am sure she will take measures to prevent it."

"She has reason to do so," said Wemyss. "But Miss Veasey is probably quite eager for me to bear a physical wound for the pain I have caused her."

"You are confusing her with other women again, Wemyss. She is a gentle soul, and if you persist in misreading her, I can only agree with Miss Lovelace that she is well out of the match. I daresay if you do wish to win her again, you will be able to woo her and she will succumb, but you must learn to treasure her and her ways." Rory pushed back his chair and rose. "If I am to rise at dawn, gentlemen, I must retire now."

This signaled a general withdrawal to their various chambers, where for once Wemyss began to think carefully about Hero. For so long she had written to him and demonstrated her affection that he had, he knew, come to take it for granted. He had flirted with Miss Sutcliffe, he had assumed the worst without questioning in the slightest whether it was plausible that a gently bred woman should consort with rough types in stables, and now he was ascribing to her vengeful tendencies for which he had no evidence.

It was as though he were rousing from a long sleep. It came to Wemyss that he had never really bothered to learn anything about Hero. It was clear that she was sweet and tender, that she was a competent housekeeper, that she was a dear and good girl and that all these attributes were desirable in a wife. But when a man such as Rory Buchanan could explain more to him about her thought processes and her reactions than he could surmise on his own, it was time to accept that he had made no real effort to understand Hero or her world.

Unused to introspection, Wemyss passed an uncomfortable night and had fallen into an uneasy doze when Macdonald came to rouse him. The duel must be fought.

It was just before five, and the day was starting hazy and gray, although there were hints that it might, for once in this summer of deluge and dreariness, be fine. A wash of blue lurking above the cloud and a freshness and crispness to the air that seemed to foreshadow sunshine suggested that the day might warm up pleasantly. But for now, it was chilly. Wemyss pulled on an oilskin coat before setting out for the space they had agreed on for the actual encounter.

Clearly, they could not meet near the house, and so much of Brackenbury's park was unkempt grass that they had to walk quite a distance to find a clearing. Finally, the men came to a grove where the ground was covered in bark chippings, leaf mold and moss. There the seconds reiterated the code they were using for the duel, offered Rory his choice of foils and signaled the start of combat.

It was apparent almost immediately that Wemyss was outclassed by his opponent. Rory, despite his greater size and age, was a good deal more agile than the younger man, and Wemyss still favored a method that included regular stamping of the ground with his right foot as he made his parries and feints. This technique sapped his stamina and opened him up to his opponent on numerous occasions. Rory was an altogether more strategic, athletic individual and had a far greater repertoire of thrusts and defenses, acquired from both the Italian and French schools. He soon had Wemyss at his mercy, standing frozen over the lieutenant in a posture that clearly showed his ability to deliver a coup de grace had they been fighting with unguarded swords.

"I demand a forfeit. A just punishment before we quit Brackenbury Park," said Rory.

"What?" asked Wemyss.

"We must go together to the assembly at Northallerton five nights hence, and there you must make it clear to the world and his wife that Hero is blameless and that you are bitterly sorry for the wrong you have done her."

Wemyss smiled up at the victor in this bout. "I shall be—well, not delighted precisely—but certainly honored to carry out this commission."

Rory tossed aside his sword and held out a hand to Wemyss, who took it, hauled himself up and dusted himself down. Together, the men walked back to Brackenbury, for the first time since Buchan's arrival, they realized, that they were all in perfect accord.

Although it was only Wemyss who had been banned from Cheveley, Rory felt a little apprehensive when he went there later that day to inquire after Rosamund. He was greeted by Anthony Veasey, in forthright mode as ever.

"So, sirrah, I hear you were cuddling my niece yesterday afternoon."

Rory looked perplexed.

"You carried her from the stables through the house. But I hear she could have walked. She walked up the stairs after seeing Buchan finally snared." Anthony gave Rory a glare of distrust. "You don't intend to treat her so shabbily as that spindle-shanks Wemyss treated my other niece."

"Rosamund asked me to stay my hand, but I have wished to come to you and Mr. Veasey for nearly a week to make my offer. Of course, she is of age and in command of her own funds, but she is still your niece, almost like a daughter to you, I believe. I have paid her my addresses, she has suggested that my attentions are not intolerable to her, and as soon as she gives me permission, I shall present the case to the world for our nuptials."

Veasey's glance traveled downward as he digested Rory's words. When he next met Rory's eyes, his own were softer. "I daresay you will be married before our poor Hero. What will become of that match I cannot imagine."

"Wemyss is most repentant. I believe that he is fully aware of his folly and is more than ready to make amends—if Miss Veasey will hear him."

"Little Hero has been to me in the depths this very morning, for brother Leonard told her of his interdict on the presence of Mr. Wemyss in our midst."

"What if they meet in public? At an assembly, for example?"

Veasey shook his head and muttered, "My dear brother is shy, very shy after that business the day before yesterday. He does not feel we should go abroad for weeks, perhaps months. I say brazen it out, and Hero seems fit as a fiddle now. But he's always been inclined to the reclusive. There is poor Rosamund's face to consider, of course. She's been badly bruised by that brute."

Rory had forgotten this and was prepared for the worst. But it seemed that while Buchan had taken his swipe at her, it was the bump on the back of her head where she had made contact with the folly wall that had caused more suffering. He entered the little parlor where she sat with Hero, now apparently entirely recovered, both girls deep in stitching. She glanced up and became quite luminous, her lips broadening and curving with a great smile as he scrutinized her for damage.

"Do you wish to send me back to the manufactory, or will I do?"

"Most serviceable and less wounded than I expected from all that your uncle said as he was leaving." He came forward and took her hand in both his to kiss it. She indicated the seat beside her and he flicked back the tails of his navy coat and sat.

"The back of my skull feels distinctly tender, but the rest of me, as you can see, has survived remarkably unharmed."

"I am delighted to see that it is as you say. I should not have believed it had I not seen you. And you, Miss Veasey, you look remarkably well also."

"You are kind to say so, Captain Buchanan, but beside our dear Rosamund, I feel something of a fraud, for I only had a very deep slumber, where she was subjected to a shocking ordeal." Hero paused. She cleared her throat, then shook her head as if to clear it of all thought and bent back to her sewing.

"You were about to say something, Cousin?" enquired Rosamund.

"No, by no means. Well, that is. Yes." She bent forward

toward Rosamund and Rory. "Captain Buchanan, how is poor Lieutenant Wemyss?"

"Very cut up."

"My father is being a little unreasonable. Mr. Wemyss was foolish not to have come to us and established the truth before making that horrid scene at our party. But his error was understandable. He had been terribly misled by that wicked man."

"Can you find it in your heart to forgive him, Miss Veasey?"

Hero nodded. "I know that he has been impulsive and wrong, but I am better pleased that he did not believe he could endure to be married to me than to continue with the engagement simply because I come dowered with Cheveley and a respectable fortune."

"Respectable fortune!" snorted Rosamund. "I have a respectable fortune. You are as rich as Croesus and far sweeter, dear Hero."

"Would you forgive him, if it were your swain who had committed so grievous an error, Miss Lovelace?" Rory took her hand in his and cradled it, mischief dancing in his eyes.

"I think, Captain, we have already established that my swain is richly endowed with common sense and a strong sense of my trustworthiness." Rosamund's tone became more serious. "Hero, are you sure you can still regard Wemyss with fondness? It is not so much the lack of trust, but his lamentable choice of location in which to denounce you that concerns me. That showed very little judgment and no kindness or consideration."

"Your swain, Rosamund?" Hero, although not noted for her intellect was not slow to catch the interplay between Buchanan and her cousin. "You have a suitor? Are you and Mr. Buchanan become friends?"

"We are more than friends, Miss Veasey." Rory raised Rosamund's hand to his. "We are contracted to be married, which means that I very much desire a reconciliation between yourself and Wemyss, for however knuckle-brained he may be, he is still my companion-at-arms and my very dear friend."

"I should be all too happy to be reconciled to my Valentine. It is my father we must convince. He is determined that there shall be no match between us and swears he will send me away if I do not abide by his ruling that Valentine must be barred the house. He almost went so far as to prohibit me acknowledging him should we meet in public."

"But he has not actually prohibited it?"

"No. Why?"

Rory smiled. "Are you planning to attend the next Northallerton assembly?"

"We are subscribers, of course," said Rosamund. "But Uncle Leonard is set against us going out at all. I am hoping that we shall send each other into catatonia and he will agree that we may go simply to liven us all up, but I am not hopeful. It is only five days away."

"Is he afraid of a scene?"

"He is afraid of whispering and mumbling and no one being quite certain what has happened. He believes that everything will blow over if we simply stick our heads in the sand and pretend nothing is wrong and we remain fixed for a space."

"You do not believe that?" asked Rory.

"By no means. We must brazen it out. Hero must be seen at balls and parties and picnics and everywhere that people gather and chat, to show that she is not guilty or shamed by that episode, that she is not in a decline, that she has nothing to be ashamed of. Only then can we overcome the gossip and give it the lie. But that is not Uncle Leonard's way and I am too rough and ready to persuade him otherwise."

"What about Mrs. Carmichael? What if she came and told him that Hero must be seen abroad for the sake of her reputation and her health?"

The girls met each other's eyes and grinned. Buchanan had hit upon exactly the right person to talk Uncle Leonard into breaking his self-imposed seclusion. He bade them farewell at once, promising to go straight to the widow to ask her to call round at Cheveley, not that very day but perhaps the next, to talk Uncle Leonard round.

Mrs. Carmichael duly did visit Cheveley, ostensibly to discover how Hero and Rosamund did. She found the family gathered in one of the lighter morning rooms, in heated debate over the vexed issue of when, if ever, Leonard Veasey would countenance their going into society. Unusually, he was subject to harangue not only from the two girls but also from Anthony Veasey, who saw which way the wind lay and clearly understood that it would be far better for Hero to be out and about, especially now that both she and Rosamund had almost entirely regained their looks. Equally unusually, Leonard Veasey was withstanding all entreaties. As Mrs. Carmichael followed the footman, she could hear quite clearly the protests and rumblings of what was becoming a full-blooded altercation. It ceased with comic abruptness as the door opened and she saw, round the bulk of the footmen, four heads transfixed by the entry of a stranger in their midst. Instantly, social smiles snapped into place, and Hero came forward, hands outstretched with a genuine air of welcome, tinged with relief.

"How are you, Mrs. Carmichael? And Daniel?"

"I have left Daniel to the delights of Pliny the Younger and the destruction of Pompeii. But I came to see how you were, my dear, for all your friends are eager for news. Half of us have you at death's door, the other half awaiting Buchan's trial like a tricoteuse at the guillotine. I am pleased to see that neither report seems to be true."

Leonard Veasey harrumphed and huffed over the indelicate nature of either rumor, but invited Mrs. Carmichael to sit and took a chair near her. There was a pregnant pause as he leaned forward to consult with her, then Anthony and the girls chatted quietly about more mundane matters while Veasey probed Mrs. Carmichael for a true account of what was being said by the county. Although from time to time they glanced toward Mrs. Carmichael, she studiedly ignored them so that they could not intervene in the conversation, for initially she seemed to be in complete agreement with all that Veasey said, endorsing his words with little "mmms" and "oh yes, indeeds" and a good deal of nodding and taking on an ever more serious air. Rosamund soon had the wit to signal to Hero and Anthony that they should leave Mrs. Carmichael to her work, for she would get on much better without the three of them making stilted conversation while actually trying to overhear the finer details. They bade her farewell and exited on various spurious errands.

It was only just as the girls came down for dinner later that afternoon that they discovered the result of Mrs. Carmichael's intervention. Leonard Veasey kept them on tenterhooks, for they knew better than to hurl questions at him. Even brother Anthony was unusually passive, but finally, as they were sharing the last of a fine port jelly with pears, Veasey finally turned the subject to socializing.

"I suppose you silly girls still wish to attend the assembly at Northallerton the day after tomorrow?"

"We do indeed, Uncle Leonard!"

"Hero? You're not afraid of going out and about and having people whispering about you behind their fans and their gloves?"

"Papa, people are forever gossiping. At least this way, if anyone is bold enough to ask me directly, I can explain exactly what happened."

"Hmm. I suppose so. That's what Mrs. Carmichael suggested, it's true."

Tentatively, Anthony spoke. "I think it wise, Brother. Otherwise people might say that there is truth in the rumors because you are ashamed of her. Especially now Buchan is safely under lock and key."

"Still, it seems a little disrespectful to the memory of that unfortunate young fellow who was his friend. I cannot like that."

Anthony here became a little more robust. "He was as much implicated in Hero's blackening as Buchan, Brother, and he was a stranger among us. It is certainly sad, but one does not go into black gloves for a foreigner who has done nothing but stir up trouble."

This comment occasioned one of the regular grousing, grumbling wrangles between brothers about protocol and etiquette and the sad want of manners in today's youth, signaling, to the relief of both Rosamund and Hero, a return to normality.

Of course, when it came to setting off for the assembly, Hero became much less sanguine. First she put on the cream chiffon, then the rose taffeta, then the jonquil silk with ecru at the sleeves and neck, then she fiddled with her hair and threw down the spray of silk flowers and replaced them with first a bandeau, then an egret feather, and even contemplated a turban that would not have looked out of place on a dowager, until Rosamund sat her down, assembled the appropriate accessories and prevented Hero from looking once again at any of her clothes, diverting her cousin instead with her own clothing conundrums. As usual, when it came to another person's ensemble, Hero was reliable in her taste and her ability to arrange the shawl, the hair, the betsy to absolutely the best advantage.

"Has Captain Buchanan spoken to Uncle Leonard yet, Rose?"

"No, I've asked him not to, not until we've settled your future."

"I think you should allow him to come forward very soon. Tomorrow or the day after. For if I do see Valentine there tonight, I am no longer so sure as I was of him. Who knows whether he is truly contrite? Who knows how constant he can be? If he is forever the sort to accuse me of misdemeanors, I should be very miserable indeed. I am still quite young, after all, and it may be that there is some other gentleman who is more trusting and dependable."

Rosamund rocked back in shock. "Hero, you have cultivated some spine!"

"Do not look so surprised. With a cousin such as you, it would be more astonishing if I were truly pliable."

"I am delighted to discover that my ways, which you have so often condemned as harsh, should have rubbed off a little. And I believe that you are right in warding off Lieutenant Wemyss. If he makes any show of affection tonight or subsequently, I hope you will not yield too swifty. He deserves to work a little and you deserve to be thoroughly wooed and won."

The girls donned their evening cloaks and departed for the assembly with hearts still somewhat uncertain and heads held high. Whatever else happened there, they would show the world that they had no cause for shame.

EIGHTEEN

Being a punctilious individual, Leonard Veasey generally arrived promptly at social events, and the Northallerton assembly was no exception. Despite their brave words and intentions, the girls were distinctly nervous by the time they arrived at the assembly hall in Northallerton. It was over a week since the disastrous gathering at Cheveley, but what with that and the sensational murder of Lowther followed by the capture of Buchan, there could be no possible rival topic of conversation. These events were by far the most interesting to have occurred in the area since the birth of a two-headed cow three years previously.

A moment's thought would have told Rosamund that as direct witnesses and victims of Buchan's villainy, the Cheveley party would be highly sought after at the assembly, but Hero's fluttering prevented even a moment of thought. Rosamund found herself entirely concentrated on calming her cousin as they shed their cloaks and slipped into a withdrawing room to make the final adjustments to their dresses before joining the throng. For all the assemblies in the area were thronged, being the chief amusement of young and old alike, despite the strict injunction on any spiritous beverages, a somewhat old-fashioned taste in musical accompaniment and a lack of ventilation that regularly caused at least one dancer and sometimes as many as five or six, to faint dead away. Before leaving the small, mirrored retiring room, Hero needed to be considerably bucked up and it was only a furious knocking at the door that forced her to emerge.

Chins held high, fans fluttering, and their pace steady, the Cheveley girls walked into the main assembly room, followed by the Veasey brothers in uncharacteristically pugnacious mode. In her heightened state, it did seem to Rosamund that all eyes had turned to examine them. But the master of ceremonies came immediately up to them to bid them welcome and was followed by their supporters, respectable and respected matrons such as Mrs. Cameron Robertson, Mrs. Allerton and Mrs. Carmichael, all agog with the news that the Countess of Rievaulx was expected to bring a party that night, inspired, it was understood, by the attendance of the family from Cheveley.

"Are we to be treated like exhibits in a menagerie or does she wish to lend us countenance?" demanded Rosamund.

"I've heard that she is not the sort of lady who seeks out spectacle and amusement from the misfortunes of others. At some time, Colonel Fitzgerald must have presented himself to the earl. I should think it is support," replied Mrs. Carmichael judiciously. The gentlemen, having assured themselves that their two charges were well protected, cleared their throats and indicated their intention to retire to the card room, although Uncle Anthony did mark down his intention to dance with his nieces one time apiece.

Mrs. Robertson led the two girls over to a group of chairs under a selection of weary-looking potted palms, where Caroline and other young ladies of their acquaintance were seated. At first there was some constraint, but as Hero displayed a willingness to be quizzed about her role in the capture of Buchan, and Rosamund a little more reluctantly imparted the tale of her imprisonment in the folly, this soon evaporated under a steady flow of questions and exclamations of wonder at their courage.

Gradually, young men trickled over, leaning over the edges of chairs to hear the tale, at once intrigued and envious that they had not had the opportunity to shine in the dispatch of so thoroughly bounderish a creature as this Buchan. They had all met him, some had admired his pose of world-weariness mixed with insouciant polish, some had envied him his war record, but now they all were keen to comment on how untrustworthy and wicked he had always seemed to them during the brief weeks he had been abroad in the county. More than one dance was ignored while this was progressing, which somewhat irked the master of ceremonies, but his amour propre was more than salved by the appearance at the door of Lady Datchet and her party from the abbey.

The countess was an elegant woman in her thirties, accompanied by three very smart ladies wearing clothes that clearly came from more fashionable modistes than were generally available to the rest of the assembly, and five gentlemen in full evening dress. Two of the gentlemen paused on the stairs to gaze round the room through lorgnettes in what Rosamund thought was a most affected manner. Her general irritation was somewhat exacerbated by the continuing absence of the officers from Brackenbury Park. Given the effort it had taken to appear at the assembly, the least her acknowledged suitor could do, she thought, was to provide his support.

Rosamund watched with skepticism as Lady Datchet swept through the room, the cynosure of all eyes, followed by a very smart coterie of guests toward the seats where she and Hero sat. She came to a halt before Hero, who stood immediately and curtsied.

"We do not know each other terribly well, Miss Veasey, for you are very young and we are so rarely in Yorkshire. I do not remember your being out the last time we were here. But I remember your cousin, Miss Lovelace, who is looking quite daggers at me. I just wished to say how very much we admire you both for enduring such wickedness at the hands of this Buchan."

Hero met the countess's open gaze with her newly discovered poise. "He is a very unpleasant individual, but we hope, Rosamund and I, that we have helped in some small way to prevent him from going about damaging any further reputations."

"Well, I hope you will not mind visiting Datchet Abbey and telling us all about the events which culminated in his arrest. It has been a great adventure, except of course for the death of that poor boy."

Hero shot a glance at Rosamund, who was doing her best to look demure and grateful for the countess's attentions. "We shall be delighted, Lady Datchet."

The countess bowed to the girls and turned, her flotilla of guests turning with her, just as the doors were thrown open once again, coinciding with a lull in the music that had so far punctuated the evening. In the sudden hush, the swift intake of breath of most of the assembled company was clearly heard, for there were the officers from Brackenbury Park, in full regalia, complete with dress swords. As one, the four men moved down the three steps into the room and again everyone made way for them as they crossed the room, headed unmistakably for Hero and Rosamund.

It seemed to take quite a long time for them to come to

a standstill before the two Cheveley girls, but it could have been only a few seconds. The musicians were clearly conscious that some unusual occurrence was under way, for they froze as they were about to launch into the next dance, their bows poised, their fingers ready.

Lieutenant Wemyss knelt down before Hero. Then he looked up and spoke so that the whole company could hear.

"Miss Veasey, I have done you a very great disservice. I have wronged you and spoken ill of you, I have made a public spectacle of you and I have repudiated you. If you never wish to see or speak to me again, it will be punishment enough, but I wish you to know that I am always in your debt, always at your disposal."

Just then, Leonard Veasey came forward. He was about to speak, but Hero looked at him. She gave a slight shake of her head. Valentine looked from her to Veasey and back again. She nodded her head at Valentine to continue.

"Miss Veasey, here before this company, I wish to declare that you were innocent of the foul misdemeanors of which I accused you, and if any slur attaches to your name, I am ready to do everything necessary to restore to you your reputation."

"If only, Mr. Wemyss, reputation was a gift to be given."

"Whatever judgment you pass on me, Miss Veasey, I shall accept."

"Thank you, Lieutenant. I shall think it over and you may call on me tomorrow, to hear my verdict." Leonard Veasey made to speak, but Hero put her arm on her father's sleeve and said, "Mr. Wemyss will not come into the house, Father. But he shall come with Captain Buchanan tomorrow and we will walk in the gardens."

Wemyss drew up to his full height, bowed from the waist and retired, leaving Buchanan, Fitzgerald and Macdonald to bow and withdraw also. Rosamund looked after Buchanan in puzzlement, understanding that he was providing support for his friend but not entirely sure why all four men then withdrew themselves from the gathering entirely.

But she had no time to ponder further, for Lady Datchet was about to open the dancing, and her two gentlemen with lorgnettes came forward to ask for the pleasure of the next dance, like the two Antipholuses of the Comedy of Errors, bowing simultaneously, speaking at once with the same slight lisp. They were unrelated, it turned out, but had grown up virtually together, attending the same schools, the same university and now both sharing rooms in London, and each turned out to be far less affected and far more interesting than first appearances might have led one to believe.

The evening passed in a pleasant haze of dancing and happy chatter, Hero entirely re-established in the eyes of Yorkshire society and Rosamund the recipient of many a sly comment about Captain Buchanan and his intentions, Captain Buchanan and his acres, Captain Buchanan and his devotion, until she was quite sick of any mention of Captain Buchanan and longing more than ever for his acerbic, amused presence.

On the way home, the Veasey brothers quizzed Rosamund, leaving Hero quite delighted that she was no longer the sole focus of their attentions. First Anthony discussed the character of the captain, then Leonard considered what they knew of his situation and his family, then Anthony chimed in with a disquisition on the distances between Yorkshire and Edinburgh and between Edinburgh and the Highlands, and together they asked in chorus whether Rosamund truly wished to marry this fellow.

"Yes. I love him dearly."

This set off another train of questions, about the previously perceived antipathy between the couple, about the nature of love and the fickleness of the military, about Wemyss and his rash assumptions about Hero.

"But Captain Buchanan would not believe any of it. He challenged the lieutenant to a duel, I understand, for he always thought that Buchan had cooked up the whole business. You yourselves saw how he was, what lengths he went to find the girl and the fellow who were party to the deception."

"They dueled?" Leonard Veasey was horrified. "My child has been the subject of a duel?"

"No one knows anything about it, dear uncle, apart from the officers at Brackenbury Park. They fought it in seclusion and no one else was brought into it at all. Honor is satisfied, Uncle, and look how handsomely Lieutenant Wemyss made his obeisance to Hero at the assembly tonight."

"Could you forgive him?" Leonard fired back at his niece. Then he looked in the dim light of the carriage at his daughter. "Tell me truly, Hero. Have you forgiven him?"

"I am not sure, Papa. I do not feel so desolate as I did. But I see him through fresh eyes. I believe it will take him some time to persuade me that my love for him can be revived. It will certainly take a good deal of time for him to persuade me that he ever loved me at all, and still longer to convince me that he loves me now."

Rosamund reached in the dark for her cousin's gloved hand and held it tight. Hero spoke so bravely, so clearly. Her whole world, her every certainty had crumbled about her and now she must rebuild the whole edifice, but this time on stronger foundations.

Hero continued. "But that should not affect us in any way with regard to Captain Buchanan. I cannot doubt his affection for Rosamund. He has behaved in an entirely exemplary way toward her, he has demonstrated his attachment in so many ways, and he is just the man for her, for I never saw her laugh or seem so happy with any other person." She squeezed Rosamund's hand in return.

"Well, if he comes to see me tomorrow morning, I shall receive him with all the ceremony that is due to him. In fact," mused Leonard, "since you are of age, it would be a courtesy on his part to come calling on me at all. If you were to elope on the morrow, there is nothing anyone could do about it. Except I beg, dear Rosamund, that you will not. We have enough to recover from what with this Wemyss fellow making such a spectacle of himself and us."

Somehow, Rosamund knew that if Hero was able to fall in love once again with Wemyss, Leonard Veasey would find a way to come round and accept his daughter's choice, even if it was not his own. But first, there would be her own wedding.

The girls rose late the next morning. After breakfast, Hero sat at her bureau, making a list of all the arrangements that must be undone now that she was not to be married in a few weeks' time. Rosamund assisted, offering to undertake some commissions, discussing how best to carry out others.

"Do you know, Ros, I think I shall still invite Mrs. Wemyss and her daughters to visit us here. There is no need to punish them just for the sake of my misunderstanding with Valentine. They could come in time for your wedding, for they know Captain Buchanan, and then perhaps they may divert me a little when you are gone on your wedding trip."

"You are going much too fast, my love. Captain Buchanan

and I have scarcely put our heads together. I do not know whether he has yet heard from his father. If Mr. Buchanan demands it, it may be that you and I together will go to his home by Loch Lomond before there can be any question of marriage. What if Mr. Buchanan takes me into great dislike?"

"What nonsense, Rosamund! Why, he will come to love you as much as we all do here at Cheveley, and then you will be immured in the Highlands and never allowed to go anywhere, except possibly Stirling for high days and holidays."

But Rosamund, as so often, was less sanguine than her cousin. Nothing had seemed normal for so long that it was hard for her to imagine a time of calm, a time where marriages might take place without intervention or concealment. But at least today, when she saw Rory, he might at last make his formal offer for her.

It was just after eleven o'clock that Jameson came to the study where the girls sat to announce the arrival of the two military gentlemen.

"Captain Buchanan says may he speak yet to Mr. Veasey, miss, for he wishes to do that at once. Shall I take him through?"

Rosamund looked at Hero. Her cousin gave a wavering smile. She turned back to Jameson. "Yes, please, take him through and ask him to meet us in the garden afterward." She stood and smoothed out her skirts, then held out her hand to her cousin. "Come, Hero, let us take poor Wemyss to your mama's walled garden and then I may conveniently lose you in some little arbor."

At first there was a little constraint between Hero and her foolish suitor. Rosamund struggled to make conversation with Wemyss, who was well aware that Buchanan was about to receive permission to become the happiest of men, who was well aware that he had thrown away his own opportunity to become the happiest of men, and who was not at all sure that he would ever be given a further opportunity to become the happiest of men. Particularly since Hero was silent and contemplative, twirling her parasol and walking a little distance away from her erstwhile lover.

Valiantly, Rosamund touched on his intentions now that Wemyss was leaving Yorkshire. He was unclear. He would go north, to Fifeshire, to see his mama and sisters, and then perhaps he would go to Edinburgh to find some gainful employment. Captain Macdonald had spoken of putting in a word for him with his brother, Aunt Lydia's husband. He fell silent. Unspoken came the thought that perhaps that offer no longer stood since he had so grievously misjudged Macdonald's niece.

"Lieutenant Wemyss, does your family ever visit Edinburgh?"

"My sisters? Yes, we have friends there, and there is some thought that my sister Caroline might become companion to one of the old ladies we know there."

Hero unbent, tucking her little gloved hand into the crook of Wemyss's elbow. "I should very much like to meet them. Perhaps I shall visit my Aunt Lydia soon, and if your sisters are there in Edinburgh, we may meet. I am sure they are quite charming."

He looked down at her, her heart-shaped face gazing up at his, no longer with adoration but now with a serenity that suddenly he wished to disrupt with kisses.

Just then, like a whirlwind, Buchanan swept into the garden, calling out for Rosamund.

"My darling, where are you?"

"We're here, Rory, by the little pond."

They heard his steps, quick, and then he appeared, tossed aside her parasol, and picked her up by the waist and whirled her about in a great wheeling motion that sent her skirts flying and her cheeks flushing. At last he gently put her down and kissed her heartily, utterly mindless of his interested witnesses. Then he spoke.

"My love, I've permission from your uncle, my father, Colonel Fitzgerald and everyone else between here and Loch Lomond to ask you formally, for the last time, for your hand in marriage."

"I think, Captain Buchanan, I wish to give you my answer in a place which is a little more private. Will you follow me?" And holding out her hand, Rosamund led her beloved officer away from prying eyes to the arbor where she had initially intended to allow Hero to speak with Wemyss.

Hero and Valentine were left looking after the happy couple as they disappeared into the distance. "They have found true love, despite seeming to detest each other. Perhaps there is hope for all of us, Lieutenant Wemyss. Will you escort me back to the house?"

Valentine nodded and held out his arm to Hero, glancing back once to where Rory and Rosamund were now safe in each other's arms.

215-4938